MIDLIFE DRIFT

DRUID HEIR BOOK 4

N. Z. NASSER

HANORA SKY PRESS

THE PLAYERS

Alisha Verma - Druid Heir
Echo - Alisha's leopard sidekick
Marina Ambrose - Alisha's best friend
Ezra Neuhoff - half-werewolf, half-wizard Minister for Justice
Orpheus Might - Vampire, Minister for History and the Today
Joshi Verma - Alisha's father
Sahil Verma - Alisha's brother
Alma Bluejay - Joshi's new love
Fei Yen and Faeza - hu hsien, shapeshifting foxes
Rajiv Chawla - Rajika Verma's brother
Gaia - Goddess of the Earth
Calypso Archer - The Custodian of the Celestial Library
Robert Jameson - Detective, Shadow Squad
Mirabel, Janey, Angelus, Xavier, Ayshah, Sage, Violet, Benny and Drew - Alisha's Wildwoods class
Phinnaeous Shine - Shapeshifter, Prime Sorcerer
Lavinia Drach - Witch, Minister for Defence
Isadora, Chandra, Ravynne and Agatha - Lavinia's coven
Rayna Willowsun - Druid, Minister for Education, Headmistress of Wildwoods School of the Wondrous
Margola Silver - Selkie, Minister for Information

Helio Woodwink - Fairy, Bestiary Minister
Gunnolf Zev - Werewolf, former alpha
Annie - a little girl
Gordon Stevens, Henry Radcliffe and Ali Sheikh - victims
Manfred - a chiropractor
Kraglek - an octopus
Mami - a tattoo artist

1

———

The streetlamp on the dark London street corner flickered, and a light drizzle fell as I pressed my phone to my ear, clear in the knowledge that I had upset my wolf.

That morning, we'd woken in a tangle of sheets in the cottage he'd inherited from his parents, the one at the end of the world, where no soul thought to disturb us. Where his pack or senate duties couldn't creep between us. Thankfully, his teleporting skills meant he wasn't tied to the pack farmhouse or Wildwoods.

We ate breakfast in the overgrown garden, warmed by the autumn sun. Ezra had bought sticky buns from the French bakery at Charing Cross. A sudden gust of wind whipped my hair into my face as I took a bite. Ezra leaned forward to hold my hair back, and I thought maybe we could make it work.

Then his phone buzzed, and he gave me an apologetic smile. Again.

Here we were again, in separate places and opposing mind-sets. Still, I listened to his worried voice, wanting to make it work. Wanting us to succeed.

Ezra drew in a ragged breath that rattled down the phone line. "With Ra, you were under my mentorship, so the buck stopped with me. With Pan, there was no real harm done. Sure, you hid a dragon, but you had also awed the senate by *animating* a dragon. With the Ravenmaster, you had no choice. Half of us made the same decision when he attacked Wildwoods." A growl. "But you can't keep jumping into the messes the gods make. I can't see you behind bars. And I can't see you hurt."

"You won't." Before he became Justice Minister, Ezra was a seeker. He had this uncanny knack of always knowing where I was. I really hoped he didn't teleport to my location.

"I mean it, Alisha. I can't be seen to bend the rules for you, even if I want to," said Ezra. "The Prime Sorcerer has warned you that he won't have it."

I heard him. That didn't mean I agreed with him.

I didn't have the smallest regret about my choices. Yes, I had fallen foul of the Magical Constitution and squeaked by without sanction, but because of me, good things had happened. Mum's killer had been punished. The elves had been proven innocent after being blamed for the tremors. And most recently, I had given the Ravenmaster his comeuppance for disrupting tech to sew discord and corrupting my brother.

It was always the same with this topic. Ezra and I talked at cross purposes but didn't shift our standpoints.

He wanted me to be safe. I wanted my nightmares to stop.

Nightmares in which I instructed the ravens to tear the Ravenmaster into tiny, bloody pieces. But instead of overcoming the god, I stood paralysed as my friends were ripped to pieces instead.

Until no one was left but me.

The only way to move forward was to arm myself with the knowledge, skills and tools to ensure I came out on top if trouble found me. Since I'd joined the Otherworld, trouble found me quicker than flies found honey. What was more, with Ezra and Orpheus knee-deep in senate business, our vulnerability was heightened.

I had to help myself.

Prickles of frustration crept into my voice. "Phinnaecus Shine is a coward."

"Just please stay out of trouble. One mistake and it can all go wrong. And these days, I can't always parachute in to help." Ezra sighed. "It's going to be a while before this senate meeting ends. I might be late back to yours."

"How about we catch up tomorrow? I'm seeing Fei Yen and Faeza for a cuppa tonight." Technically it wasn't a lie. They served tea whenever I visited.

"Okay. I miss you."

"I miss you too." A pang of guilt ran through my stomach. Ezra Neuhoff was the man of my dreams. I'd tell him everything as soon as we were back.

I ended the call. My trainers squelched on the pavement as I crossed the street and walked into Shanghai Moon, the local tea and occult shop run by my fox friends. Inside, curls of incense wafted through the air, and three bodies gathered at a sumptuous, candlelit tarot table, draped with a velvet tablecloth.

"Everything okay?" Echo purred. He perched on the chair intended for my best friend, Marina. In the bright light of the shop, his golden leopard coat with its rosettes was a kaleidoscope of different shades.

I sat down next to him. "Ezra wants me to stay out of trouble. But sometimes, a little trouble in midlife is just what the doctor ordered. He'll be proud of us when this is done."

Fei Yen and Faeza sat across from us in solemn repose, card deck ready and waiting.

"We better get started then," said Faeza, ever the blunt one of the two. "But please, try not to make a mess. It's been a long day, and I could do without having to get the hoover out."

Fei Yen nodded. "A little consideration goes a long way. Even on adventures."

The journey to and from the Celestial Library was a little rough and tumble. The last time we attempted this feat, I'd ended up somersaulting through the galaxy and crash-landed a dragon in their shop. They hadn't forgotten.

A second later, Marina tumbled through the door in a black leather catsuit and a flash of rainbow hair. A swirl of autumn leaves followed her into the shop. For once, her plentiful tattoos had been covered, but the catsuit left nothing to the imagination.

Jessica Rabbit, eat your heart out.

Echo's lips split into a grin, revealing tombstone teeth in need of flossing. "Marina Ambrose, the queen of grand entrances."

Marina grinned and pulled up an extra chair. "Sorry, I'm late. I have the Rose of Jericho book. Do you have your mum's necklace, Alisha?"

"It's right here." The necklace nestled at my collarbone, an oval amber stone on a choker-type gold chain, just hidden from view under my hoodie. For a hefty piece, it was surprisingly light.

Faeza leaned forward conspiratorially. "Now you're all here, we wanted to double-check. It's not been a moment since we put the whole Ravenmaster thing behind us. Are you sure you want to go through with this? Maybe it would be sensible to take things easy for a while. A new Chinese takeaway just opened around the corner. We could have a quiet meal instead."

My body sagged. My intuition and my hips told me now wasn't the time to rest on my laurels and indulge in a Chinese takeaway. Why did everyone want to put the brakes on and pretend life would potter along without hiccups?

It was only a matter of time before another god came knocking.

Gaia had told me as much.

"That's a wonderful idea," said Fei Yen. "There is nothing

wrong with a quiet life. No jumping through portals, no shifty senators, no battle-training, no ripping an immortal god limb from limb. How about some chicken in oyster sauce, a tofu noodle dish, maybe a spring roll or two and a fortune cookie?"

A dollop of drool trickled down Echo's jaw. "I am always in the mood for food. And singing. How about chow mein and karaoke?"

Marina edged forward to look past Echo at me. We had discussed the risks. The Celestial Library didn't stay at a fixed point, and the journey was perilous. There was a chance we wouldn't make it past the entry hall, or we'd be unable to find our way back home.

Echo's head dropped. "Anyone would think I'm invisible. You know it's an emotional wound of mine after years of being seen as a Bengal cat."

I scratched his ears. "Without you, I wouldn't know who I am."

Marina hugged him. "You know how much we rely on you, but we have to make this trip. We witnessed the Ravenmaster's attack. We've comforted Alisha after a nightmare. The only way to protect her is to complete Rosalie's work on the Rose of Jericho project. For that, we need more information than is available to us in this world." She drew in a deep breath. "Forget the spring rolls, Fei Yen and Faeza. We're off to see a library amongst the stars, guarded by a dreadlocked woman in blade runners. Doesn't get much better than that."

Faeza sighed. "Very well."

A heavy, midnight blue curtain hung from a circular ceiling rail. She pulled it around us, enveloping us in silver sequins reminiscent of stars.

She picked up the deck of cards and shuffled them with the fluidity of water. "This is your journey, Marina Ambrose. Tap the cards and spread your energy through them."

It wasn't the same deck we had used for my last journey to the Celestial Library. The foxes couldn't work with an incomplete deck, and I had burned the previous gateway card. This deck was hand-drawn cards with blood-red edges.

Marina's blue eyes widened. Unlike me, she truly believed in the power of the cards. She took a deep breath and gave the cards a wallop.

Faeza continued. "Now concentrate, Marina. To get to the Celestial Library, you must ask a question of it—an open, undemanding one. Learning takes humility, after all. Approaching any library, let alone this one, with a selfish heart is a fool's errand."

Marina considered her options for a moment. "How can a library amongst the stars help me keep my best friend safe?"

Fei Yen beamed. "Well done." She spread the shuffled cards across the table with a flourish. "Now clear your mind and choose two cards that draw you."

Marina tapped two cards in quick succession on opposite sides of the spread.

Faeza flipped the cards. On one, a handheld wand was sprouting with shoots, with rolling hills in the distance. "The Ace of Wands speaks of family and inheritance, of invention and creation. It is telling you to follow your heart and make a plan. This plan might take great effort, but you should surrender yourself to it."

"I'm not scared of hard work," said Marina.

The other card lay upside down. It showed a semi-clad woman stepping forward, a laurel wreath on her head.

"The World reversed signifies extended travel," said Faeza. "You stand at the precipice of a large project. It warns against shortcuts and tells of the cyclical nature of life's seasons." She tidied the remaining deck and pushed the two cards from the reading into the middle of the table under the flickering light of the candelabra.

I'd hoped for a clearer sense of an upcoming victory, but

that wasn't the point of tarot cards. They provided guidance, not answers.

Fei Yen cleared her throat. "One of these cards is a gateway to the Celestial Library, and although Alisha has taken this journey before, it is you, Marina, who must take the first step and pull her after you. The journey is yours. Choose the door. Once you step through it, we will guard the card until your return."

Marina stared at the cards, her bright blue eyes drawn time and again to the Ace of Wands.

The candles danced and twitched, and then with a fizz, one went out.

The foxes looked at one another in alarm.

"Quick. The chance of passage is shrinking," said Fei Yen as the second candle fizzled out.

"Hurry!" Faeza's eyes widened as the final candle began to spit.

"Echo, stay here and guard the portal until we return," I said.

Marina dove for the Ace of Wands with her right hand and reached for me with her left hand.

Echo's roar met my ears as we slipped into the card with its blood-red edges. Marina's body jerked away from me, her eyes prised unnaturally wide, but I clung on. My eyes were also open, yet I couldn't decipher the shapes before me. I couldn't see further than our bodies being sucked upwards and sidewards, jolted like riders on the world's worst buckaroo.

Hadn't the Custodian told me that no journey to the Celestial Library would be the same?

I winced as heat hit my skin. Unbearable heat. Heat from the unyielding sun. Heat from a dragon's breath. Heat from the Earth's core.

"Trust in the journey. Don't feed the universe your fear," came Faeza's voice from worlds away.

Marina, too, shrivelled in the intense heat. Her body curled into a ball, but her rainbow head jerked backwards, strands of bright hair spooling as if she were a supernova shooting across space and time and not a mere woman, a fragile cargo of all the things I loved best in one person.

I ached to protect her, but I was as vulnerable as she was—a ping pong in a machine. My mouth gelled shut, but I willed her to hear my thoughts.

Just hold on.

I clutched her tighter, intertwining our fingers like a Ziplock as we zigzagged across the universe.

2

I needn't have feared she'd give up. The universe might knead us like dough and whack us over the head with a rolling pin, but women in midlife were tough. We responded to anything that hurtled our way. We had learned to be malleable, resilient and strong. And we weren't scared of being soft.

Marina's eyes locked on mine as the stars flew by, as the dark became blacker and deeper than I ever imagined it could be. We allowed the universe to pummel us. Just when my breath had become a mere wisp, and my fingers ached from clinging on, the universe spat us out.

I landed on my hands and knees on a concrete floor. Without a blanket or yoga mat to pad them, it bloody hurt, but the cooled temperature was a relief. Marina, with a dancer's instincts, rolled a turn and then emerged in a standing position beside me. I almost expected her to perform a finishing pose, but instead, she offered me a hand and tugged me up.

"That was wild, but we'll need therapy," she said, only the hint of a quiver in her voice.

In the Otherworld, trauma came as frequently as a London bus.

Our hair looked like we'd been through a wind turbine. We patted it down as best we could and looked around. The great hall, with its marble pillars, no longer held an armchair and fireplace.

Instead, two striped deckchairs and a cocktail bar awaited us on a bank of sand.

Awe filled Marina's face. She took off her rucksack and her Dr Martens. "After the scorching heat out there and the boob sweat underneath this catsuit, this is exactly what I need. Come on."

I started after her, then lurched to a halt at the clip-clop of hooves across the floor and a whinny. Joy bubbled in me.

"Nightfall." I rushed to the black stallion, whose trust I'd gained to win access to the inner halls of the library.

He whinnied again, nuzzling his silken head against me.

I smiled up at his rider. "Hello, Calypso."

Calypso slid down from the horse, taking care her blade runners didn't strike him. "Hello, druid. I had a feeling I might see you both today." Not a scrap of makeup covered her skin. Crescent shadows pooled under her eyes, and her braids were untidy as if her mind had been too busy to care about mere appearance. Tonight, she wore a tracksuit rather than a trouser suit. "I've been preparing for your arrival."

Marina gave the deckchairs one last longing look and inched over.

"You have come to help your friend, empath," said Calypso. "Rosalie Verma couldn't have hoped for a better ally for her daughter than you. Perhaps that is why she laid down her life without regrets. And yet your path within these hallowed walls won't be easy, Marina Ambrose. I hope you can draw on your inner strength when the night seems dark. First, your trial. Because no soul may enter these hallowed halls unless the library deems you worthy."

I shuddered. Blind courage when it came to myself was one thing, but I wouldn't survive if anything happened to Marina. She was my found family, as important to me as my biological family. "Let me do this for her."

Calypso shook her head. "This is the empath's burden to carry. Each of us has a part to play for good to prevail."

Marina gave me a bright smile. She pulled out a four-leaf clover from her bra to match the newly tattooed one on her wrist. It peeled away from her clammy skin. "See? I came prepared. I have luck on my side."

Nerves churned in the pit of my stomach. I'd move heaven and hell to help her if she needed me. I didn't give a damn about the rules.

"That's the spirit, empath," said Calypso.

Marina frowned, suddenly uncertain. Then great lumps of marble rained down on us as the ceiling crumbled.

"Marina!" I surged forward.

Dust and stone fell around us, yet Calypso, Nightfall and I were unharmed as if the library had carved out an island of safety for us amidst the carnage. As if it intended only to attack Marina.

Calypso's hand clamped around my arm like a vice. "Breathe, druid. It will soon be over."

I fought to calm myself. "Libraries are places of safety and comfort. They aren't capable of doing real harm."

"Actually, this one can." Calypso's cheerful voice contrasted with the horror painted on my best friend's face. "But Marina Ambrose isn't on its hit list. She might lose the tip of a finger or two, maybe a toe, but no need to fear any real damage."

My insides twisted as Marina executed a roly-poly to escape plummeting concrete. Her fitness regimen of dance classes, swinging on bedroom poles and the odd walk to buy wine didn't make her especially strong, but it did make her agile. Although, the catsuit impeded her full range of movement.

"You can do it." I gave her a thumbs up, resisting every sinew in my body that strained to help her.

"I have seen hundreds of trials staged by the Celestial Library during my time as the Custodian, and one thing is always the same," said Calypso. "The library is fixated on what we do when we are isolated and whether we choose to protect strangers. I think it's symbolic of the library's own loneliness. It holds the stories of countless beings. It sees what happens across galaxies. And yet its halls are almost always quiet."

Nightfall whinnied and tossed his mane.

Calypso eyeballed him. "Apart from your racket, Nightfall."

By now, Marina looked green around the gills. My own feet might have been steady, but the floor beneath Marina rocked like the deck of a ship on the high seas. The striped deckchairs lay in wretched pieces amongst the rubble. Slithers of night crept into the great hall through cracks in the floor and ceiling.

Marina leapt over them in survival mode, but her exertion had taken a toll. Her leaps were smaller, her breath came faster, and the fierce determination on her face slipped into hopelessness with every passing second.

How could she bring this to an end?

I scanned the room, my pulse thundering. When I had faced my trial to gain entry to the Celestial Library, I'd protected Nightfall with a cushion of wind ahead of myself, gaining the horse's and library's trust in the process.

But Marina was an empath, not a warrior. Her skills were based on intuition and emotions, not on the elements or raw physicality. She couldn't piece this broken hall together. She didn't have a shield like my werepigeon brother, Ezra's teleporting skills or speed like Orpheus, the vampire. What could the library possibly expect of her?

Then I remembered Faeza's advice. *Approaching the library with a selfish heart is a fool's errand.*

I blinked as a fine layer of dust covered my head and hoodie. We weren't protected anymore. We were sitting ducks. I swallowed hard and spun to face Calypso. "You knew this was coming. That's why you didn't wear your posh clothes."

Calypso's brown eyes gleamed. "The library and I can read each other's thoughts. It's not always detailed. More a vague understanding of our mental trajectories. A bit like having a sibling. I know its patterns, but it can still surprise me." A blanket of dust had turned her black dreadlocks grey and dulled her smooth skin, like a premonition of who she would become four decades into the future—a badass granny with blade runner prosthetics who awed neighbourhood children. "I had an inkling it would get messy. Expensive dry-cleaning bills make me grumpy, but this tracksuit can be tossed into a forty-degree wash and spin cycle, no problem."

Her talk of laundry was so casual I wanted to shake her. She didn't even attempt to dodge the falling debris. Neither did she bat an eyelid at the crumbling of the ceiling, hand-painted with images of angels and cherubs.

I whirled around to track Marina's progress, more concerned about her fate than my own. We stood ten metres apart, maybe more. The ground had become a patchwork of broken, uneven slabs and nothingness. A crack sounded as the pink-veined pillars gave out at last, like the spilling of sugared candy as they disintegrated, bringing the ceiling down above our heads.

Marina's blue eyes widened as our gaze met, revealing her worry not for herself, but me. Resolve sparked in her. She kissed the cross that she wore on her neck.

Then she took a leap of faith.

My best friend, who always managed to find her courage —sprang across the floor, where the void had opened up, and darkness waited. She propelled herself onto the patch of dwindling ground I occupied, pressing Calypso and me down as her body shielded us from further debris.

Sweat lined her face. "Get on the horse, both of you."

I shook my head. "He'll never make it."

Calypso watched us, an enigmatic smile on her lips.

My heart slammed against my ribcage. Soon there would be no ground left.

"I have a hunch." Marina stood and coaxed Nightfall over, deadly focus in her eyes. "Hurry."

Calypso sprang onto Nightfall, though he didn't wear a saddle, and pulled me up behind her. I wrapped my arms around her waist and clenched the horse with my thighs, but they were like jelly. I should have done more lunges and squats when I'd had the chance. I shuffled forward to make space for Marina.

She shook her head. "He can't carry the weight of three."

"What about you?" I cried out. A jagged piece of concrete came from nowhere. I raised a hand to send my winds to flick it away from her, but my powers fizzled, blocked by the cunning library. The stone scraped her cheek, and a cut bloomed like a rose in its wake. My fear amplified. Was I really unable to help her?

"Trust me." She stepped through the cloud of dust to Nightfall's head. Her lips formed a word I strained to hear. "Fly."

Beneath my dangling leg, the horse's flank shuddered. Where it had been a sleek satin to touch, it rippled. Plumes of black feathers emerged from his sides.

I gasped, rearranging my legs to accommodate the wings. They began to beat, a caress of feathers at odds with the scream wrenched from my throat. I shook Calypso. "Do something. We're not leaving her behind."

The Custodian remained stoic, in cahoots with the library.

Nightfall soared into the air, leaving my best friend amidst the collapsing hall.

Marina smiled and clasped her hands to her heart as we rose higher in the air. Her face shone with pure love. She took solace in our escape, even if it meant her own doom.

A wail wrenched from my throat.

"Keep your knickers on, druid," said Calypso.

At that very moment, a strange sound met our ears, cutting through the beating of Nightfall's wings—it was like the shuffling of poker chips at a casino. Nightfall hovered in the air as the great hall rebuilt itself around us, piecemeal.

I held back tears of relief as the floor around Marina repaired itself. The pillars re-emerged from pools of candy-pink dust. The painted cherubs and angels danced on the ceiling once more, and the deckchairs returned to their splendid form. The cracks knitted together as if their creation had been merely a temporary blip of the imagination. Dust from the great hall and our bodies faded away, leaving us squeaky clean.

Beneath us, Marina clapped in glee. "I did it."

Nightfall landed, retracting his wings.

I ran to Marina, enveloping her in a hug, the kind of never-ending hug that rocked back and forth. "You stubborn, brilliant woman. How did you know Nightfall could fly?"

Marina's eyes twinkled. Only her catsuit showed evidence of her toils, with a rip on her right knee and at her hip. "I thought he looked a little chubby around the middle when we said hello. I figured there was more to him than met the eye."

"Of course there is. That horse was animated by Rajika Verma," said Calypso.

Nightfall's hooves danced with glee.

"We're practically family, Nightfall," I muttered.

Marina hopped from one foot to the other in elation, still

high on adrenalin. Either that or she needed a wee. "So, did I pass?"

The Custodian nodded. "Yes, Marina Ambrose, you proved you have an unselfish heart. The inner sanctum awaits."

3

Marina had a handful of healthy fetishes, and libraries were one of them. Her jaw hit the ground at the sight of endless rows of cherrywood shelving holding first editions and lost tomes. She browsed without hurry, knowing that neither Calypso nor I would scold her for her excitement. Only a pitiful soul could walk in the Celestial Library without awe, and there was nothing pitiful about Marina. She burst with colour from the roots of her rainbow hair to the purple goth nail varnish on her toes. Her love for life and learning seeped out of every pore.

The sound of Nightfall cantering through the library faded into the background as I turned my attention to the bookshelves myself. One particular volume sprang forward as if it had been pushed under my nose by invisible fingers, startling me. As thick as an encyclopaedia, it had a chestnut-brown leather cover and gold embossed lettering on its spine. I tilted my head to read the lettering.

A GENEOLOGY OF THE EUROPEAN OTHERWORLD

My heart pounded as the book shuffled towards me of its

own accord and then tipped into my hand. It was held together by a crimson ribbon and blanketed in a thin layer of dust. I blew gently to dislodge the dust and tugged on the ribbon. Brittle parchment pages opened to reveal a hand-inked family tree, with clouds of annotations filling any white space.

One word leapt out at me.

Verma.

How strange for a record of our family to be tucked away in this place amongst the stars for all of perpetuity. The spiky cursive lettering made reading painstaking. I sucked in my breath and traced my finger down the lines of ink that wove up and down the page, wishing I hadn't pooh-poohed the optometrist when she had suggested reading glasses on my last visit. My entire family was represented here—Mum, Dad, Sahil and me—together with Mum's French family from Brittany, names I recalled from Mum's patchy retellings of her past. There was my grandmother, Rajika, and my grandfather, Sohail Verma, after whom Sahil had been named. Each name was followed by a bracket denoting date of birth and date of demise, where that had already happened.

Tears filled my eyes at Mum's date of death, but I read on, anxious to soak up all the knowledge.

My parents had hidden the Otherworld from me until I reached middle-age.

There was so much still for me to learn.

I attempted to take a picture with my mobile phone, but however hard I tried, the image blurred into an undecipherable mess. Instead, I doubled down to absorb all the information, frowning. My great-grandparents had two children: their daughter Rajika and a son called Rajiv. The bracket that followed his name noted his birthdate to be 1933.

But there was no date of passing.

I squinted at the family tree, light-headed from the discovery. My legendary grandmother had a brother I hadn't known about. And he lived. I screwed up my face as the creaky cogs in my maths brain churned. That would make him eighty-eight years old.

A voice at my shoulder made me slam the book shut. I spun around.

The Custodian's eyes lingered on it. She blew out her breath in a puff of irritation, then stuck out her hand. "Oh, hell. Hand it over."

There the senate went again, pretending to protect us by hiding the truth. Didn't they realise by now that knowledge armed us to make better decisions in the future?

I jerked the book out of her reach, my heart beating out of my chest. "Not a chance."

Hiding dirty laundry meant it piled up all the same. I was living proof of this fact. Dirty laundry was the bane of my life since joining the Otherworld. I'd had enough of family secrets. She could spill the beans or prise it out of my cold, dead hands.

Calypso's eyes narrowed, and she shook a balled fist but not at me. She shook it at the building like a crazy woman.

"Are you okay?" I soothed, but I took a step back in case she was on mushrooms. Who knew what the diet consisted of in the Celestial Library? Come to think of it, I hadn't once seen the Custodian eat. It was possible she existed on fumes, and it had messed with her mind.

She rolled her eyes. "No, I'm not okay. There it goes again, sticking its nose where it's not wanted."

I followed her gaze to the bookshelf that shuffled the book towards me. "The library?"

"Yes, of course, the library. What else would I be talking about? There is a time for knowledge and a time for patience, but this mischievous beast of a library likes to alleviate its boredom by skipping forward a few steps." She glared at the bookshelf. "It really is an awful habit."

The bookshelf behind her launched a stealth attack, sending a steady stream of book missiles directly at her.

I leapt out of the way. "Look out."

She batted them away with a haughty flick without a care for broken spines or torn pages. "It'll have to do better than that."

The books flapped in what looked remarkably like an F-you dance, then returned to their positions with a hop, skip and jump.

I locked my eyes on Calypso. "Did my grandmother have a brother called Rajiv?"

She sighed. "I see Pandora's Box is open. You already got to the good part, huh?"

"But why have I heard nothing of him?"

Dad had never mentioned a peep about his uncle, nor had Echo. I would have liked to have travelled to India to meet him. We could have wired him money or sent him a haul of Cadbury's chocolate and invited him to come and stay with us for the holidays. Families were supposed to stick together, weren't they? What possible reason could Dad have had for keeping this from me?

The Custodian shrugged. "Rajiv was a black sheep. He wasn't easy to work with, but he was brilliant. Who did you think your grandmother's illustrator was all those years before your father took up the role? It was he who drew Nightfall. But Rajiv had many flaws. He didn't like how your grandmother received all the praise. Being an animator is an ostentatious role. An illustrator is altogether different. They work all cooped up, forever at the whim of the animator. Rajiv didn't like being in the supporting role. He wanted the reins."

"So my grandmother just abandoned him?"

That didn't fit with what I knew of Rajika. She was a badass. She fought for her family and her community. Why would she have walked away from her brother?

I'd been tempted to walk away from Sahil, but I couldn't imagine forsaking him entirely. Sometimes my eyes watered from biting my tongue around him, but he was still my brother. Every werepigeon feather of him and every ambitious bone. He was my kin.

Calypso's brow creased. "It was before my time, druid. My knowledge is gleaned from stories passed down through the ages and the odd snippet in the dusty books held in the library. By all accounts, it was a relief for your grandmother when your father's illustrator skills emerged."

"All the same, I would have liked to have known Rajiv. To have made up my own mind about him." An idea sprang to mind. There were many perks to dating a teleporting werewolf-wizard. "Maybe Ezra can whisk me to India to find him."

"Actually, he's not in India. Once an illustrator has seen his creations come to life, seeing stagnant art on the page is a little difficult. Whatever his criticisms of your grandmother, Rajiv could never bear to be apart from her. When she came to South London, he did too. But I don't think it's a good idea for you to seek him out, Alisha. He's notoriously volatile." Calypso's gleaming, almond eyes met mine, and she held out her hand for the book again.

This time, I relinquished the book to her. After all, I had my answers. Some of them, at least.

"For what it's worth, my advice would be to steer clear of Rajiv. After all, the eternal girl has bigger fish to fry."

My mouth dropped open, and the words fell out, tiny rocks of denial. "I'm not the eternal girl."

Only those in my dragon's cave had heard Gaia's revelation.

Marina, Echo and Ezra would never have betrayed my trust. The Earth goddess had let me grow at my own pace. She guarded the secrets of the universe. She wouldn't have outed mine. Tielbu, the dragon, hid in Bulgaria still, far from the grasping fingers of the senate.

Besides, there could be no certainty I was the eternal girl. It's not that I was calling the goddess a liar. It was just that we wouldn't really know unless I stepped into a tank with the magical octopus, and I'd had quite enough of batty Wildwoods rituals, thank you very much. I'd never forget the barbaric ceremony when Mirabel and other Wildwoods girls had been forced into a tank with Kraglek, the octopus.

The truth was, I wasn't ready to be the eternal girl. I'd never be content to sit on the sidelines, but leading the whole charge was another matter entirely. I'd only succeeded so far because of my allies. The thought of having to lead the charge made me want to hide in the corner with a bottle of gin. Or at least a huge bar of Cadburys.

The Custodian smiled. "I see the shine of truth in your eyes, druid. Thank goodness you know. For a moment there, I thought I would have to explain the Chameleon Tale to you."

Lavinia's words had been branded into my head the first time I had heard them in the Wildwoods reading nook. *There will come the eternal girl, who blends in even though her talents are brighter than the sun. When Death opens the door, only the eternal girl may stop the coming Dusk, together with a disintegrating tome lost to the world.*

Calypso tossed the genealogy book across the aisle, where it slotted into place. "It took me a while to piece it together, but now it all makes sense. You passed the Celestial Library's trial with flying colours with barely a lick of magical experience. You have repeatedly outwitted, if not outgunned, immortal beings. You're the culmination of both a Hindu and a French druid line. And for all the waiting across the centuries for the eternal girl, you come in the shape of a middle-aged woman, with all the compassion and life experience that entails. It couldn't be more perfect."

Yeah, because what the world needed was a saggyboobed, rapidly ageing woman like me—who'd rather be flat on her back on the sofa eating biscuits—to save the world. The major thing I had going for me was that I actually gave a damn about the world. Too often, those with power seemed content to focus on filling their own pockets and peacocking about rather than making the world a better place.

"There is no proof I am the eternal girl," I said.

The Custodian grabbed my shoulders and squeezed. "Proof is overrated. It's self-belief and courage that will see us through. You've seen them come thick and fast: Ra, Pan, Hermes. It's only a matter of time before another god comes your way. Do you see now why you can't be distracted by Rajiv?"

A pang of regret permeated my stomach. As much as I hated to admit it, maybe the family black sheep had to wait. I already had Sahil to wrestle back from the dark side. With the Ravenmaster torn to shreds and buried in pieces, we had a window of opportunity to get my brother on our side.

What was more, Calypso was right: a new threat was rising. I could feel it in my waters.

4

When the peak of Marina's excitement at entering the inner sanctum had settled into a gentle fizz, she came to find us, her eyes wide with wonder. "It's wonderful here, but don't you ever get lonely?"

The Custodian shook her head. "Even in crowds, I've always sought out solitude. I don't need anyone else to feel whole. In fact, *solitude* is my favourite word in all the languages I know, and I can speak many. Besides, how can I be lonely? I have my books. I have my freedom. My purpose. And I have a winged horse. What more can a woman want?"

Ezra flashed into my mind. His crinkly, grey, copper-flecked eyes. The feel of his arms around me as the universe became mere molecules around us. The timbre of his voice vibrating through me when I laid my head on his bare chest in our bed. Well, technically not our bed because we hadn't moved in together. But I loved him, and I knew in my bones it was heading that way.

The Custodian frowned. "Alisha?"

"Don't mind her." Marina laughed. "She's fallen into a reverie about Ezra. I can sense the love hearts from here."

"I was not thinking about him." I blushed. "Okay, maybe I

was. But he's busy with his new dual duties as alpha of the pack and Minister for Justice on the senate. We're lucky to even spend a few waking hours together these days."

"The books in these halls have all taught me one thing. Romance spells trouble," said Calypso.

In the dying days of my marriage, I hadn't thought my calcified heart would be able to love again, but my feelings for Ezra had caught me by stealth. I believed in love again. But I also knew not to make love my everything, and I knew there were other loves that meant just as much to me as romantic love. Sisterly love, for example.

Marina grinned. "In my experience, romance—whether with a man or a woman—is always worth the trouble."

I shrugged. "When I'm with Ezra, I feel there is nothing we can't achieve."

Calypso harrumphed. "I've never liked it when a woman ties up her accomplishments with a man's. As far as I remember, it wasn't Ezra Neuhoff who triumphed over the Ravenmaster. We were all bit players that evening. It was you who were the god's literal undoing, druid. You'd do well to remember that."

A low whistle sounded.

Calypso's head jerked up as a paper plane flew towards us, made from the torn pages of a book. She plucked it out of the air and unfolded it, her brow furrowed as she deciphered the message inside, made from circled letters.

"How odd." She turned it over in her hands. "It looks like the library's messaging system, but the paper is more crinkled than usual. It must be a glitch. Still, it's come from Wildwoods, so there's no ignoring it."

I peered at the undecipherable message inside, made from circled letters. "What does it say?"

She screwed it up into a ball. "The werewolf needs you in London, druid. There's been an oddity at a shop called Black Lotus Inkings in Waterloo that he needs your help with."

"That's where I got this." Marina pointed to the clover tattoo on her wrist. "It's run by a woman called Mami. She has a velvet voice and designs tattoos to die for."

She'd wanted us to get matching tattoos but had gone ahead by herself when I wavered. I liked to think I made my own luck.

I shook my head. "I can't leave. We haven't achieved what we came for. What about the Rose of Jericho project?"

Calypso pressed her lips together. "Hurry then. Once you see what the library has to offer, maybe you'll feel better about leaving your empath friend in its care." She strode forward into the bowels of the library, through endless rows of stacked shelves, neither slowing her pace nor checking to see if we loitered. "Keep up. We have no time to lose."

Doors appeared left and right between the aisles, each different in colour and material: a dented steel one, a narrow arched one, one with the bronze carving of a mermaid on it and another decorated with constellations that flickered against a matt black swipe of paint. Odd scents caught my nose: the musky whiff of Nightfall, the scent of freshly baked bread, pungent wines and the salty ocean.

Eventually, the Custodian laid her hand against a peeling green door hidden between the aisles and whispered a Gaelic phrase. The door popped open with a sound reminiscent of the uncorking of a champagne bottle. We stepped over the stone threshold to find a small room tiled white in its entirety, with tiny slithers of window revealing the galaxies outside. It held a very basic laboratory set up: two bench tops with stools, a refrigerator, a sink, an incubator, a Bunsen burner, a microscope, test tubes, beakers and an oven. A row of lab coats and scrubs hung from a rail in the corner.

Marina placed her rucksack on the bench and looked around, her enthusiasm draining quicker than a bathtub. "Huh. It's not what I was expecting."

Calypso raised an eyebrow. "This equipment is state of the art."

"Oh, don't get me wrong. I'm very appreciative. But even with EvolveTech resources at her fingertips, Rosalie didn't manage to finish her Rose of Jericho project. This set up is a bit minimalist." Marina frowned. "And what's the oven for?"

Calypso pulled her silver-threaded dreadlocks over one shoulder and pursed her lips. "That's not an oven. At least, not *only* an oven. Although one year, according to the diaries of the 48th Custodian, it did cook a Christmas turkey."

I walked over to the gleaming oven, opened the door and peeked inside.

"Probably best not to put your head in there, Alisha. The oven has a habit of recycling objects. There's been many a body part lost in there over the decades. The senate's Defence Minister once lost his entire toupee, and it came back as a squirrel," said Calypso.

"How does it work?" I said.

"Place a slip of paper in it with your requirement. Shut the oven door. Wait until the hullaballoo stops, and then see what it spits out. You'll find you can work your way around most problems if you think inventively enough."

Marina's eyebrows shot up. "That's quite some gadget. Maybe I can see Rosalie's project through after all."

Calypso turned to me. "Now you must go."

A stab of anxiety in my stomach. "She can't stay here without me."

Marina was always my default call when anything was wrong. She could soothe my ruffled feathers or buoy me with just a few words. We were one another's support system. With her at my side, I was more than the sum of my parts.

"You can't keep going up against immortal beings without a shred of protection. Let me do this for you," said Marina. "Don't worry. I have the surgery to run. I won't be here forever."

"Forever is a relative term," said Calypso. "Time passes differently in the Celestial Library. You won't be missed at the veterinary surgery while you are working on the Rose of Jericho project. In fact, not even your boyfriend will notice you are gone. Time will pass, but it's as if the universe leaves space for you to slot right back into when you return."

Marina frowned. "That makes me sound expendable. Like it doesn't matter if I'm there or not. I quite like being the centre of Rob's universe. It makes up for all the time I've ended up dating Neanderthals who didn't know my chin from my clitoris. If I'm not there, I'd like my bloke to miss me at least."

A burst of laughter escaped me. Marina brightened up whichever room she was in, but how would she fare alone cooped up in a hidden laboratory at the Celestial Library? How could she survive alone, without even an animal at her side? "If I have to leave, let me at least animate a creature for you. A lab assistant. A listening ear. A warning system. A creature whose purpose it is to have your back. Since Rajiv was an animator, there must be some archived drawings around here."

Marina met my eyes. "No need. I'll be engrossed in work. You have to let me do this."

I turned to Calypso. "You'll take good care of her?"

She nodded. "I will."

My heart fell like a stone in a well. "Then I guess it's goodbye for now."

I unhooked Mum's necklace from around my neck, pressed it into Marina's palm and pulled her into a lingering hug.

She whispered into my ear. "I'll be all right, and so will you."

"Quickly, druid," said the Custodian. "The werewolf waits for you at the portal in Shanghai Moon."

5

Nightfall danced outside the laboratory. He gave an impatient whinny when I appeared. I leapt on his back and gripped his coarse hair as he galloped through the Celestial Library at full pelt. He came to an abrupt stop at the deckchairs in the great hall, where a lone glass of Baileys on ice waited.

I slid off his back, unsure of my next steps. The Celestial Library had no earmarked exit. Each journey to and from it was different.

Having true sight meant my eyes always had to be open to possibilities and signs from the universe. When Nightfall blew hot air from his nostrils and pushed his muzzle against my back towards the Baileys, I didn't wait. The ice clinked as I gulped the sweet concoction down, grateful for the burn of alcohol that temporarily blunted my sadness at leaving Marina behind.

The Celestial Library melted away as the liquid flowed down my throat. A sigh from Nightfall met my ears.

I gasped as I fell into a channel between the worlds, filled with surging water. A moment of shock and spluttering before I took a deep breath and settled into a steady breaststroke, that inelegant, froggy stroke beloved by middle-aged women. The current carried me forward. I kept my chin above the water, loathe to taste its depths. My skin crawled in the dank waters, and my limbs tired. I fought not to lose faith, holding on to an image of Mum at the poolside during childhood swimming lessons. My body toiled, my clothes heavy around me, my arms and legs pushing, and my breathing thin.

I squealed, startled, as a lone jellyfish coursed by, followed by a shoal of toothy, pink fish and then a gush of eels. My brain fired unhinged thoughts. Slimy bodies next to me. Slithering through me. Devouring me. A sticky end far from home. My body floating in nothingness. Nobody to mourn me.

I froze with fear.

Swim, you silly cow, said the logical part of my brain.

"That's Alisha," came Faeza's voice. "She's nearly through."

My loved ones waited for me in Shanghai Moon: Ezra, Echo and the foxes, all willing me on, willing me to be safe. I heard them, a cheering, a coaxing, and it chased away my doubt.

I had made this journey before. I could do it again. This time, there were no half-measures. I started front crawl and dipped my head under the black frothing swirl despite the eels and toothy fish and the electric glow of the jellyfish. I pushed until bile crept up my throat. My nostrils filled with the scent of exotic teas and Chinese takeaway just before the channel spat me out on the floor of Shanghai Moon. I landed in a heap; a rag doll drenched from head to toe.

Ezra's strong arms closed around me. His worried voice rumbled through his chest. "Quick, get a towel. She looks half-dead."

I spluttered, leaning into the familiar contours of his chest, and peeled my eyes open. "I just need a minute. I'm fine."

"I beg to differ," said Echo. "You look like you've just been pushed through a birth canal. You're lucky not to have a cone head."

Ezra gripped me tighter and tucked my head under his chin. My wet body soaked his crisp, white shirt. He'd swapped his T-shirts for dress shirts since becoming a senator. But he still didn't quite fit the mould of the other senators. He'd grown his hair longer in subconscious rebellion. It curled at his collar, and he raked his hands through it when it slipped into his grey, copper-flecked eyes.

"Damn it," he said. "Always taking risks, Alisha. If something happened to you…"

I stood up, supported by him, my knees shaky and my clothes clinging to me. Heat coursed through me as his eyes scoured every inch of me, checking for injuries.

Faeza trained her eyes on the Ace of Wands, the portal card Marina had chosen. "Where is she? Where's Marina?"

"She stayed behind." My voice was flat.

Echo unleashed a fierce growl.

Ezra's muscles tensed. "She what?"

"She's working on Mum's necklace. You know what she was like after our run-in with the Ravenmaster. She wouldn't take no for an answer. If she combines the healing properties of the Rose of Jericho with the necklace, she thinks I'll be safer."

"Let's look on the bright side," said Echo. "Marina Ambrose passed the trial, and she is not dead."

Faeza sighed. "Visits to the Celestial Library are supposed to be fleeting for all but the Custodian. We must keep the portal card safe, or Marina won't be able to return. I'll lock it away."

"Let me take it to the Wildwoods vault. There is no more secure place in London," said Ezra.

Faeza shook her head. "The card has to stay here. It is dangerous to move an open portal. Marina could be discombobulated or her spirit torn from her body. Or her head hair could end up on her bottom. You get the picture."

That mental image was going to be hard to shake.

"Lead me to your personal vault, fox. I will check it is secure," Echo purred.

Fei Yen returned with her hands full. She handed me a threadbare towel and a steaming cup of green tea and began mopping the floor. "Our safe place is under the mattress, leopard, but we will not keep the card there. Rest assured, there is no safer place than with us. Foxes are hoarders. We have a hundred different tarot card sets in this shop. For someone to compromise the portal, they would have to know exactly which card Marina had picked."

I wrapped myself in the towel. "I tried to talk her out of it. I would have stayed with her, but I got your message, Ezra."

He frowned. "What message?"

"The paper aeroplane that Calypso read to me in the Celestial Library."

His frown deepened. "I didn't send a message, hellfire."

"Then why are you here?"

The copper in his eyes sparked. "I came here because I'd had enough of ministers bickering and missed you." Ezra puffed out his chest. "The senate's considering a new law to allow only sanctioned trips to the Celestial Library. It can't come too soon, as far as I'm concerned."

My eyebrows snapped together. The power must have gone to his head. There was no way my freedom-loving, teleporting Ezra would have put his weight behind this before he became a senator. "You can't be serious. A law to ban access to knowledge unless peculiars have permission? Can you hear yourself?"

He flushed and pushed his hands into his pockets when all I wanted him to do was hold me.

I turned imploring eyes on Fei Yen and Faeza. "It doesn't feel right. If the message wasn't from Ezra, who was it from? Can't you open a new portal so I can go back and get her?"

Faeza's slight hands made butterfly movements. Fei Yen dropped the mop and held her wife's hands. They shook their heads, speaking in unison, like a mantra. "It is not possible. One portal is risky. Two is suicide."

"How about a message?" I turned to Ezra. "There must be some way the senate gets messages to Calypso."

Ezra nodded. "There is a rudimentary system at Wildwoods. But if Calypso is a bad egg and suspects she has been discovered, it could put Marina in more danger. You need to tell me exactly what was in the message."

Either someone else had sent the message, or Calypso had manufactured a reason for me to leave Marina behind. I had trusted the Custodian and considered the Celestial Library to be both a safe haven and a place of truth.

But history taught us that the library could be compromised. My own grandmother had died that way.

I shivered. In trying to protect me, my best friend had left herself defenceless.

But there was one more person I trusted enough to ask for a view on the Custodian.

I PICKED up the telephone to call Orpheus.

He had his hands full during casino night at his gentleman's club in Charing Cross. He'd confided to me that it wasn't the drunk human punters taking heady risks with their money that he worried about. It was the vampires he had to keep a close eye on. A smashed glass and a drop of humdrum blood were all it took to send some of the younger vampires into a frenzy, and there had been more than one occasion on which he'd had to wipe the minds of all the revellers.

It was tiring work, which ruined the night's takings and made him seem a killjoy, but he had strict rules about who could be drained. The Metropolitan Police and Her Majesty's Prison Service liked to keep the vampires greased up. It killed two birds with one stone: vampire hunger and preventing the waste of taxpayers' money on the pricks who didn't deserve a second chance.

Only I thought everyone deserved a second chance—even pricks.

What was more, my ex-husband had lost our savings due to gambling. I would have preferred Orpheus to have staged a book club evening over a casino night. He was a man who read and would do womankind a service by encouraging men to follow his example. Men who read were hot.

Not that he was having any of it, judging by the raucous noises coming down the phone line. Orpheus's voice boomed, impatient and gruff. "Don't be silly, Alisha. I grant you that there are question marks hanging over the Prime Sorcerer's intentions, but Calypso is entirely trustworthy. I looked into her background myself before she became the Custodian. I'd stake my life on it."

That was an unfortunate term for a vampire to use— especially this vampire, given his history.

Orpheus sighed. "It was a turn of phrase, Alisha. And no, I'm no longer suicidal."

I grinned. He was lucky I hadn't used my usual trick of thinking about random things just to derail his train of thought. I didn't know yet how to keep him out of my mind. I sure as hell wasn't going to make it easy for him to be in there. Call it a defensive manoeuvre. Meat and two veg. Python. Sausage. Beaver cleaver.

Judging by his tone, his eyebrows had disappeared into his hairline. "What on earth are you doing?"

Oops. At least I'd taken his mind off his depression. What were friends for? "Sorry. The thing is, people change. They can be corrupted, their priorities change, or trauma drives them to take a different track."

"You and the empath are family. You must do what you think it right. The bottom line is I trust Calypso. Unlike you, she's not an open book, but she is honourable."

"Thanks for the advice." I bit my lip. His certainty eased my anxiety, but that still left the question of who sent the message. I had to follow the clues.

Orpheus huffed. "Of course, you're going to follow the trail. I can't leave the club." A pause and then a gruff edge to his voice. "I take it the wolf is with you at the occult shop?"

Ezra and Echo prowled the shop floor while Fei Yen and Faeza scurried around them.

"Yep," I said.

A crash of glasses made him curse. "I have to go. Don't do anything stupid."

The line went dead.

I cleaned myself up and changed into a new pair of jeans and a jumper I'd left at Shanghai Moon. In fact, I'd left a toothbrush, matching underwear and a change of clothes at all my usual hangouts: Marina's, Ezra's parents' cottage, Dad's, Shanghai Moon, and even Ezra's office at Wildwoods and the pack farmhouse. Anyone would think I was a hussy, not a stealth heroine. By now, I anticipated ending up with some kind of body residue or murky fluid on me every time I got into a scrape. At this point, even bathing in bin juice wouldn't surprise me. One of the advantages of becoming a peculiar at forty was there wasn't much that could make me queasy. As a young woman, even a rogue fart would have made me retch. Now, I could fight off an army of witches' rats and rip chunks of flesh from a seething god if that was what the moment required.

Who needed grades to track progress when our own

reactions to the world taught us all we needed to know? Although, as a teacher, I would be keeping that particular thought to myself.

My focus in the classroom had been lacking these past months as my brain was wired to look for the next threat. Just as anticipated, here I was, with damp, smelly hair and squelching trainers chasing down a lead with Ezra and Echo.

"I'm ready," I said. If we couldn't open another portal or send a message to Calypso, then there was nothing for it but to head to the tattoo shop.

The world turned monochrome, and my breathing shallowed as Ezra teleported us across London. His lingering anger showed in the way his body didn't mould entirely to mine. When the cobbled street solidified beneath us, and he released me from the circle of his arms, his hand lingered on the small of my back, a promise we would reconcile.

Echo vomited up a puddle of partially digested dumplings. "You barely held me, wolf. I could have ended up in the Thames, and then where would you be?"

Ezra raised an eyebrow. "Next time, I'll be more alert to your need for closeness, leopard."

"Well, it has been a long time since I've had the pleasure of a harem of moggies." Echo sniffed the ground, his tail swishing. "This family works too hard."

The starless sky lay thick with clouds above us. I rubbed Echo's ears, and within seconds, a satisfied purr rumbled through him, more Ferrari than pussycat.

Waterloo was many things. The name of a battle at which Napoleon was defeated in 1815. A Belgian town where said battle took place. The third busiest station on the London Underground. And my personal favourite: an ABBA song which used the Napoleon battle as a metaphor for love. Because love often meant war.

It was also a district in London where Black Lotus Inkings was situated.

Ezra peered at his phone under a flickering streetlight. "Black Lotus Inkings should be just around the corner. According to this entry, it's been up and running for about a year."

I bit my lip. "Maybe we should reconsider. We could call Jameson first thing to see if he has any intel on the shop before blundering in. Isn't it you who says I should be less spontaneous?"

"I also know you won't get a wink's sleep while you're worrying about Marina. And the detective would be the first one to charge into this shop if he thought it would help her," said Ezra.

Echo stalked the pavement, nose down, whiskers twitching. He raised his head and looked over his shoulder at us. "I can smell beer and piss and fish leading away from the river. It's most unusual."

I sighed. "We go in carefully."

"Agreed," said Ezra.

Echo bounded ahead of us, as careful as a bull in a china shop.

I pinched the bridge of my nose. "Dad's working on my catalogue of creatures. I don't have it with me."

"This is a recon mission, not a battle. We'll be fine. Besides, you've got other skills up your sleeve. Not to mention life experience. If you can inspire a room of adults at your evening classes when most humdrums are bingeing a boxset, you've got this covered." Ezra paused. "I've..."

"Spit it out. What's on your mind?"

"I've always wondered why you stayed with your husband as long as you did."

I frowned, my eyes trained ahead on Echo's leaping form in the shadows. My body brushed Ezra's as we walked side by side. "Shall we pick this up later? We should probably focus on the shadows and the rats and the leopard charging ahead."

Ezra raked a hand through his hair. "Yeah, I know. We don't seem to have much time alone anymore. I decided not to wait when I have something to say."

I sighed. "I stayed with Alex because I thought I could change him. I was wrong."

"You infuriate me sometimes, but I wouldn't want to change a hair on your head."

His words made my skin tingle, but I kept my voice light. Now wasn't the time to get mushy. "Just as well. I have really stubborn hair."

He laughed, and the tension evaporated between us.

Maybe he was right. Did waiting for the right time to say something ever really change the outcome? Maybe all of us would be better off saying what was on our minds.

We lost sight of Echo around a corner, and both of us instinctively picked up our speed. Ezra undid the top button of his shirt for easier access to his charm necklace, and I rubbed my hands together, ready to channel the familiar tingle, wishing I had my catalogue of creatures with me.

The leopard came bounding back, a scowl etched on his handsome face. "The shop is lit, although it is past midnight. There is a beautiful woman in there."

I shrugged. "There are beautiful women everywhere if you look closely. Beauty isn't just the outer shell. It's passion and knowing. It's scars and wrinkles that tell stories. It's the light in the eyes, a tilt of the head, a guiding hand or the twitch of a mouth."

Emerald eyes glinted. "You misunderstand, Alisha. The beautiful woman saw through the glamour. She saw me as I am. Not as a Bengal cat, but as a leopard. Come. There is magic afoot."

Every nerve in my body told me to turn back. But when Marina swam before my eyes—her rainbow hair, her ridiculous unicorn tattoo, her ocean-blue eyes—the choice had already been made the first time I met her. Sisters would never choose anything but to run towards the fire for each other

6

———————

Tucked away between a rundown sushi takeaway and a vintage clothes shop, Black Lotus Inkings glowed, even at this late hour. A grubby window made up the front facade. The name of the tattoo studio hung in neon blue lettering there, suspended within a black metal heart. Inside the shop, uneven, turquoise walls reminded me of the Atlantic Ocean. An unchained, rusting red motorcycle leaned against the shop front.

But it was the African woman who stood beside the counter that captured my attention. She had large, steely eyes —so dark they could have been black—set in an unwrinkled face. Her lips were mauve, and her fingernails short. Her thick, natural hair had bounce and length. A floor-length dress clung to her shapely body. Though the dress brushed the floor, it did nothing to preserve her modesty. Made of fisherman's nets, it allowed her dark areola to poke through. My eyes dropped to a tattoo of a snake that started under her cleavage and ended just above her belly button. She wore silk panties under the dress rather than the big cotton granny ones I preferred.

She was both beautiful and terrifying.

"Wowsers." Ezra's mouth fell open like a fish on a hook.

I elbowed him in the ribs, although, to be honest, she had the same effect on me.

The woman assessed each of us in turn. Wolf. Leopard. Druid. Her hooded eyes lingered on me.

There could be no doubt she had true sight. I ran my fingers over Echo's thick coat. Stroking him always calmed my nerves. "Echo, stay out here in case something goes wrong. No wandering off to hunt poodles or spaniels."

The leopard lifted his chin. "Your protection is my first priority. If she harms a hair on your head, I will tear her limb from limb."

I took a deep breath. "I wouldn't expect anything less."

Ezra issued clipped instructions, a vein throbbing in his cheek. "This is a fact-finding mission only. Strictly no wind powers, animation or kickboxing, Alisha. I mean it. Stay behind me."

I pushed ahead of him through the decaying door. I liked him wanting to protect me, but I was strong enough to protect myself too. Although, having him as a backup helped my confidence.

The pungent smell of rubbing alcohol hit me. I gave the woman a bright smile, deciding to suss her out before putting our cards on the table. "Sorry to disturb you at this late hour."

"Welcome," said the woman. "I am Mami."

Her voice was as smooth as honey, just as Marina had said. It was impossible to guess her age. She held her head high with the confidence of someone who had lived long enough to know herself. She was the kind of woman you hoped your husband would never meet.

Next to me, Ezra shuddered.

I focused on Mami, taking care not to stare at the nipples that stood literally front and centre. They'd take my eyes out if I got any closer. "We wondered if you'd spotted our friend walking past."

Mami's smile revealed pearly teeth that contrasted with deep brown skin. "We're not in a dusty village. You'll have to give me more to go on than that."

"You'd have noticed her if you'd seen her," I said. "She's almost forty. About five foot six inches and curvy. Has armfuls of tattoos and hair that is pink at the crown, turquoise in the middle and purple at the ends. She never goes out without lashings of eyeliner."

Mami's dark eyes gleamed. "The woman you speak of came in here a few months ago for a four-leaf clover tattoo. I remember her well. She didn't flinch once, which tells me she's probably into kink. You must be the best friend she mentioned when she was in the chair. She said you both needed luck but that you had refused matching tattoos." She swivelled to point her boobs at Ezra. "What about you, sweetie? Fancy some ink? I think you'd enjoy the feel of my hands on you."

Ezra flushed. His words jerked out as if his self-confidence had drained out of him. "Nope. No. Not for me. Thank you, ma'am."

I stared at him.

Ezra—orphan, teleporting werewolf-wizard, seeker, now pack alpha, and the senate's Minister for Justice—who had learned long ago to be true to his own compass, floundered in front of this woman like a pubescent boy.

"Suit yourself. I'm here if you change your mind." Mami's eyes narrowed. She turned around, her buttocks on glorious display through the fisherman's net dress. "It's not every day I come across a wolf, a leopard and a druid on the streets of London."

There was the proof of her peculiar nature. My senses heightened. "You have true sight?" My conversations with Fei Yen and Faeza taught me that peculiars didn't always choose to be part of the Wildwoods community. My friend Flinar's experiences as an elf showed that they weren't always welcomed.

"Are you new to London?" Ezra's words were stilted as if only sheer focus propelled them out. "It is rare for a peculiar to live in this city without our paths crossing."

Mami's black eyes held his gaze for a long second that made *me* the outsider. "There is nothing new about me. I am as old as time itself." She smiled as if making light of herself. "At least, that's how it feels sometimes. I have been in London long enough to know the colours of its skies and the desires of those who walk its streets. I followed the ships that brought my people here."

Well, that was a weird thing for a tattoo artist to say. She must have been one of those poetic types who made and lived their art and wove pretty words together like a string of pearls. Why else would she be dressed in a fishing net?

I cast an eye over the framed photos of her tattoo art on the walls. An intricate blue whale caught my eye. "Do you have any peculiar talents, Mami? You are obviously a talented artist."

"That's kind of you to say."

I blinked as the snake on her stomach tilted its head and then put it down to a trick of the light or exhaustion. These days I was always either exhausted or in need of a burst of caffeine.

"If that is all, the hour is late, and I have a guest waiting for me at home," said Mami. "It was nice to meet you both at last."

My eyebrows snapped together. "That makes it sounds like you were expecting us to come."

I reached into my memory for the wording of the message Calypso had read out. The summons. *The werewolf needs you in London. There's been an oddity at a shop called Black Lotus Inkings in Waterloo that he needs your help with.* Ezra had already ruled himself out as the sender of the message, and Orpheus had gone to great pains to vouch for Calypso.

Could Mami herself have lured us here? The Ravenmaster had infiltrated Wildwoods once. Why not her?

Mami arched an eyebrow. "You dare to pick apart my words? You came here to enquire after your friend—a favour well after closing time. And yet I see you have decided to leave your politeness at the door, as well as your leopard. Not only that, but you come in here stinking of your swim with otherworldly eels. At the very least, you could have covered the stench with some talcum powder or perfume."

Ezra snatched my hand as if Mami's weird hold on him had been broken. "I don't like this. I don't like it one bit."

A chill ran up my spine. I hadn't even told Ezra the details of my swim back through the portal yet. How did this strange woman know about it? She had a point, though. I definitely needed a shower, and there wasn't any judgement in her tone, at least.

My intuition was like a hot poker, urging us to flee, but my curiosity won out. "How did you know where I was?"

Mami's mauve lips curved into a sly smile. She shrugged. "It's not exactly a mystery. I could smell it on you the moment you walked through my door. It's very distinctive. Very starry. A bit zesty. A bit pongy. With a swirl of Baileys on ice."

The Celestial Library was a myth to most people in the Otherworld. A slice of history they read about in textbooks. The journey to the Celestial Library was unique to each adventurer, yet Mami had homed in on the details of my passage.

She was an unknown entity who was armed with knowledge. And that made her dangerous.

Mami pouted. "It was very naughty of you to start our relationship based on a lie. We all know where your friend is, don't we, Alisha Verma? She's alone without your protection at the Celestial Library. All alone, unable to be the present, loving friend you've always relied on."

My blood ran cold.

I swallowed the urge to grab the earring display on the counter and flick them at Mami one by one until she told me everything she knew. But spontaneity in the Otherworld could lead you to the grave. We still didn't know what we were dealing with. "How do you know my name?"

Mami's tone was light and playful. "I always remember a face. And you and your father are so alike."

Ezra gave a warning growl. He cupped my waist, ready to teleport us out of there at the first sign of danger.

I willed him not to haul us out of there. He'd said it himself; this was a fact-finding mission. "You know my dad?"

"A long time ago, we went to art school together, didn't he tell you?" Mami's soft laugh echoed through the studio. "I'd love to meet him again. Yes. That's exactly what I plan to do."

Why did her words sound like a threat? She was smiling. She hadn't used any violent words. But the gleam in her eyes made me want to scoop up my loved ones and slap tracking devices on them that I could monitor twenty-four hours a day.

Love could make you crazy.

"It's time to go," said Ezra in my ear.

I met Mami's gaze and held it for an uncomfortably long moment, knowing she had summoned us here and held all the cards. "Goodnight, Mami."

"Goodnight, druid." She spun on her heel, her sandals slapping against the floor, and headed into the back of the shop as if we weren't any threat at all.

We left the shop, minds whirling. The night air welcomed us into its cool embrace as we stepped onto the road, illuminated only by the streetlamps and the ominous blue glow of the tattoo parlour. Echo paced, his swishing tail carving shapes as he went. His body language changed at our approach.

He rushed to us and rubbed himself against our legs. "Who is she?"

"Trouble," I said.

A hiss from Echo. "There's something you need to see. Or rather someone."

I groaned. "Our priority is Marina right now."

Emerald eyes demanded I change my mind. "We can't leave this little one out here alone."

The city slept. Instead of getting some much-needed beauty sleep or upping my night class earnings, here I was, chasing ghosts from the Otherworld. Wildwoods was going to have to start paying me a salary to make up for all the lost earnings. We followed as Echo padded a few metres down the street to a bench within a recess shrouded by an overgrown evergreen bush.

There sat a little girl, no more than six, clutching an empty polystyrene cup. Tendrils escaped her messy, blonde ponytail. Her blue eyes were wide and fearful. Her little legs, clad in striped tights, swung. When she saw us, she shrank back.

I bent down to her height. "Whoa, darling."

She wrinkled her nose at me, or rather, the stench of me. "Daddy said we should have a shower every day."

I nodded. "Your daddy sounds like a sensible man. Where is he? It's very late to be out here by yourself."

The little girl pressed her lips together.

"You don't talk to strangers, huh?" I said.

"Her name is Annie. She told me her father went into Black Lotus Inkings to make an appointment and never came out," said Echo.

Annie's words burst out in a wave of enthusiasm. "That cat's my friend. He miaows a lot. My daddy sent him to me when I got scared of the dark."

My heart contracted. She had a pink rain jacket, but it

wouldn't shield her from the biting wind as the night reached its apex. "Annie, your daddy wouldn't want you to stay out here. It's cold."

Annie stared at me, her blue eyes narrowed in suspicion. "Who told you my name?"

I pointed at Echo. "The magic cat."

She nodded as if that explained everything, made a clicking sound with her tongue and beamed when Echo responded by coming to her side.

Ezra knelt and raked a hand through the hair that fell into his eyes. "Hi, Annie. I'm Ezra. How about we take you down to the police station, and we can call your mummy?"

She shook her head. "Daddy told me to stay on the bench. The magic cat can keep me warm. He's good at that. I like his purr too."

"What if the magic cat comes to the police station with us? We can ask the nice officers to get you another hot chocolate while they find your parents?" I said.

Echo miaowed and rested his head on Annie's lap.

She considered my offer before breaking into a gap-toothed smile. "With marshmallows?"

"Deal." I rose to my feet and held out my hand.

Annie slipped her small hand into mine and slid off the bench. "Do you think my daddy's okay? I'm his favourite thing. He likes me better than teddies. He'd never leave me behind."

A pang of trepidation made me hesitate. "I'm sure he's fine, Annie. Why don't you and Echo go to pick a flower from that planter over there? We can take it to the police station to cheer up the officers. Only one, or we'll find ourselves in hot water. I just need a second with Ezra here."

She ran towards the planter, shepherded by Echo.

I faced Ezra. "We'll take Annie to the police station at Southwark, and then I'm heading to Dad's. I don't care what the hour is. Mami might have been smiling, but her words sounded like a threat. And she knows far too much about us for my liking."

Ezra clenched his jaw. "I agree. I'm not sure what happened in there. She had a weird hold on me like I struggled to maintain control over my own body's reactions. As soon as there was a distance between us, my hackles went up. I'm going back to Wildwoods to check if she's already on someone's radar."

I nodded. "I'll ring Jameson from Dad's house to see if the Shadow Squad has any leads. Ezra, we have no choice but to send a message to the Celestial Library to check on Marina."

"I know."

I hesitated. "We used to have this game when we were kids. Silly, really. We used it if we were with adults and wanted to check on each other. We'd say, 'Who is your Hollywood crush?' If we were fine, we'd name our real crush. If we needed rescuing, we'd name someone we absolutely wouldn't fancy in a million years. A sort of code that could have a hundred different answers but only meant something to us."

Ezra blinked. "Blokes would never do that. We'd just give a thumbs up or down or an appropriate grunt."

"Will you message her?"

"I will." He slipped off his shirt.

My cheeks grew hot at the sight of his bare skin. "What are you doing?"

His grey eyes sparked copper. He left a lingering kiss on my cheek. "I need a run. I'll call in the morning."

I darted over to Annie and Echo at the planter. We walked in the direction of the police station as bones cracked behind us, and Ezra Neuhoff ran into the moonlight night.

7

Echo and I dropped Annie at the police station as promised. The little girl didn't mind parting from me, but buried her head in Echo's fur. He let her rest her forehead against his and didn't complain when she tugged his tail. Their goodbye made me remember how important a role he had played in my childhood, and I felt a pang that I didn't have any children of my own to experience the joy of a loving, forgiving, protective animal.

Annie might not have trusted strangers enough to tell us her address, but she had no such qualms about the police officer who brought her hot chocolate with marshmallow sprinkles and a heavy dollop of cream.

We left, knowing her mother waited for the police car to bring her daughter home.

Unable to explain what had happened to her father.

"He's probably drunk," said Echo. "He'll stagger home when he's sobered up, and his wife will give him an earful he'll never forget. If someone abandoned my cub, I know my teeth would rip into their sorry behind."

I voiced the sense of foreboding that I'd hidden from

Annie. "Annie seemed adamant he'd gone into Black Lotus Inkings to make an appointment."

Echo growled. "He left her alone in the middle of central London. She could have come to a sticky end, fallen into the Thames or been taken by child traffickers."

I grimaced. "I don't know. Annie didn't paint him as a bad dad. She was dressed well. He'd bought her a treat and told her not to speak to strangers. My gut says whatever happened was out of his control."

Emerald eyes glinted. "We make excuses for those we love. The child was lying to herself. Eventually, the scales will fall from her eyes about her deadbeat father."

The early fingers of dawn had broken through the sky. We hopped on a night bus towards Tooting Bec as the sun came up over the city, showering smoking chimneys and tiled roofs in golden light. At this hour, with passengers scarce and zombie-like, sleep-deprived drivers paying little attention, Echo slipped on board with me. He found it infinitely more dignified than squeezing into a cat carrier.

I curled my fingers into his thick coat. "Echo? Why didn't you tell me about my great-uncle Rajiv?"

The leopard's tail swished. "There is nothing to tell, Alisha. Rajiv was history once your father discovered his illustrator powers. Rajika shone far more brightly without him. I was glad to leave him in the past."

I stared out the window as the bus bumped along the worn tarmac and sighed. "We'll check Dad's okay, and then I need a rest. No frolicking with the koi, okay?"

At the next stop, we jumped off the bus and headed for my family home. An explosion of new flowerpots decorated the block-paved drive. It took a full five minutes of incessant knocking before Alma opened the front door in a frilly nightdress and a flowing dressing gown, bleary-eyed with sleep. Mum had been a pyjama type of woman.

Alma squinted at me. "Alisha? I thought your father had

forgotten to pay the milkman. It's six-thirty a.m. What are you doing here?"

She stayed over at Dad's house most days and only swung by her own house to delve into her pantry, which was stashed full of decades-old yeast and chocolate sprinkles for her baking or to feed her goldfish. I found it strange that a woman in her sixties would have goldfish, of all things. They died so easily. As a child of the eighties, I knew them as trainer pets for small children that didn't live for decades or take much commitment to the relief of parents everywhere.

"I'm sorry to wake you," I started.

"Your dad is still snoring. Not even an earthquake would make him stir," said Alma.

"I had the sudden urge to check in on him."

Alma shook her head. "Dads and their daughters. I was like that with my own father; God bless his soul." She looked down at my feet. "You brought the cat?"

Echo gave a plaintive meow for dramatic effect. I had to hand it to him. It was BAFTA-worthy.

I nodded. "The cat's attached to me, a bit like a surrogate child. You know how it is."

Alma wasn't peculiar. She was just plain old Alma, her Spanish flair a little dulled by age but still evident in her olive skin and the red lipstick she sometimes wore. A neighbour I'd known forever and who now happened to be in love with Dad. Tidy, caring, obsessed with baking and an award-winning maker of doilies. That fact alone was enough to make me want to put her in the bin. But she made Dad happy, so there was that.

"Can we come in?" I asked.

"Of course, dear. It was your home before it was mine. You could have used the key under the planter."

I grimaced. "Privacy's important. I didn't want to catch you in a compromising position."

I had no idea what the sex life was for newly intimate

sixty-year-olds, but I wasn't taking any chances. I was too fond of my retinas to burn them off at the sight of Dad as Tarzan swinging for his new Jane.

She tried to pick up Echo, gave up and scooped up a letter instead. "Let's wake your father with a cup of tea, shall we? It'll do him good to have his favourite ladies here."

"Wait until I pounce on his chest with my claws out," said Echo. "That was a much-loved pastime of mine when you were younger after he bound your powers. It was very cathartic."

I held my fingers to my lips. "Shh."

Alma pottered around the kitchen, oblivious to his mewling, completely at home in the space that used to be Mum's kingdom. A pang of sadness hit me. I didn't know if I'd ever be able to interact with Alma without thinking of Mum, but the feelings were complex. I wanted Dad to be happy. But Alma could never fill the space Mum had left in *my* heart. If she tried, I would blast her head with wind so fast she'd have a permanent mohawk, to hell with the consequences.

She handed me a mug of tea. "Do you mind bringing this up? My hands are a bit shaky these days."

"Of course not."

The tea slopped in the mug as we trudged upstairs, Echo winding between our feet.

"The cat really does follow you everywhere." Alma pushed open the door to the bedroom.

"I wouldn't miss this for the world." Echo charged into the room, took a flying leap and landed on Dad's belly as promised.

Dad sat bolt upright. "What the flying duck?"

The covers slipped down, but luckily, he wore his trusty Y-fronts.

"I think you'll find I'm a leopard, not a duck," said Echo.

"Alma, why are there foreign objects in our bedroom? A

man's bedroom is sacred." Dad shoved Echo off with difficulty before turning his astonished eyes on me. He rubbed his eyes. "Oh, Alisha, it's you. Can't you keep this… cat under control?"

I kissed his wizened cheek and set the tea on his bedside table. "Hello, Dad."

"Are you here for your catalogue of creatures? I'm almost through with the upgrade."

He'd decided it made no sense for me to use the illustrations intended for my grandmother. Not when I could only animate winged creatures. I didn't have the heart to tell him I was attached to my grandmother's book. Using it made me feel closer to her. She was less the grand Custodian, beloved of the Otherworld, than my grandmother, reaching through time to help me in my hour of need.

For now, my grandmother's catalogue of creatures remained in Dad's studio as a template for the new one: a ring binder with sheets that could be unclipped. He said it would be lightweight and easier to use. I didn't want to break his heart, but this old gal had a penchant for beautiful books, and a ring binder didn't cut it.

I shook my head. "I'm not here for the catalogue of creatures. I came to ask how you know Mami."

Alma drew open the curtains and handed him the letter from the doormat. "Whose mummy?"

Dad froze, and when he spoke again, his voice quivered a little. "No, dear. She said Mami. It's been a long time since I heard that name." A sigh. "Let me pull on my robe, and I'll tell you everything."

Echo and I retreated to the kitchen, leaving Dad and Alma to get dressed. Muffled voices filtered through the house. I pulled out a chair and sank into it. I decided to leave my own ablutions until I got back to my flat. Dad didn't have the lotions and potions I used, and it wasn't like I could dip into Alma's washbag like I would have with Mum's. When I hit forty, I adopted a skincare routine. Applying my fluffy soufflé face cream was like meditating. I almost didn't mind the price tag.

Echo's ears pricked up. "Ten minutes tops, and they'll be down, judging by the bowel movement that just landed in the toilet."

I screwed up my face. "That level of detail isn't necessary."

"My ears are one of my greatest gifts. I can even hear small animals darting through stalks of grass or digging their burrows. I can hear foxes skulking at the backs of houses for toys their cubs can play with. I can hear rats running up pipes. It's how I heard Annie sobbing on the bench." His eyes widened in innocence. "I spent so much time in this household that I know Joshi's routines as well as I know my own. Or yours, for that matter. Every other day, isn't it?"

"Heaven help me. Put a sock in it, will you, Echo?"

Echo slunk away into the corner, whistling a tune from *Footloose* to while away the time, even though his whistling rarely hit the right note and almost always unleashed a shower of spittle.

I pulled out my phone and found a message from Ezra.

Got a message back from the Celestial Library. Marina's Hollywood crush is Jessica Chastain.

The anxiety calcifying my heart fell away. I sent Ezra a quick reply. *She's okay. But I'll feel better when she's home.* I took a moment to fill my lungs with breath and my heart with gratitude, then dialled the detective.

He answered on the third ring and groaned. "Alisha Verma. A call from you at seven a.m. means trouble."

I smiled. "That's what I like about you, Rob. Always straight to the point."

"No rest for the wicked. I've got my hands full right now following up on a missing person's case. You've got sixty seconds."

I could just picture him in his grubby puffer jacket, rubbing a hand over his shaved head. No need to beat around the bush when the man was busy. Not when Dad and Alma would be downstairs any minute. "I need intel on Black Lotus Inkings in Waterloo and the woman who runs it."

"What's this about?" said Jameson.

"I don't know yet. I thought maybe you could poke around your files and see if she's come up at all. Maybe send around a local bobby to ruffle her feathers to see if she has anything to hide."

"You're going to have to give me more than that. I can't use the Met's resources to go and harass a civilian, based on your say-so, however much I trust your instincts."

"Her name's Mami. She's a peculiar, Rob. She knew I'm a druid and Ezra is a wolf. She saw Echo for what he is. She knew the Celestial Library and about Marina. She spun me a story about knowing Dad and made a veiled threat about going to see him. I just want a heads-up about what we are dealing with."

"Marina? I've not thought about her since yesterday. I usually think about her all the time." Jeers erupted in the background. "Pack it in, Wheeler. The only woman I've ever heard you talk about is your mother." A sheepishness coloured his voice. "Sorry about that. Wheeler brings out my immature side. I better go. I've made a note of the tattoo parlour. I'll look into it."

"There's something else. Do you think you could get an address for a man called Rajiv Chawla for me? He's an Indian national, born in 1933, and lives in London."

A sigh. "Why not? I'm already bending the rules for you. What difference can one more favour make?"

"Thanks, Rob." I hung up, frowning. Calypso had said Marina wouldn't be missed while she was away, but the universe would hold space for her return. That didn't hold true for me. I missed her already, and Jameson seemed confused. I made a mental note to check in on him in her absence.

Dad hobbled into the kitchen, his body curved like he hadn't yet stretched it out after the night's sleep. He set down his empty cup, grumbling. "That cat really does make a racket."

He was right. Echo's tuneless whistling had reached the depths of a dentist's drill.

"Tell me about Mami," I said.

Dad sighed, sank into a rickety kitchen chair and picked up a doily to play with. They were literally everywhere. "It was the 1970s, and London was changing."

Alma rushed in, floofing her hair. "Don't mind me. I'll just potter around you."

I took the chair opposite Dad and shot him a quizzical look. Surely, he'd have to guard his words with humdrum Alma in the room?

Dad gave her a fond smile. "You go ahead, love. I have nothing to hide."

He'd obviously become more comfortable with telling porkies overnight.

Echo gave a plaintive meow. "Joshi's thinking with something other than his brain."

Dad's look of disdain would have made a lesser cat shrivel, but Echo held his head high, undaunted.

I leaned forward. "Go on."

"London in the 1970s felt like a truly cosmopolitan city and nowhere more so than our halls of residence. Your mum had arrived from France on a scholarship to study Natural Sciences at University College London, and I was there at art school. Our eyes met across the cafeteria, and we gravitated towards each other. We smoked pot, played Pink Floyd and Led Zeppelin and soaked up the freedom of being at university in one of the best cities in the world. We were married within a year, but there was a blip. And Mami was that blip."

Goosebumps raced up my skin. "Blip?"

Behind us, Alma's arms foraged elbow-deep in the washing-up bowl.

"Mami was a fellow student in the art department. She made waves as soon as she arrived. The rumours spread about a dark-skinned, bikini-clad goddess swimming lengths in the university pool. She had a snake tattoo on her stomach. It made her a legend before she even unpacked her bags."

Alma squirted some soap onto the sponge. "Good thing you don't know her anymore, dear, or I'd be worried."

I grinned. Apparently, Alma had told Dad his moustache made him look like an Indian Tom Selleck, which was quite frankly absurd, as he had neither Selleck's build nor height. Still, I wasn't about to knock Dad's confidence or lose a chance to tease him.

I waggled my eyebrows. "I'm getting vibes here, Dad. Was Mami a notch on the old bedpost?"

Maybe that was all Mami was, a flame from Dad's past. That would be weird but, in many ways, a relief. I could chalk all the weird message stuff up to Mami being a jilted lover or going a bit bunny boiler.

He cringed. Indian fathers liked to think of their daughters as chaste and shy creatures who had only reached first base, not women capable of giving and receiving all-night orgasms. He spluttered, so embarrassed he could barely get his words out. "If you weren't forty, I would tell you to wash your mouth out with soap and water. I apologise, Alma, for this wayward child of mine."

"No need to apologise, dear," said Alma. "I'm quite enjoying this insight into your youth."

I felt a pang of nostalgia for the times Mum and I had ganged up on Dad.

Dad grunted in defeat. "In any case, we only coincided for that one year. Every man or woman at the university knew Mami. Wherever she went, she'd have people fawning over her, even tutors. Her dorm room became this place of refuge. Sportsmen would go to her with an injury, which she'd miraculously heal with a kiss. Awkward, gangly, spotty students would find their way to her, and an hour or two later, they'd be transformed. But it wasn't just their outer selves. They were different somehow. More confident. More beautiful. They'd splash about money they never had." He shook his head. "I don't know. I think what I'm trying to say is she understood people's deepest desires. It was uncanny. They'd bare their souls to her, and when they left her, their problems would be solved."

I frowned. "Maybe she was just a good listener."

"It was more than that." He shook off the dark cloud of his memories. "Or maybe I'm just getting senile in my old age."

There was more to the story. I could see it in the depths of his brown eyes. It takes a child a while to read the body language of their parents. Age and self-absorption all play their part. But when a child matures and *really* tries to look, a parent is easy to decipher by how tightly or loosely they hold their body, the clench of their fists, and the lingering or distancing of their eyes.

And right now, Dad was bricking it like he had dodgy sphincter muscles.

I held his gaze and didn't waver. "Is that all that happened? You were just a little weirded out by her?"

He broke our eye contact. "Of course, I was in love with your mother. A year later, your mum and I were married. We had our studies. We had each other. Nothing else mattered."

"And Mami?" Why did I have the feeling he was hiding something?

"We were paired for a project in the art department. She left the university soon after, and I never heard from her again."

I chose my words carefully. "She wants to meet you, Dad. There was something about her tone that made me worry."

"Funny to think all these years later, she is still in London."

I swallowed hard. "I didn't tell you that. Did you overhear my conversation with the detective?"

"No, darling." He pushed a letter at me.

I unfolded the thick, cream paper to find words written in a swirly, blue fountain pen ink with the skill of a calligrapher.

Dear Joshi,

It's been decades since our paths crossed, and yet fate saw fit to send your daughter to me. Do you remember the portraits we painted of one another? I would love to do another study. Come and see me at Black Lotus Inkings in Waterloo to reminisce about the olden days.

Yours, Mami.

A flush crept up Dad's throat, but he took refuge in the familiar rhythms of fatherhood. "You weren't thinking of getting a tattoo, were you, darling? I know Marina loves them, but I've always been rather pleased you gave them a wide berth. Hideous things."

A ball of dread gathered in my stomach. "You can't go to see her. What's this about the portrait?"

He shrugged. "It was a kind of goodbye ritual between artists when one of us moved on. Her painting of me has been in the loft for years. It made your mother uncomfortable. I should have thrown it out, but it's rather good."

I blinked, recalling an impressionist painting with an M scratched into the bottom righthand corner.

Dad reached across to pat my hands, the beds of his nails caked with paint from his latest project. "Mami is used to getting her own way, Alisha. But I'm not the boy I once was. I am perfectly capable of saying no to an invitation."

Alma turned away from the sink and wiped her hands on

the tea towel. "I wouldn't worry about your father, dear. He can look after himself. And he has me to look after him too."

"You see? We have it all in hand," said Dad.

I bit my lip. "There's one more thing. I was reading about our family line and came across your Uncle Rajiv. Why did you never mention that my grandmother had a brother?"

A storm played across his face, deepening his frown lines. "My uncle hated me and didn't want me to succeed. My mother told me she'd been making excuses for him all her life, and she freed me from doing the same."

Indian families tended to pull everyone into the fold. Second and third cousins, uncles and aunts by marriage, wily old farts or precious maiden aunts. What had Rajiv done to be cast out?

"But he was an illustrator too. He could have taught you so much," I said.

Dad's brown eyes skirted to Alma, who was checking the bowl for mouldy fruit like only Stepford wives did at seven a.m. The rest of us were too busy glugging caffeine. "Rajiv was talented, but I've never known an artist with such darkness. Some lessons are the wrong ones."

He was hiding something about Rajiv. I could feel it in my bones. I rubbed the crick in my neck. "I don't know. Edvard Munch's 'The Scream' is pretty intense, but you would have jumped at the chance to learn from him."

"Leave it alone, Alisha. You stay away from him, you hear me?" A sharp tone of warning. Dad's emotions rarely got the better of him. He was usually the very definition of solid, stoic and dependable.

Echo unleashed a low growl, startling Alma. "In this family, the women make the decisions, or had you forgotten?"

Alma straightened the doily underneath the fruit bowl and swung around, holding two oranges to her chest. "Some fresh juice, Joshi?" She turned to me. "Your father is very talented. He needs to keep up his strength."

Dad perked up. "Yes, please. It was kind of you to check on me, Alisha. A father likes to think he looks after his daughter, but sometimes it's the other way around, eh? I'll see you to the door, shall I? The light is beautiful. I've got the urge to finish the paintings for a show I've lined up and then complete work on your catalogue of creatures." His chair scraped against the kitchen floor as he stood.

I followed him across the hallway, but he blocked the entrance to his studio.

"Can I see it?" Maybe I could make him understand the niggling feeling I had about Mami. Maybe he'd let slip some actual stories about Rajiv.

He folded his wiry arms across his chest. His eyes darted over his shoulder to the cabinet in the corner of the studio where he kept the catalogues under lock and key, as if guns, not books, hid there. In the right hands, the paintings were weapons, after all. "Nope. You know what they say. Anticipation makes the heart grow fonder."

He'd muddled the saying up, but I liked his version. I took the hint, despite my reservations. I'd tell Jameson about the invitation and leave it at that. I had to get out of the habit of always thinking I could jump in and solve problems with my magic.

"Sure thing," I said.

At worst, Mami had a crush on Dad and was looking to stir the waters after all these years. Maybe she'd heard Dad was a free agent and was hoping they could give it a go. Dad could handle that.

He brushed his dry lips against my cheek. "Make sure the cat doesn't terrify the koi on the way out. Last time, I found one who'd suffered sudden death from the shock. And darling…take a shower, will you?"

8

I laid my head against Ezra in the reading nook at Wildwoods. With him a senator now, we had to be careful about public displays of affection. At this precise moment, however, the pupils were in their lessons. The humdrum school day might have ended, but Wildwoods was only just coming to life. Its cabins beckoned, dressed this term in bright plumage that reminded me of rainforest birds.

It should have been quiet amongst the trees, but noise buzzed around us. It was a typical autumn day in Crystal Palace Park, with dog walkers squelched in their wellies, prams with chattering toddlers wrapped up against the cold, runners pounding the pathways around the park and the tinkling music of an ice cream van's arrival.

My hearing had deteriorated over the years. Either age, blaring music or a build-up of wax had ruined my hearing. Perhaps by middle age, the body started giving you little reminders of the ticking clock. It was poetic, really: an in-built mortality reminder to ensure you took a picture of blue skies and got on with your bucket list.

All this had changed with my wind powers, although it had taken me a hot minute to realise it. My affinity for the wind meant that when the wind blew in the right direction, it amplified my hearing. Right now, it carried the shrieks of children playing in Crystal Palace Park to my ears. Of course, sometimes I heard nothing at all and was grateful for it. Who wanted the sound of Echo pissing against a tree to be in stereo? A fireman's hose had nothing on that leopard's release of his bodily fluids.

I turned my head to where a golden coat nestled amongst the verdant foliage. "Thanks for being my wingman for this "

Unblinking emerald eyes met mine as Echo sharpened his claws lazily against the tree. The afternoon light obscured the three-inch scar at the corner of his eye. "It is my honour to be of service. When Rayna Willowsun asks you to teach a class at Wildwoods School of the Wondrous, you better show up with your A-game. And I am your A-game, Alisha."

"No marking territory. No karaoke. No whistling. No weird tangents about meeting Ursula K. Le Guin," I said.

Echo's claws stretched in and out. "Tonight, I shall have choice cuts of deer meat that are equal to my body weight."

"That's daylight robbery," said Ezra.

Echo bared his teeth. "Mind your own business, dog. On top of that, I'd like free rein to hunt down the mutt who has been keeping me up all night with her howling."

I shook my head. "Yes to the deer. No to the mutt."

His whiskers quivered. "You drive a hard bargain. Party pooper."

A gong reverberated, like from an ancient Tibetan monastery.

Echo leapt out of the tree, clean over our heads, and landed on the rope bridge behind us. "A class of hungry peculiars awaits."

I laughed. "Remember our deal."

He might have his quirks, but Echo's big ego was backed by brilliance. There was no doubt in his decisions. If I fell, I knew I could save myself by cushioning my body with gossamer layers of the breeze, but I still feared the fall. Echo trusted his instincts and effortlessly leapt into the unknown.

"I'll be your warm-up act." He bounded off across the rope bridge, paying no heed to the students who emerged between lessons and had to hold on for dear life as Echo ricocheted past.

I bit my lip. I hadn't told Echo yet that Jameson had already pinged me a text with my great-uncle's address. It would have put him in a bad mood. To my surprise, he agreed wholeheartedly with Dad that inviting Rajiv into our lives was a rotten idea.

Ezra grinned. "He's right about one thing. I've been working in my office, hearing excited whispers from the pupils all day about the great Alisha Verma coming to teach them."

I snorted. "Let's hope I live up to their expectations."

When Rayna had asked me to teach a weekly class, it had made sense for many reasons. Not least that it might stop peculiars from wandering into my night class and wreaking havoc under the noses of humdrums. I'd been flattered by her proposal. When I initially discovered the Otherworld, I thought it had given me a higher purpose. I realised now that it mostly made my life more chaotic. The trick was to find out how to live a more meaningful life amidst the chaos. Maybe closer ties with Wildwoods could be a part of that.

"Oh, you will. You will. Especially off the back of the belching leprechaun teaching them about ethics." He picked a leaf out of my ponytail and then traced my bottom lip with his calloused thumb before leaning in for a lingering kiss.

I sighed when he pulled away. "We haven't had a quiet moment for days. How about I make a ratatouille at the cottage tonight, and we can crack open a bottle of Merlot together? Then you can fill me in on the pack and how it's going without Gunnolf."

His grey eyes darkened. "I miss him. And the pack does

too. I know it was right to stop him, but he was a father to us. Whatever he did, he was a father to us. To me." He stood up and gingerly stepped out of the nook onto the rope bridge, then held out a hand to me.

A frisson of pleasure rushed up my arm at his touch. I squeezed his hand as I jumped barefoot from the nook and bent to scoop up my heels. I slipped them on and reached up to kiss the corner of his mouth, my hand flat against his hard chest. "It'll be okay."

His eyes softened. He ignored the passing swarm of pupils and gently turned my arm over and trailed a featherlight forefinger over the circle of eleven dots on the soft flesh of my inner arm. "Rayna had something else up her sleeve when she asked you to teach, didn't she?"

I shivered. "She offered to help turbo-charge my druid training."

A wounded look flashed across his chiselled face. A flicker of rejection.

I kicked myself for my poor choice of words. "You're the perfect mentor, Ezra. But you said yourself you're busy. And you're not a druid."

He dropped his voice into a whisper. Up amongst the trees, Lavinia's ground network of rat spies might not be able to hear us, but it was possible that even the trees could hear at Wildwoods. Magic was all around us. "It's not me I'm worried about. We decided to keep your place in the prophecy under wraps. You risk outing yourself."

"That's not fair," I hissed.

Was I supposed to hide in the shadows because it was possible I was the eternal girl? That was a coward's choice. I wasn't going to sit on my laurels while Marina did all the hard work to protect me. I was going to grab the opportunity to train with a learned druid with both hands. I'd put in the hard work to enhance my magic because who knew what was around the corner?

That didn't make me a crappy girlfriend. It made me a kick-arse girlfriend who, at the very least, deserved some hanky-panky after sharing a bottle of red wine with her boyfriend that night.

Ezra's eyes flashed a warning. His lips made a grim line. "You better get going."

I flattened out my pencil skirt and straightened my blouse. "How do I look?"

But he'd already gone.

FOR YEARS, I'd taught English language and culture at my night class for immigrants. What I provided there was a sense of family and confidence so my students could establish roots in a new culture.

"You'll be fine," said Rayna when she noticed my frayed nerves. "They are fascinated by you. Whatever you teach them, as long as it is within the laws of the Magical Constitution, will be inspiring. Others might need more steers, but you are a teacher. You have the instincts, training and thick skin for this."

Only after stepping into the classroom did I realise the emphasis should have been on thick skin.

I walked into the allocated cabin, a beaming smile on my face.

Nine pupils, aged from about twelve to fourteen, were dressed in the Wildwoods uniform of slim grey trousers with a crisp white shirt, topped with short, hooded robes in navy velvet with the school crest—a golden W, crowned with posies of plants—placed above the heart. Their attire didn't bother me, but their behaviour did.

A wall of noise assaulted my eardrums. Only a handful, including Mirabel, sat patiently with folded hands, waiting for instruction. A girl who could only have been a banshee made the most horrendous racket, and her shenanigans had sent the rest of the class into a frenzy. I was pretty sure her scream foretold her own impending death if she didn't shut her gob. A group of sporty types repeatedly whacked a ball against the ceiling. A boy with a badger's face burrowed with human hands in the soil that carpeted the floor in a misfire of the Wildwoods rainforest decoration. Echo had been driven to despair and had climbed a desk in the corner and was now fenced in, being prodded by two girls with blunt raven fringes and a ghostly pallor, although in London, that had no bearing on their talents and probably meant they hadn't had enough sun. To top it all off, Orpheus lurked in a corner perched on a high stool, his dark hair slicked back, a smug smile on his lips.

The smile slid off my face. I dropped my bag on the floor.

I was pretty sure this show of disrespect wouldn't have happened if I hadn't been a spectacular failure during the display of animation powers in the Wildwoods arena. Margola Silver had given me pretty decent headlines in the aftermath of the Ravenmaster showing up at the school, and my subsequent victory, but a little birdie had told me that the clips of me looking dejected on the arena stage had gone viral on social media, with much further reach than *The Otherworld Herald*.

I scowled at Orpheus. *You couldn't have dealt with this?*

His lips twitched. *I am here to observe only. Imagine I'm not here.*

I drew myself up to my full height—all five foot five of me—and used every ounce of my restraint to swallow the profanities on my tongue. "Quiet! Return to your seats. Or I will instruct the leopard to give you a mauling you will never forget."

The noise stopped as abruptly as lifting the needle on a record player.

The class stared at me.

"Echo, come down from there."

He unleashed a roar and leapt to my side.

"A warm-up act, was that?" I muttered.

Mournful green eyes met mine. "They are heathens, I tell you. With no inclination for learning."

"We'll see about that." I raised my voice, pointing to the sporty group. "That ball is mine. Hand it over."

A freckled boy with a mischievous glint in his eyes lobbed it at me.

I caught it with ease, raised my hands and sent a stream of wind across the classroom, tucking in the chairs so the pupils sat upright and ready to learn.

That's my girl, said Orpheus.

I rolled my eyes at him. "Listen up. I'm Alisha Verma, teacher, druid, granddaughter of the lauded Custodian Rajika Verma and winner of the Wildwoods Medal of Honour during my very first year as a peculiar." I cocked my head at Echo. They didn't have to know I was the eternal girl to show us some respect. "This is Chanakya Gunbir Hredhaan of Maharashtra, a descendant of a man-eating leopard, otherwise known as Echo. He was a trusted adviser to and protector of Rajika and fought at her side during the Battle of the Celestial Library."

I paused for effect. Teaching was as much about performance as it was about having knowledge to impart.

I fixed my eyes on the freckled boy. "Do you know what that means?"

He gulped and shook his head.

"Come here ready to show respect and learn or walk out the door. Time-wasters are not welcome." I picked up my bag from where I'd dropped it in the soil, flung it on the desk at the front of the cabin and picked up a piece of chalk from the ledge of the blackboard. "Now, the theme of today's lesson is teamwork. I'm going to give you a problem, and together we're going to analyse your strengths and weakness as a peculiar and work out the best way for you to solve the problem as a team. Are you ready?"

"Yes, miss," said the class in unison.

Mirabel shot me a grin.

Echo paced through the desks, his head raised at a jaunty angle now we had wrangled control.

The blackboard screeched as I wrote up the task. "Here is the problem: a powerful werewolf has gone rogue, prowling the streets and killing anyone in his path. You and your friends corner him in the car park of a supermarket not far from here, but his loyal pack are not far behind, and there are no adults at Wildwoods to help you."

"But miss, you're talking about what happened to the Justice Minister. He went on a killing rampage and stole a selkie skin, and now he is in prison," said the banshee.

My mind flashed back to Ezra taking Gunnolf down in the grounds of the Windsor farmhouse they had shared together. Blood and betrayal. Broken bones and so much pain. "Yes, it's a twist on what happened. But you might find another way to solve the problem. Your own way. You must stay within the parameters of the Magical Constitution, and each of you can perform only one task. The werewolf must be captured, not killed."

Echo purred. "You must participate equally. You may use the blackboard. You may stroke me if it aids your thinking."

Forty minutes later, a white scrawl covered the blackboard. The banshee came up to present the group's ideas, the procession of her loafers muffled by the thick soil underfoot. Orpheus watched from his stool, his dark eyes hooded, his long fingers clicking the end of a glossy ballpoint pen.

Anyone would think you are nervous, I said.

Hardly, he retorted. One eyebrow lifted a tiny fraction. *Just bored.*

You could be in your office playing with your sausage and veg.

A cough took hold of him. *There is only so far you can taunt a vampire, Alisha.*

I suppressed a grin. "Well, come on, Janey. We'll be here until tomorrow at this rate. Go ahead. Make your case."

Janey, the banshee, pushed her frizzy blonde hair over her shoulder. "It was like a riddle, but we got there in the end, thanks to Xavier." Her eyes darted to the freckled boy with a penchant for balls. "Our first task was to clear the car park to prevent humdrums from stumbling across the Otherworld. Benny would be the first on the scene. He's a stink badger. We'd peg our noses. Then Benny would spray the car park to ward off any onlookers with the stink. Ayshah's voice sends everyone to sleep when she hits the lowest octave. She'd knock out the werewolf, and Xavier would cloak us with his invisibility cloak to make sure we weren't discovered. Sage and Violet have super strength when they work together. Sage would take the werewolf's legs, and Violet would take the upper body. If the loyal pack turned up, my banshee scream would paralyse them, as wolves have sensitive ears. Angelus's dad is a seeker. He knows the shortest route anywhere. We'd follow him back to Wildwoods, the safest place in London for peculiars. Drew knows the Bestiary inside out. He'd lead us to the empty cages and is able to open any door. That's where we'd put the werewolf while Mirabel flies to find a member of the senate. Or you, Alisha. Because we think you'd help us too."

Echo roared in approval.

I gave the class a round of applause. "Well done, all. You may return to your seat, Janey."

She beamed and bounced through the aisle, a far cry from the screaming banshee I'd met at the start of the lesson.

"Your inventiveness impressed me. I wouldn't have thought to use the cages in the Bestiary. Bonus points for using human skills as well as peculiar ones. Angelus, what are your magical talents?"

A ring of thick kohl lined his blue eyes, his posture like a plush toy that had lost its stuffing. "I can make rainbows."

Poor kid, said Orpheus. *That's why he dresses as a goth when he's not in school uniform.*

"How wonderful." I infused my words with the encouragement he needed. Hopefully, Angelus knew how to steer clear of predatory leprechauns.

Orpheus made a sound like a choking donkey.

I leaned against the front of my desk. "Do you know why I set you this task, everyone?"

Mirabel's hand went up lightning-bolt quick. "You wanted us to learn how to work as a team."

I nodded. "And I wanted you to think for yourselves. Following the crowd, even depending on leaders, can sometimes lead you down the wrong path. Think for yourselves. Be true to your internal compass." I threw Xavier his ball, using my magic to loop it through the air and land it cleanly in his bag. "Class dismissed."

An inner glow filled me. I'd enjoyed myself more than I expected.

The gong sounded, marking the end of the school day. With reflexive urgency, the pupils stuffed their possessions into their bags. The class filed out with shy glances at me, escorted by Echo, still chattering about their solution.

I locked eyes with Orpheus. *Satisfied?*

His dark eyes gleamed. *Very.*

Hiding my smile, I turned to wipe the blackboard. Euphoria filled me at how far I'd come in the past few months. I was now a trusted part of the Wildwoods community. Trusted enough to teach here, despite pushing back against some of the rules of governance. It meant that Wildwoods had changed me, but I had also changed it. Next time I'd dress less formally like I did for my night class. The heels I wore weren't high, but my back twinged all the same. I swept the duster across the board, generating a cloud of chalk dust as I worked.

A rustle behind me made the small hairs on the back of my neck stand on end.

When were you going to tell me that you're the eternal girl?

The duster fell from my hands, sinking into the soil underfoot with a muffled thud. I spun to face Orpheus, my mouth slack. He stood millimetres away, and I cranked my neck up to take in the thin line of his lips, his pale Roman nose—did I imagine it?—the pride in his dark eyes.

A low rumble came from Echo at the door.

I fixed my eyes on him. "I need a few minutes alone with Orpheus. Wait for me at the reading nook."

"The vampire is not the only one who can draw blood," Echo paused. "I like you, vampire. But the druid is my world."

Orpheus nodded. "Much obliged."

I barked the command. "Echo. Go."

His tail swished as he padded away.

I drew in a haggard breath. "You know."

9

Orpheus smirked. "I can read your mind, Alisha. When you entered the cabin, your admittedly complex mind cartwheeled around strategies to regain control of the class. In among it was a rather interesting titbit about how you couldn't win their respect by revealing you were the eternal girl." He paused. "I'm relieved to put the pieces together. The wolf has been caging his mind from me at senate meetings. Now I know why."

I sighed. With every passing day, it seemed that more people discovered my secret. First Calypso and now Orpheus, to add to those who had heard Gaia in the cave: Ezra, Marina, Echo and Tielbu.

Still, as mistakes went, it could have been worse. I trusted Orpheus. I couldn't imagine what Lavinia would do with this information had she found out.

A smile softened Orpheus's stern visage. "It is good that you trust me, Alisha."

All the same, spikes of anxiety flared in my belly. "Why haven't you revealed me to the senate?"

"Because we are friends, and your choices are your own.

And because I have underestimated you before, and I won't make that mistake again."

I caught a whiff of the dark chocolate and cherry scent of his beard oil. "Thank you. This is our secret, Orpheus."

He inclined his head like a gentleman from a long-expired century. "Of course."

A rummage at the door made us both whip our heads around.

"Echo, I told you to wait at—" I frowned.

Ezra stood at the door. Grey eyes darted from me to Orpheus.

I stepped back a few paces to break the charge of electricity between me and Orpheus. A charge that came from shared secrets and friendship. After our little spat earlier, the last thing I wanted was for Ezra to grab the wrong end of the stick.

I hooked my bag over my shoulder. "We're done here. Is everything okay?"

He glanced at Orpheus again.

I mean, Orpheus was hot if you liked your men centuries old. Especially when he respected my decisions or drove his Lotus. Or opened the door to his club barefoot while nursing a glass of whiskey, having had his nose buried in a first edition of classic literature. Especially then.

But I noted this from the perspective of a neutral observer, completely in love with my own man.

Behind me, Orpheus had a coughing fit. *You will be the death of me.*

I winced. Oops.

Ezra gave the vampire a nod of greeting. "Orpheus."

Orpheus nodded in response. "Neuhoff."

I didn't like male power dances. They were weird. I much preferred bromances.

Ezra's brow furrowed. "You didn't answer your phone, Alisha."

"My phone is always on silent in the classroom. Teaching 101. What's wrong?" I delved in my bag for my phone to find three missed calls. Two from my brother. One from Ezra. My chest grew tight with fear. I searched Ezra's face, my voice shaky. "It's Dad, isn't it?"

A vein throbbed in Ezra's cheek. "Alma went out for some flour, and when she returned, the studio had been turned upside down. The loft hatch was open, so she thought Joshi was up there, but he wasn't. That's when she realised."

My heartbeat thundered like a horse across the plains. "What?"

Ezra's hand went to his charm necklace as if the mere act of touching it meant he'd be ready to fight what came next. "Your father is missing."

I blinked and then sank into the soil on my knees. "I should have followed my instincts. I knew he was in danger."

Ezra crouched down next to me; smart trousers be damned. "Your brother's there with her now."

Thoughts carouselled through my mind, but one face kept floating to the fore. "It was Mami."

"We can't know that for sure," soothed Ezra.

I fought to hold back my tears. It'd only been a day since Marina had been gone, and things were already falling apart. "What does your gut say?"

He clenched his jaw. "My gut's not important. We follow the evidence."

I pushed myself to my feet. "You never would have said that before you became a senator."

We will get your father back, said Orpheus.

Ezra glanced at the vampire. "You'll have to take the meeting with the Prime Sorcerer without me, Orpheus."

Orpheus shook his head. "You were the lead. I'm ill-prepared. We might not get another chance to make this move."

Ezra frowned. "Okay. I'll wrap things up as quickly as

possible. Then we can teleport to your father's house, and I'll use my seeker skills to help bring him home. We'll figure this out together, Alisha."

The yew tree now allowed him to teleport within Wildwoods. It was one of the perks of being a senator. Still, there was no way I was waiting to get a start on this. I gave a half-hearted nod.

"You said it this morning. It will be okay." Ezra kissed my forehead and strode away.

Orpheus sighed. "Poor Neuhoff. He has no idea what goes on in your head."

I glared at him. "I can't wait."

"I know." We left the cabin, and I was thankful the pupils had departed, and all was quiet.

"Want a ride in a Lotus? It's much faster than the bus." He was a brilliant friend.

"Yes, please."

"The leopard can't come. He'll scratch the seats."

"He'd do much worse than that. I'll tell him to wait for Ezra on the way out. I'll meet you at the car."

"I left the car on Thicket Road." He strode over to the cable cars to make his descent to ground level.

I made for the reading nook. There, I discovered Echo in a great oak with a squirrel captured between his paws, licking its terrified head. Rolling my eyes, I lifted my hands. With simultaneous gusts, I held Echo back while I sent the squirrel on his merry way. It chattered in my direction before bopping Echo on the nose with an acorn.

"How rude," said Echo. "It should be grateful I didn't take a bite from its juicy thigh."

I beckoned him over to the rope bridge. "Why didn't you?"

He landed at my side. "I was working up to it. I've choked on squirrel hairballs more than once. I don't wish that experience on anyone."

"Echo, Dad's missing from his house. I'm heading there with Orpheus to check it out. I need you to wait here for Ezra."

A growl. "Joshi is often a fool. But he is my fool. Let me help."

I left behind a disgruntled leopard and called Dad's mobile phone on the way to Orpheus's car. As expected, it went straight to answerphone. Dad's phone was inevitably either on silent or stuffed in a drawer with no battery. He preferred landlines. Mobile phones intruded on the focus needed to be an artist, apparently. A few minutes later, I buckled up in the Lotus as Orpheus pulled away from the kerb.

Orpheus programmed the sat nav and pressed the button for heated seats.

My bottom warmed almost immediately. "That's sorcery."

He chuckled. "No, that's all the extras. You wouldn't catch me on a London bus."

I slackened the seatbelt against my chest, kicked off my heels and arched my back to iron out the cricks.

Orpheus threw me a glance. "Your back is hurting. I'll set you up an appointment with my chiropractor."

I frowned. "Will you stop reading my thoughts?"

"If I didn't think you enjoyed our connection, I would stay out of your mind. That is a privilege I reserve for friends."

All I could think of was Dad. He'd been happy when I'd seen him. He'd had Alma to fuss over him and purpose in his work. He had finally reached a kind of equilibrium after Mum's sudden passing. What could have happened for him to leave his studio in such a state?

I lurched forward to retrieve my handbag from the footwell. Jameson had to have some intel on Mami by now.

"I'll put him on speaker phone," said Orpheus. Ashen fingers deftly worked the menu on the central console.

Part of me liked the effortlessness of our communication. The other part felt taken advantage of. I kneaded my neck with my fingers. What was it about worrying about loved ones that made a sea of knots spring up in my body? "You have his number?"

"Of course. We do a spin class together at Baba Yaga's. Don't look at me like that. This physique might look impressive, but it takes work, especially at my age."

Didn't I know it. My metabolism had slowed to a snail's pace by the time I hit thirty-five. I only had to look at a bar of chocolate to put on three inches around the hips.

All the better to grab you with.

"Stop it. The banter we have is fun, but we're not slipping into innuendo. One, what kind of man first propositions a woman when she's stuck in a car with him and can't escape? It's creepy. Two, you sound like the Big Bad Wolf who's about to eat granny. Three, I'm in love with Ezra, the sexy, werewolf-wizard love of my life."

"Relax. I was trying to take your mind off your father." A pause. "If I was coming onto you, believe me, you'd know. That said, both your heartbeats were elevated in the cabin. There was a slight difference in the rhythm that told me the elevation stemmed not from anxiety but anger."

Mum and Marina had always been my go-to gals for conversations about relationship woes, and they weren't an option. The nosey vampire could stick his pasty schnozzle in his coffin.

I took a deep breath. "Can you hit the call button, please?"

The detective answered on the second ring. "Orpheus Might. Our thighs took a pounding last time. I'm not sure I'm ready for another round yet. Chandra might seem like she has the serenity of the moon, but underneath, she has the instincts of a sadomasochist."

"I quite agree, Jameson. Better to rest your legs and leave it to us to ride on in glory." Orpheus smirked. "...I have the druid here with me. She needs a word."

Jameson muttered something inaudible that made Orpheus's smirk deepen into a grin.

I filled the detective in on Dad's disappearance.

The detective's gruff voice filled the car. "So Alma called Sahil, and Sahil called Ezra, who called you. Are you sure Joshi is missing and not having a knees-up in some London pub?"

I frowned. "Have you met my dad? He's not exactly the boozer type. A glass of shandy sends him into giggle mode. He rarely ventures away from home for long."

Like most older people, Dad preferred to use his own toilet. Call it a need for privacy or 3-ply, lavender-fragranced toilet roll.

"Maybe he had a hissy fit about a painting that wasn't working out and stormed off."

"There's no chance he damaged his studio. It's his pride and joy. And there's even less chance he'd want to worry Alma, Sahil or me. He's a worry wart. He always lets us know where he is." Desperation crept into my voice. "It can't be chance Mami issued her invitation just before Dad's disappearance."

"You said Joshi turned down her invitation."

Panic rose in me like a wave. I clenched my fists, imprinting my palm with tiny crescent moons. "He did, but I have this awful feeling I can't shake."

The detective swore under his breath. "I was going to wait until I had something concrete, but it's time I updated you on the digging I've been doing for you. Text me your father's address. Don't go in without me. It could be a crime scene. Have you heard from Marina? I found some of her hair dye in my bathroom, and I couldn't for the life of me remember when the last time I saw her was. She wasn't at the surgery. On holiday, is she?"

I kept my voice light. The universe would find a way to

tell me if my bestie wasn't okay. I had to believe that. "I miss her too, Rob. She'll be back soon."

"I'll see you at your father's." He hung up.

I blinked back tears as the streets rushed past. I couldn't lose Dad so soon after Mum. I'd never survive the loss. Why had I let him persuade me everything was okay? I'd never forgive myself if something happened to him.

You're not going to lose him. Orpheus pressed his lips into a thin line, bone-white knuckles clutching the steering wheel. He pressed his foot to the accelerator, running a red light as if he understood the urgency bubbling in me.

I sent the detective the address. Then I leaned back against the seat and closed my eyes, trusting Orpheus's skill behind the wheel despite the rumble of the engine and swerve of the car as he pushed it to its limits. In fantasy stories, closing your eyes in the vicinity of a vampire was plain stupidity—a death knell.

Rewind a few months, and I never would have realised I could feel so safe with Orpheus. "Aren't you worried about speeding tickets?"

"Druid, I can wipe minds. I have no need to worry about trivialities like fines." His voice would be perfect for a bedtime book. When he talked to me, he tempered the harshness he used with others.

A nugget of information surfaced from the recesses of my mind, from one of my earliest training sessions with Ezra. "But what about The Jailor's Law? It's forbidden to interfere with the compos mentis of another peculiar."

"I've never come across a traffic officer who is a peculiar. Our kind don't tend to serve in humdrum governments. We have our own codes to live by."

I opened my eyes. He'd taken us down the A214, and we'd hit Streatham already. Mum and Dad's house was a stone's throw away from here. "Orpheus, why aren't you angry at me for hiding my place in the prophecy from you?"

"I'm a private man. How can I judge you for keeping a secret?"

"I appreciate that. You know we could be running into danger right now, but you haven't tried to talk me out of it."

The traffic slowed.

He shifted into second gear. "Through my centuries of life, I have suffered inertia, depression and loss. The single thing that has pulled me through my days is finding something to fight for."

We pulled up outside Dad's house. My palms grew clammy with anxiety even before I'd unplugged my seatbelt. My breath came in short rasps. Jameson waited for us, leaning on the bonnet of his dark blue Ford Focus, his face a frown. Sahil's car, a black Range Rover with tinted windows and a personalised number plate, was there too. I crammed my feet into my heels and slung my bag on my shoulder. I stepped out of the car and slammed the door shut.

Orpheus, at the opposing door, winced.

My palms tingled, and the autumn leaves swirled around me. They gathered pace, becoming a twister on the suburban street.

Stay calm, druid.

My palms burned. The leaves swirled ever higher, reaching past the rooftop of my family home. *Help me. I'm losing control, Orpheus.*

A teen boy on a bicycle drew to an emergency stop and gawped at the phenomenon. Then he pulled out his phone and snapped pictures.

Orpheus strode to my side and pulled me into an embrace. *You don't need my help. You're the eternal girl, aren't you? Preserve your strength. Or your father is deader than a dormouse.*

10

With a deep inhale of breath, I disentangled myself from Orpheus, although it would have been easier to stay against the wall of his chest. Dad needed the logical me rather than the emotional me. I fought to ground myself. Images of my loved ones swept through my mind's eye. Marina giggling after a night out. Smudges of paint on Dad's face. The stillness in Ezra's grey eyes when he told me he loved me. Echo's purr of ecstasy when he rested at my side.

I exhaled, imagining my fear leaving me. It was a technique that worked a treat with constipation.

The leaves floated to the ground and landed in a mound in my parents' driveway.

The teen boy shrugged, stuffed his phone into the pocket of his tracksuit bottoms and resumed his journey.

I glanced at Orpheus. *I'm ready.*

We strode over to the detective.

Jameson pushed himself off the hood of his car. His clothes were rumpled like he'd been doing overtime. It didn't help that the Shadow Squad was a minuscule unit.

The men shook hands.

I got straight to the point, my voice curt. "I appreciate

your help, Rob. You need to tell us the facts out here. My brother's inside, and we can't trust him. He has betrayed me one too many times."

Orpheus sighed. "The werepigeon's mind and bowels are indeed full of shit. We have yet to find out the colour of his soul."

Jameson rubbed his hand over his shaved head. "Your tipoff about Mami turned up more than I expected. It's early days in an ongoing investigation, and usually, I wouldn't share any information at this point. But Joshi's disappearance changes everything."

I chewed the inside of my cheek. "Go on."

"The officer I sent to check out her premises came back with tattoos. Greenest fella ever too. Definitely not the tattoo type. He wouldn't say boo to a goose. He'd only just come off traffic duty, and came back with a Viking across his back. Very odd. So I did some digging."

Fear snaked inside of me.

"Mami's a hard woman to get a history for. She uses a number of aliases. She was Mami Webb at university, where she met your dad. We made a possible link to a Mami Wade, a calligrapher. Black Lotus Inkings is registered to Mami Wills. She's been a bank manager, an art gallery owner in Brighton and the founder of a cosplay shop in Lewisham. Each time, she's circled through the same identities. Each time, she moves on after a year or two and surfaces somewhere else. My gut tells me it's only a matter of time before we uncover a crime, but at this point, I don't even know if the crime is a matter for the local bobbies at the Met or the Shadow Squad. She's a conundrum." His voice trailed off.

"There's something you're not telling us," said Orpheus. "Come clean."

Jameson's angular face grew tight. "Don't forget who keeps your food stores topped up."

The slightest rise of Orpheus's eyebrow. "I can extract the

thoughts from your head quicker than a monkey picks a flea out of its mate."

Jameson winced. "When you put it like that...You remember that kid you dropped at Southwark police station, Alisha?"

My eyebrows pinched together. "Annie? As cute as a button. Abandoned on a bench. You know about that?"

"I do my homework. Annie's story checked out. We have the CCTV footage to prove it. That part of London is covered in them. Her dad is holding a hot chocolate. He takes off the lid, blows on it for a good minute, then puts the lid back on and settles her on the bench. A minute later, he looks over his shoulder and smiles at her while he goes into Black Lotus Inkings. Twenty minutes later, the kid is picking out the marshmallows from the hot chocolate when her dad leaves the shop and walks towards the river without a glance at his daughter. Nada. We tracked CCTV footage a bit further but lost him thirty minutes later. And he's not been home since."

I frowned. "What kind of man does that? Cares enough to make sure his six-year-old doesn't burn her tongue on a hot drink but then clean ignores her a few minutes later."

Orpheus shrugged. "Some men are not meant to be fathers."

Jameson drew in a ragged breath. "I went through the missing persons records, and Annie's father is one of half a dozen men who've gone missing in Waterloo since Mami showed up there. We're not talking about homeless men here. That would be bad enough. God knows this city has enough of them. These were family men integrated into their communities. They left their loved ones and dropped their responsibilities overnight. With no explanation. We scraped the footage from the cam across the road, and each of them has gone into her shop in the days preceding their disappearance."

My chest tightened. "Bloody hell."

"I'm working all hours on this with nothing to hold her on, but if I were a betting man, I'd say she's at the centre of it. I just pray to God that Joshi's not her latest victim."

"It's time to find out." I turned fearful eyes on my parents' front door and started up the driveway.

The chime hadn't ended before Sahil flung open the door with Alma behind him. He threw his arms around me. "You're here. I've been going out of my mind with worry. You didn't answer my calls."

I returned his hug with the enthusiasm reserved for random grannies at the temple. "I came as soon as I heard. Dad still hasn't turned up?"

A wall of minty breath hit me as he drew back. His brown eyes filled with worry. "Afraid not."

Sahil's hair—once his pride and joy, coiffed by high-end gentleman's barbers who offered eyebrow and designer stubble shaping at the same time—grew more dishevelled each time we met. His legs had grown spidery. Little wonder, given he could transform into either a spider or a werepigeon and had a weird luminous shield to boot. Shifters needed easy-access clothing. Gone was his Saville Row suit, replaced by a T-shirt and slacks that the previous incarnation of him wouldn't have been caught dead in.

"Did he take his phone and wallet?" I asked.

"I found them in his bedroom." His eyes flicked to Orpheus and Jameson behind me, and he stepped into the house to allow me through. "You've brought the calvary."

Orpheus inclined his head. "Werepigeon."

Sahil cocked his head, pigeon-style. "Vampire."

Alma didn't baulk. She must have put their exchange down to the insults men traded. Friendly banter, apparently. Her pinched expression and a lopsided buttoning of her cardigan reflected her distress. "I just don't know what happened, Alisha. He was so looking forward to a Victoria sponge with raspberry jam for afternoon tea. And his studio…it's ruined. I promised I'd look after him."

"He'll be home before dinner," I soothed, gesturing to her wonky buttons. There were fewer things more lowkey humiliating than going through the day with lipstick on your teeth, a hole in your crotch or your skirt tucked into your knickers, and nobody telling you.

Alma sniffed and fumbled with her buttons. When she looked up, her bloodshot eyes lingered on Orpheus, who hovered on the doorstep. "Who are these strapping young men? You're not really called Vampire, are you? I know Alma's is not en vogue anymore. But Vampire seems a bit farfetched."

Orpheus loomed over her. "Orpheus Might, at your service."

"Oh my. Well, do come in, Orpheus. I'm Alma Bluejay."

He stepped over the threshold.

Jameson flipped his Met badge. Seemed he had one, even though most ordinary officers didn't know the Shadow Squad existed. "Detective Robert Jameson, madam. Metropolitan Police. Alisha filled me in. We're here to get to the bottom of your friend's—"

"My life partner," said Alma helpfully.

"Your life partner's disappearance," said Jameson.

"We've checked his favourite local haunts. The common, the library, the baker that sells custard doughnuts." Alma extracted a well-used tissue from the cuff of her cardigan and blew her nose with gusto. "You know what your father's like. A hermit unless prodded out of his cave."

The woman needs a lie-down, said Orpheus. *Do you want me to put her to sleep?*

I glared at him. *You will not drink a drop of her blood.*

I wasn't going to kill her, you cretin. Just put her out of her misery for a half hour while we look for clues.

"I put up a missing person's notice at the community centre, but I haven't filed a missing person's report with the police. I'm not really family, you see," said Alma.

"You did the right thing, Mrs Bluejay," said the detective. "I'll take it from here."

Alma trumpeted into the tissue once more and checked what fluids she had evacuated before tucking it away again. "There's something you should know. Joshi was wearing his weekend clothes when I left."

Jameson frowned. "You mean his Sunday best?"

Alma flushed. "Not exactly, detective."

"Tell her, Alma." Sahil's beady eyes met mine.

I cottoned on in an excruciating flash of memory: Alma posing as Botticelli's Venus, painted by Dad in tights and a cape, giddy with excitement. "He was wearing the Superman outfit?"

Alma nodded. "I looked in the wardrobe and the laundry hamper. He definitely still has it on."

A few feet away, Orpheus—presumably reading my mind —cringed so hard his body almost curled into a ball.

"Jesus. Well, we'd better get started. I assume you've left everything where you found it?" Jameson handed out some latex gloves that Orpheus eyed with disdain and pulled his on with a snap. "Gloves on, and we'll crack on."

We made our way past the shrine in the hallway with the garlanded picture of Mum, her expression downcast.

I gasped as we entered Dad's studio. The damage was irreversible. Years of work lost in one fell swoop. Canvases tipped from their easels lay on the floor, many torn. Others had been drenched, leaving the paintings a hodgepodge of pooled colours and erased details. Paint brushes were strewn across the floor.

Jameson spoke first, his policeman's practicality cutting through the atmosphere of unease. "As far I can see, the walls and floorboards have no water damage. The pipes are intact."

He picked up a curled page from a trestle table laden with oil paints, watercolours, sketching pencils and jam jars of dirty water. "This is Mami's invitation?"

I nodded. Barely legible, the blue ink had a washed-out look, although the invitation was days, not decades, old.

He took an evidence bag from his jacket pocket, eased the letter into it and sealed it tight.

"You don't think he's been kidnapped by a spurned lover, do you? He's not exactly in his prime," said Sahil.

"I beg to differ," said Alma. "You should see how many women pretend their baskets are too heavy at the supermarket, so he'll help them to their car. One even dropped her scarf and batted her eyelids lasciviously at him. It was almost entrapment."

Jameson gave her a puzzled look and peered at the doors to the garden. "No forced entry?"

"No," said Sahil. "The front door was intact, as were the entry points here and in other rooms. I checked myself."

Jameson scratched his jaw. "Then the question is, *if* there was an intruder, where did they gain access? And where did the water come from?"

My brow furrowed as I looked at the paintings. "The only ones that have been soaked are the ones of winged animals." I couldn't be frank with a humdrum hanging onto every word. "Alma, would you mind checking the water meter in the utility room?"

"Of course, dear, I'll turn over the towels on the drying rack while I'm there." She scurried off.

I stepped across the floor and knelt by the cabinet in the corner. The lock had been ripped off. I eased the door open, a clamp tightening around my heart. "The catalogues of creatures Dad had been working on. They're both gone."

Orpheus swore with enough skill to raise the dead.

"You know what this means," said Jameson.

My heart hammered as I stood. "This isn't just an ordinary crime. It's an otherworldly one."

Sahil's thrust his chest out. "If the illustrations are gone, it means that *you* are the reason Dad is missing, Alisha."

Orpheus's flashed a cold smile. "I've always found it unsavoury when the guilty point fingers."

Alma stumbled through the door. Her foot went clean through a sketch of a peregrine falcon. "Oh, dear. I am sorry. I've checked, dear. The water meter is as steady as my monthly cycle used to be."

The men squirmed and looked pointedly away. I would have thought a vampire would have been comfortable with talk of blood.

"Thank you for checking, Alma," I said.

"I really do think you should check the loft, dear." She blew into her overloaded tissue. "Your father doesn't like going into the loft by himself these days. I found it a little strange that the hatch was open when I got back from the shops. I checked that he wasn't up there, of course, but a second pair of eyes wouldn't hurt."

She was right. Dad's balance had deteriorated with age. He preferred to outsource the task or have someone accompany him up there for moral support. I glanced at Jameson. "Follow me."

"I'll stay down here and put the kettle on so we can have a think about what to do." Alma crumpled. "My poor Joshi, out there in the world with just a thin sheath of Lycra to accompany him."

With the light fading quickly, I grabbed my phone for the torch function, kicked off my heels at the bottom of the stairs and grabbed a pair of Mum's old canvas shoes from the shoe drawer. Then I trudged up the stairs past family portraits that made my heart ache.

Sahil bristled behind me. "And they say *I'm* the one who's trouble. He'd be okay if it weren't for you."

I held a finger to my lips, my voice a hiss. "I know you're angry at me, but put a sock in it at least until Alma's out of earshot, will you?"

The loft hatch hung open with the ladder extended. A slight draught from the poorly insulated loft sent a rush of goosebumps up my arms. The ladder creaked in protest as I climbed ahead of the men, with my brother on my heels. Next came Jameson, and Orpheus brought up the rear, tripping on the gentleman's coat he wore.

Hope flared in me.

"Dad?" I called as I pushed myself up. Maybe he'd be there, a bit dazed under some boxes. But when we emerged into the dusty, boarded loft space, my heart sank anew, plummeting like a lift into the deepest basement.

Sahil walked the wobbly boards, ducking his head behind stacks of empty suitcases and sheer boxes filled with childhood mementoes. The rest of the space was an explosion of art. Endless stacks of water colours in frames and oil paintings on canvas. "He's not here."

I frowned at the flickering light bulb and turned on my phone torch as we looked for clues. "Dad's a stickler for saving electricity. He would have remembered to switch it off."

"There must be something that jumps out at you both. Something unusual." Jameson nosed around, gloved fingers picking up the odd painting, including the frog on the lily pad I had failed to animate before I realised my animation skills were limited to winged creatures.

That was when I noticed it. A painting that stood propped up alone against the wall. A painting that wasn't one of Mum or Dad's favourites. For years, it had been hidden at the back of a stack. An afterthought. A piece of the past. Something that he might have considered throwing into a skip but never had.

In it, Dad had a full head of hair, slightly parted lips and light falling across his face in a way that illuminated both his intelligence and humanity. "A M" had been scratched into the bottom righthand corner with coarse strokes.

I stooped for a better look at it. "Mami painted this. It's my father at university."

Orpheus's voice boomed behind me. "Is that what I think it is?"

Disbelief filled Orpheus's voice. "Your father kept this in his loft all this time?"

I nodded, edging even closer to the painting. *Call it nostalgia.*

Call it stupidity, said Orpheus.

The M pulsed with an eerie glow that made my skin crawl. "Is anyone else seeing this?"

Sahil leaned closer with me, gawping.

"I see it," said a sombre Jameson. "I think it's pretty clear by now that your father's disappearance is not a humdrum matter." He pulled out the evidence bag. "I'm going to get back to headquarters and have this processed. We'll put a watch on Mami and double down on our leads."

The painting beckoned me. I sensed it. Not a sound but a tug, impossible to resist.

I reached out my hand to touch the M. The letter grew more dazzling. It widened, and a sudden, icy cold snaked up my hand.

A sharp tone of worry from Orpheus. "Pull back, Alisha."

The painting sucked my wrist in.

I wrenched it back in horror, but it captured me all the same, pulling me into the dark, inch by inch, until my head and shoulders were through, then my waist. Into the pitch blackness I lurched, and even the hands clawing at my calves couldn't hold me back. I let out a blast of wind, but it tore into the void with no enemy as its target.

A thrust of energy dragged me fully onto the other side of the painting, where I landed in foot-deep water, together with someone else whose hands still clutched my calves.

"What the hell?" I kicked him off and glared at him. "Sahil?"

11

S ahil threw a horrified glance at his slopping wet shoes and clothes and scowled. "I couldn't exactly just let you go, could I? Now that Mum and Dad are gone, we must stick together."

A flashback of the Ravenmaster ricocheted through my head: blood and bones, dust and dank soil.

"Dad is *not* gone." I clenched my fists and pushed the memory out of my head.

I shone the phone torch—mercifully still in my grip—behind us and shuddered with dread. Whatever portal we'd stepped through had closed, leaving only a wall slick with grime. We were in some kind of sewer, judging by the brick tunnel and the stench of stagnant water. A quick check of my phone showed I didn't have a cat's chance in hell of reception down here, let alone using my map app to track our whereabouts. Still, I'd seen a BBC documentary on London sewers once, and I was pretty sure we were standing in one. That didn't mean I was happy about it.

I glowered at Sahil. "You could have tried to keep us on the other side of that lousy painting."

"Yeah, well, I've not had much time for the gym recently,

and a werepigeon and spider don't exactly have optimal upper body strength," said Sahil. "My Tinder rating has gone right through the floor since all this Otherworld malarkey, and I've been sprouting hair in the most disgusting places. Not to mention the random bowel ejections. Not only that, but my tenants can't understand why I refuse to install pigeon spikes. It's a real problem."

I rolled my eyes, ignoring a scuttling rat with superhuman effort. Hopefully, the toothy vermin wasn't one of Lavinia's spies.

Once, the river Thames had been an open sewer, giving rise to cholera epidemics. Nowadays, a modernised Victorian sewer system blocked at some points by fatbergs—mounds of wet wipes, fat and grease deposits—ran under the city's streets. I pegged my nose against the stink with my thumb and forefinger. It made me retch just thinking about wading through here.

I wished I'd waited for Ezra. He'd protect me until his dying breath. And it'd be damn hot. Instead, I was stuck in a sewer with my deadbeat brother and no phone signal.

Still, I wasn't going to mope. I'd learned long ago that I could move mountains if I put my mind to it. Usually mountains of laundry, but I had to start somewhere. It was time for big girl panties, not squeamishness or melodrama. "Come on. Dad must have gone through the painting. I hope we've got the wrong end of the stick, but if this Mami is responsible for the missing men, we'd better find him."

Sahil grabbed my shoulder. "You really think he's going to be okay? I'm not ready to be an orphan."

Putrid water sloshed around my ankles as I turned to face him and swung the light in his face. The smart-arse response evaporated from my lips as I took in the real worry in his eyes. Mum and Dad would want us to work together. Maybe this is what we needed to heal our fractured relationship.

A bonding experience in a rat-infested London sewer.

"We're going to do everything in our power to bring him home, you hear me?" I said.

He looked around. "Where are we, anyway? That portal could have taken us anywhere."

I sighed. "The London sewers. You're the property magnate city boy. I thought you would have realised."

His voice jerked in surprise. "Hardly. My portfolio is full of penthouses, sis. Not rat-infested dumps."

I wasn't sure if I'd make it through the next thirty minutes without throttling him, let alone a rescue attempt. To top it off, Sahil's past shenanigans meant that—brother or no brother—I'd be a fool to trust him.

I kept my tone even. "So, have you still got Mum's car then?"

Not only had Mum left him her car in her will, but said car had turned out to be a conduit for the gods. It was the sole reason Sahil had been able to make a Faustian deal with Hermes for his powers. Well, that and the fact that my brother had the moral compass of an angry warthog.

"Yeah, you know how sentimental I am. I couldn't get rid of the last thing Mum gave me."

Heaven help me. He was anything but sentimental. The sort of person who threw out a birthday card as soon as it arrived.

"It's in my garage," he continued. "I call Hermes's name every now and then, just out of habit, but he hasn't answered. Discombobulation has that effect." A pointed pause. "I'm lucky all the sawdust is out of my lungs."

Was he fishing for an apology? My gaze snagged on something floating in the water. I picked it up and turned over the ruined suede in my hands, my pulse accelerating. "It's Dad's moccasin slipper. I got them for him last Christmas."

Sahil inched closer. "Oh shit. He loved those things. He was really down here."

I nodded and peered down the tunnel, where the dark stretched for miles. "We need to check the rest of the tunnel quickly. There's no time to lose. I need you to shift into your werepigeon form." Not only would he cover the ground quicker, but he'd have a 340-degree field of vision, so he would be less likely to miss stuff.

He baulked. "You shift into a werepigeon."

I sighed. "I can't. Only you can."

His eyes gleamed. "So you need me, now, eh? Well, okay. But only because without me, this mission would be a complete failure. You have to hold my clothes, though. There's nowhere to put them down here."

I turned my back on him. The shadows cloaked him anyway, but a view of my brother's package after the day I'd had would just about finish me off. A rustling of clothes met my ears before he thrust them at me, his stiff boxers topping the pile. A pop, a few coos and a fluttering of wings later, and I turned to find the werepigeon hovering inches from my nose.

"Thank you," I said.

Tufty feathers poked from the werepigeon's muscly chest and grey-greenish cranium. He opened his orange beak, and I recoiled at the teeth that loomed. They might be well-cared for—my brother had an exemplary flossing regimen—but teeth on a pigeon gave me the heebie-jeebies.

"You'll come after me if things go square?" he asked.

"Of course." I meant it. Our sibling bond might be complex, but I loved him. We were in this together. I clutched his clothes and shone my torch in the direction of travel. "Now find Dad and report back."

The werepigeon cocked his head and focused on me with one fiery red eye. "What's the magic word?"

He didn't wait for a response. Instead, he offloaded his bowels into the water and flew down the tunnel.

"Pretty Polly?" I called after him.

Avoiding the white splodge Sahil had ejected, I plunged forward through the dark waters, maintaining a speedy pace not to fall too far behind. I'd long given up trying not to inhale the smells. My nostrils twitched with the onslaught, but finding Dad was worth any discomfort. The tunnel was eerier still without Sahil at my side. I listened for his grunts or the beating of his wings.

All was quiet, apart from the slopping of the stagnant water as I waded through it. Fear rippled through me and became a scream in my head.

There was barely any wind in the sewers. My druid powers didn't work in a vacuum. The catalogues of creatures had been stolen. My sword lay in my knicker drawer at home. There was no Echo or Ezra at my side. Marina, my sister and support, was caught in a library amongst the stars. I was just a middle-aged woman, friendless and alone.

But a middle-aged woman fighting for her family was a force to be reckoned with. She was a lioness, ready to walk barefoot through fire, wind and rain.

Or sludge.

A flash of colour caught my eye on the tunnel wall, and I directed the torchlight at the image of a woman with deep colouring, dressed in hues of rich orange and sea-green. She had a bare torso and thick, dark hair. A fat snake lay across her shoulders, its serpent tongue inches from her own. The woman had a mermaid's tail.

I tore my eyes away, repulsed yet drawn to it.

A few steps further revealed a different but not dissimilar woman stencilled onto the sewer walls. This African woman had dreadlocked hair and blood-red lips. She stretched out her mermaid body on a bed of corals and held a mirror. A snake had wound itself around her torso and her legs.

A frisson of fear jerked up my spine. The resemblance to Mami was undeniable.

Despite where we found ourselves, I couldn't shake the

fact that there was something shrine-like about the images. I shook my head. That was stupid. Mami was a peculiar, not a deity. She was a bunny boiler who had gone to university with Dad, that was all. Sure, she was a few sprinkles short of a sundae, but there was nothing to say she had harmed a hair on the heads of the men who'd gone missing.

Either way, if Marina ever asked whether we could go for matching tattoos again, we'd stay well clear of Black Lotus Inkings.

My brother appeared in a sprawl of wings with a haphazard trajectory. He perched on my shoulder, breathing heavily. "It's not good. It's not good."

I struggled against his weight, but the poor bloke was exhausted. "Calm down, Sahil. What's not good?"

A minty werepigeon wail in my ear. "I don't see how we'll get him out. He said she'll be back any minute."

I dropped Sahil's clothes and the slipper in the sewer with a plop and picked my brother off my shoulder so I could look him in the eyes. Well, one eye because the side positioning of his peepers made normal eye contact impossible.

The air grew thin and still. "You found him. Where is he?"

He squirmed in my hands. "Follow me."

I ran after him, not caring if anything slithered in the rat-infested sewer. It didn't matter that I was in a skirt and blouse. It didn't matter that I ran through darkness in an eerie, stinky tunnel beneath the city.

Dad was alone. He needed us.

He said she'll be back any minute. Angry thoughts pounded through my head, metre after metre, through the revolting sewer. I'd give that loony-toon tattoo artist a taste of her own medicine. How dare she take our dad from us. From his home.

Sahil's nasal werepigeon voice floated back to me. "Hurry, Alisha. We don't have much time."

I caught up at last and skidded to a halt next to him. Sahil perched on a set of bars that sealed off a small chamber adjacent to the main tunnel. He peered inside, grunting, flapping in distress. My eyes acclimated to the shadows in the chamber just as a weak voice spoke.

"My children. You shouldn't have come."

"Dad?" My hands pulsed as I tried to shift the bars with my wind powers, but barely a light breeze emerged. I gripped the bars in frustration and shook them violently. I squinted, and at last, my blurry vision deciphered the blues and reds of his Superman costume.

He slumped against the left-hand wall of the chamber, his cape torn. His hands and feet had been bound. He wore one slipper, and underneath the costume, his ribs seemed concave. His frailty hit me with such a force that I trembled with fear for him.

"She did this to you? Mami?" I searched in vain for an opening, then lifted my hands, cursing when the wind wouldn't come. Cursing the airlessness of this place. "Has she hurt you? What does she want?"

Dad shook his head. "Go. Leave now. She is more than a woman. More than a peculiar. She is—"

"She is a goddess." How had it taken me so long to see it? Her strange pull on Ezra in the tattoo parlour. Her all-encompassing knowledge of my loved ones when I'd not heard a hoot about her. The immortal disdain with which she walked through the world, secure in the knowledge that no rules applied to her. The reverential images in the tunnel.

A cry of anguish from Dad. His wiry white moustache hung limp. "There are other men in the chambers. I can hear them. They say no one stays in one place for long. She's already moved me once. And she is never gone long. Please, my children, go! Save yourselves."

"I'll leave you my phone. We'll put it on silent. That way, we'll be able to track you," I said.

He glanced at his Superman outfit in woe. "It's no good,

love. This wretched thing has no pockets. Sahil could put it in my smalls, but the last chamber I was in filled with water."

My helplessness overwhelmed me. How could I be powerless to help my own dad? The man who had kissed my tears away, who had made me pancakes for breakfast and mopped my bloody knees when I stumbled. The man who, even in old age, would drop everything to help me move a wardrobe. The man who fretted when I walked the streets of the city alone, even though I was forty years old and hardly an ingenue. Who had tolerated sharing my childhood home with a cat he loathed because he sensed our bond. Who had felt so alone since Mum's death and had only just found love again with Alma.

I closed my eyes and prayed for help. For Gaia.

I don't have an offering for you, goddess. All I have is an open heart. Please help us. Only Gaia could get us out of this. Only her goodness could be a match for a warped goddess.

The air shifted behind me, and I spun around with my phone torch, my empty fist clenched, my stance wide in case it was the other goddess. Mami. The one who made my elderly father tremble. Powers or no powers, I could still unleash the full force of my kickboxing on her. I'd kick her to Timbuktu for what she'd done.

"Hellfire," said Ezra. "Thank Christ. I've been pinging all over the place after Jameson triangulated your last phone single." Grey eyes narrowed on the scene behind me. "Joshi?"

I'd never been so pleased to see anyone in my life. "Mami's a goddess. We have to get him out of there."

"Hurry, werewolf," said Sahil.

Ezra nodded and closed his eyes, like he did just before he teleported, picturing his destination to minimise accidental landings on top of teapots or in rivers or on steep mountainsides. But he didn't fade like he usually did. "It's not working. Dammit, why isn't it working?"

"How about your charms?" I glanced at them. A moon for

light. A thistle for healing. Binary code for tech. "There must be something that will help."

Ezra shook his head. He gritted his teeth and rammed the gate over and over until his shoulders must have been black and blue. "It's magically enforced. I'm so sorry, Alisha."

"It's no good," Dad's parched voice called out before waning into a whisper. "Don't you see? Your mother's death was my fault. You have to go. Before Mami ensnares you in her net too."

I looked around for something, anything to help him. I didn't even have any drinking water for him.

"No. No, we refuse. You're coming home with us." Sahil squeezed his werepigeon body through the bars with grim determination, heaving and wriggling until he popped out the other side and landed on the dank floor. He threw himself at Dad's feet and wrists, clawing and biting the restraints. He jerked back and spat a liquid out in disgust. "I don't get it. Chains made from water? What kind of black magic is this?"

It wasn't going to work. I turned to Ezra with urgency. "Water. He needs water."

A vein throbbed in Ezra's neck. He disappeared and returned a moment later with bottled water.

By now, Sahil had shifted back into his human form, but the chains of water couldn't be broken, however much he tried. He collapsed onto Dad, butt naked and weeping. "You've been there for us our whole lives. We are not leaving you."

"I told you, son," Dad whispered in anguish. "It won't work. Her magic is too strong."

I shoved the water bottle through the bars. "He needs water."

Sahil strode across, grabbed the water and returned to Dad.

Dad gulped it down like he'd been in the desert. "There's a spell to release the bindings, spoken only by water creatures, but they are loyal to her. Maybe if Alisha could animate one, it could work, but without the catalogues of creatures, what chance does she have?"

Soft singing wove through the darkness, a mysterious grouping of notes that didn't sound like any song I'd heard on the radio or any choir in a church.

Dad crumpled. "Oh Ganesha, oh Ganesha. I can hear her." Fire filled his voice, a fatherly instinct to protect us that overrode his sense of self-preservation. "Go now, or I will never forgive you."

Tears clogged my throat. I drank in the sight of Dad, terrified we'd never see him again. But our only chance of getting him out was if we recouped and came back stronger with the tools to get him out. "Sahil, we have to go."

My brother's voice was an open wound. "We can't leave him."

"It will kill him if he sees you die here." Glass in my throat that cut deep. "We love you, Dad."

"Now, Alisha," hissed Ezra at my ear.

My brother staggered to the bars as the singing grew ever louder.

I pushed my palm through. "There's no time. Shift into the spider."

Our brown eyes met as his body twisted, stretched and shrank. A hairy, bulbous spider scuttled into my palm. I darted to Ezra's side, and his arms closed around me as he teleported us between the worlds, holding me as I cupped my brother in my palms.

We left Dad behind, my brother and I united in the wretchedness of abandoning him.

12

———

We materialised in Dad's kitchen. The evening sun filtered across the tiled floor. It was a pretty ballsy move of Ezra's, bringing us to the heart of Dad's home, where humdrum Alma could be pottering in any corner.

I tossed the spider at the counter. No sane woman wanted to touch a hairy, bulbous spider for longer than necessary.

The spider squeaked in a voice that was still recognisably my brother. As in, Sahil before his voice broke. "No need to be so rough. I thought we were bonding there."

I shuddered. "Count yourself lucky I didn't give into my first instinct to flush you down the loo."

Ezra lent against the fridge, energy spent. "Might be a good time to shift, werepigeon. We've got a lot to talk about."

The spider grew before our eyes into my brother, his bare bottom on the worktop.

I averted my eyes, gagging. He hadn't lied about hair sprouting in odd places since he'd become a werepigeon.

Alma bustled into the kitchen with a tray of tea and biscuits. She squealed in horror. "Sahil Verma, get your nether regions off that countertop. I've only just wiped it. It's going to need bleaching now you've rubbed your behind there."

Sahil slid off the counter, his bare bottom giving a last humiliating squelch against the surface before he landed on his feet and cupped his balls. "I'll grab some clothes from upstairs."

"Why did he take them off in the first place, dear?" Alma stared after him, bewildered.

"You don't want to know." I sighed, closing my eyes. *Gaia, I need you.* Nothing.

"Well, each to their own, I suppose," said Alma. "I wondered where you and your brother had got to."

I peeled off my sodden shoes, considering filling her in on Dad's whereabouts but decided it would break the Founder's Law to reveal the existence of the Otherworld to her. Not to mention the possibility of fracturing her humdrum mind by revealing it. Not every mind expanded enough to cope with reality shifting. "Have you seen the detective and Orpheus?"

"They are discussing your father's disappearance in the living room. Your cat turned up, Alisha. He's very clever." She gave Ezra an admiring glance as he unburdened her of her tea tray. "It's nice to have so many strapping young men in the house, even if they do have a tendency to leave it all hanging out. I do miss my Joshi."

Tears clogged my throat at the thought of Dad all alone and in need. "He'll be home soon, Alma. I promise."

She dipped her hand into a bag of flour and scattered it liberally over the work surface, stared at it for a moment, and then smiled at me. "I believe you, dear. Go on through, and I'll bring you some tea."

I gave her a wan smile. Baking was obviously her safe space. "No need for tea. We'll let you get on."

She popped the kettle on. "Suit yourself. I learned a long time ago that a cuppa at a moment of anxiety is a blessing."

Ezra and I made our way to the living room, with its comforting pair of shabby green tartan sofas which had accompanied me through childhood. An uncomfortable silence reigned, similar to the atmosphere in a hospital waiting room. Jameson sat on the sofa closest to the television, where usually Dad watched *Countdown*. Echo had commandeered Mum's sofa next to a reading lamp with a flowery shade, leaving a grumpy Orpheus to perch on the rocking chair in the corner.

He sprang up before we came through the door frame. *I am not grumpy. I was worried. You disappeared through that blasted thing, and I couldn't hear your thoughts anymore.*

That's how it should be. Out loud, I said, "Gentleman, we have work to do."

Echo raced towards me. Emerald eyes widened with joy, but his voice pulsed with hurt. "I am tempted to put a training lead on you, Alisha. How am I supposed to protect you if you tear off, leaving all of us in the dust?"

Jameson, too, had taken to his feet. "You were gone nearly an hour. Your phone signal went batty once you went through the portal. Luckily, we managed to triangulate it. Your wolf worked himself to the bone trying to find you. He seems to have quite an instinct for the scent you leave on the fabric of the universe. I'm not sure he would have found my granny so fast."

Orpheus came to our side in a blink. *I should spank you for disappearing like that.*

"Well done, Neuhoff. They don't call you our best seeker for nothing." He reached out to Ezra. They shook hands like I was a prize they'd won at a fair.

Ezra pumped his hand. "It was pure luck. I don't get to do much seeking these days with my skin in the senate game."

"A dog is useful if he is well-trained," purred Echo. "But an armoured leopard is unparalleled."

I frowned. "Will you all stop peacocking? We found Dad."

"Alisha, I think we've put it together," Jameson frowned. "If you found Joshi, where is he?"

Sahil strode into the room, thankfully dressed. We

gathered in a huddle in the middle of the living room, mindful of Alma overhearing. Echo, conscious of his height disadvantage, leapt onto the sofa to be at eye level.

I willed myself to keep my emotions at bay, though they threatened to spill over. "He was locked in a chamber in the sewers. We didn't have the strength or the magic to free him, but we did speak to him. Mami's not a peculiar, Jameson. She's more than that."

Jameson nodded. "She's a goddess. I don't know why I didn't see it sooner."

I shrugged. "It's okay, Rob. This city is full of gods. They've hidden in plain sight for centuries. You're just a man with limited resources in a city where even immortals can be anonymous. What matters is working out what we are up against and how we get Dad out."

A catch in Sahil's throat. "We need him home."

My heart went out to him. For the first time in forever, I understood him. Not only that, it felt good being on the same side.

Echo's whiskers twitched with emotion. "How was Joshi holding up? A man like him, with marshmallow at his centre, isn't good on the battlefield."

"You do him a disservice," said Ezra. "It takes a core of steel to be a good father, and though Joshi was afraid and vulnerable, he insisted we abandon him. He put his children first."

"I tried so hard to free him, but he was bound by chains of water," said Sahil. "My beak just went clean though them."

"Your beak? A portal in a painting. A goddess in a sewer. Magical water chains. This job never fails to surprise." Jameson shook his head. "We were helpless while you were gone, Alisha. I went through your parents' mythology books, cross-checking with what we had already. They have quite a stash. Anyway, hidden in some obscure text, I found her. I know her true identity."

I leaned forward, my heart pounding in my ears. "Who is she really, Rob?"

"Mami Wata, a water goddess. The earliest mentions of her are four thousand years ago. She was beloved by African societies. I think she came to England across the Atlantic with enslaved people. She's a protector and nurturer but also has the capacity for destruction."

"I think we know what bend she's on right now. What are her powers?"

"She's a provider of riches, a healer of physical and spiritual ills. She can protect rivers, seas and oceans. She can provide fish or a cure for impotence. She can make you beautiful. Fill a barren womb or protect abused women. She can give you the house of your dreams. Or she can steal your husband and demand he is faithful only to her. One smile from her, one sniff of her perfume, one touch of her hand or song sung, and the trap is open. She commands loyalty. To deny her means death. She can expend sexual energy until nothing is left but a lifeless corpse."

Sahil paled. "Bloody hell, that's horrific. But one way to avoid Viagra, I suppose."

Jameson ploughed on, his policeman's mind intent on gathering all the clues. "Tell me, was Joshi drugged?"

"No. He was lucid…He could hear other men's voices who were trapped in adjacent chambers." A catch in my voice. I couldn't break down in front of them.

I have a handkerchief in my pocket if you need it. Not a mocking twitch to be found on Orpheus's face.

"We need the location. Neuhoff, you can get us back there, can't you?" said Jameson. "We'll take your Aunt Lavinia and her coven. There's not much she can't handle."

"Dad said Mami keeps moving them around," said Sahil. "And she's never gone long."

Jameson's jaw tightened. "I'll get the plans to the sewers. We'll find the missing men if we have to search every square mile of that putrid pit. We'll need to do some digging and find out her exact powers. See what we're up against."

I thought back to the kernels of information I had filed away in my mind for this very moment. The clues I had held onto that might be the key to freeing him. Hope bloomed in me like a flower. "There's a spell to release the bindings, spoken only by water creatures, but they are loyal to Mami. The coven could replicate the spell, I'm sure of it." I turned imploring eyes on Ezra. "Mami has this pull on men, even on Ezra. I think that's why the men have been taken so easily. But Lavinia could help. She doesn't like me, but would help if you vouched for us, Ezra."

Orpheus tore his dark eyes from my face. "I can't speak for Neuhoff, but you're forgetting one thing. It is still a fraught matter amongst the senate that peculiars choose to challenge the gods. For centuries, we have turned a blind eye to their manoeuvres. Some would be sympathetic to your plight after the Ravenmaster trespassed and shed blood on Wildwoods territory—"

"But others are less amenable to tear up the old ways." Ezra sighed. "As Justice Minister, what I risked this evening for you was in a personal capacity. Orpheus and I can't operate openly against the gods without jeopardising our standing."

How cold and calculating Ezra sounded. I wouldn't ask questions if he asked me to bend the rules for his family. I'd do it for love, even if my conscience twinged.

That isn't strictly true, druid. You were keen to put the boot into Gunnolf Zev, and yet wasn't he a father to your wolf? said Orpheus.

Get out of my head, Orpheus. This is the hill you're going to die on?

Using Christ imagery with a vampire isn't the done thing, Alisha.

My brother drew himself to his full height. "Your

standing? Well, that's a load of bollocks. We're not just going to let my dad rot down there!"

Ezra's grey eyes sparked copper. "Steady on, Sahil. That's not what I said. We're working on it."

"The wolf is right," said Orpheus. "The wheels of office move slowly. It is a chess game that cannot be rushed."

Echo leapt off the sofa and nuzzled my legs as if he could sense the ache in me. "It sounds to me like the wolf is enjoying the trappings of power too much."

My anger flared, mirroring my brother's. "There's no time. Who knows what Mami wants or how long she'll keep those men alive? The Pragmatist's Law can go to hell. What's the point of rules if they protect the powerful?"

I balled my fists. How could I be surrounded by allies yet feel so alone? I would have given anything for Marina's counsel at that moment.

Jameson continued. "Looks like we're at a stalemate here. We should reach out to Gaia. Find out what she knows."

"I've tried. She hasn't been forthcoming." My brow furrowed. "We should burn the painting in the loft. We can't risk the goddess having an access point. We can access the sewer system the old-fashioned way."

Orpheus gave a curt nod. "Consider it done."

"I'm going to head back to the office and do some digging. I'll call you as soon as I have something new." Jameson frowned. "I used to have someone to go home to, but she's not there anymore."

I hugged him, feeling the bitter pill of Marina's absence keenly.

Ezra held out a hand to me. "Let's go home and talk this over. We have to recoup and get more information. If we rush in there again unprepared, we'll do more harm than good."

Sure, there was logic in his words, but was love for family logical?

There was nothing to talk about. I had to save Dad. "Actually, I need a moment with Sahil."

And just like that, the werepigeon regains his place in the family, said Orpheus.

I turned to my brother. "Fancy a walk to clear our heads?"

My brother's brown eyes met mine. "Sure, sis."

"I'm in," said Echo, untroubled by the lack of invitation.

His loyalty touched me. Even if I knew that a choice cut of meat or braised salmon, not to mention a well-coiffed poodle, would turn his head.

"Gentleman." I nodded at the three men, avoiding Orpheus's eyes, frightened he'd unravel every last secret I shielded from him.

Ezra followed me into the hallway. He looped his fingers around my waist—the slightest touch. "I'm on your side. I know this is hard. I wouldn't want you to lose Joshi. He is a good man. A good father. And we all need one."

He missed Gunnolf. I could see it in his pauses, even when he didn't say the words. It should have made him tear up all the rules for me.

Ezra grasped my arms. "I know you too well to think you're going to rest on your laurels while your dad is in danger. It cuts me up that I can't jump straight in there with you. But there's this spell Lavinia knows. I think it can help."

"You'll talk to her?"

He nodded and then kissed me hard. "Don't do anything stupid. If you need an extraction, I'll drop everything to help. You're my girl."

In the hallway, I lingered at Mum's shrine. It wasn't time for Dad's photograph to stand next to hers. Not yet. We needed him. Squeezing my eyes shut, I called for Gaia with all my might. But when I opened my eyes, the rustle behind me was only Sahil and Echo, impatient to leave. Loneliness washed over me at the thought that Gaia, too, had abandoned me.

We said our goodbyes to Alma and walked away from the house in silence. The crisp night air was a relief.

Then Sahil turned to me. "Spill the beans."

Emerald eyes glinted in the shadows. "We know you have a plan."

13

I faced them, fists clenched, eyes full of fire. "I'm not going to sit on my butt waiting for lightning to strike. Not while Dad is in a London sewer, thinking we abandoned him. I won't have it. But we'll have to be better prepared this time."

Echo's whole demeanour changed at the prospect of a battle. His head lifted, his chest puffed out, and his eyes shone. He lived for moments when he could slip the shackles of pretence that he was a household moggie. "It will be magnificent. She's going to call in the dragon. The dragon will raze that sewer down to ashes, and Joshi's jail will be molten metal. There will be immortal blood spilt, and I will lap it up like milk. And Joshi will be free."

"What a lovely fantasy, but Tielbu is safe and sound in Bulgaria. That's where he's staying."

Sahil looked at the leopard, aghast. "And we prefer our father to be whole rather than a charred husk."

Echo dipped his regal head in disappointment. "More fool you. It would have been quite the spectacle."

I stalked the asphalt between the two of them, my hand coiling in Echo's fur as my thoughts churned. Streetlights flickered overhead. "My wind powers didn't work down there. Dad said if I could animate, I might stand a chance, but I can't animate without an illustrator. Echo would have to get close to Mami to do any damage. And your werepigeon and spider selves have limited offensive capability, Sahil."

Sahil pursed his lips. "I could always jump on her face."

He wasn't even joking.

"Yeah, then she'd drown you in a puddle. The chains tell us Mami has water abilities. Dad said she had control over water creatures. That marries up with paintings I spotted in the tunnel of an African woman with a mermaid's tail."

Echo growled long and low. "I swallow fish as easily as I draw breath."

I drew a shaky breath. I'd studiously avoided thinking of the stolen catalogues of creatures during the meeting in case Orpheus caught wind of it. "I do have a plan, but it's a risk."

Sahil nodded, his lips set in a determined line. "I'm staying at your side until we bring Dad home."

The genuineness of his tone chiselled away at my anger about him teaming up with the Ravenmaster. Maybe it wasn't beyond the realms of possibility that we could be close one day.

Echo roared, and the leaves of the oak tree edging the pavement quivered in response. "As am I."

I drew in a deep breath and exhaled slowly. "There's nothing to say that an animator can only be paired with one illustrator. Our family history proves that. Rajika was paired with both her brother and Dad, after all."

Sahil cocked his head, birdlike even in his human form. "What are you saying?"

Hope fluttered in me, cautious and small. "Sahil, we have a great-uncle we never knew about. He was Rajika Verma's illustrator for decades before Dad was born. But he and our grandmother parted ways."

Echo slapped me with the back of his paw like I was a cub. "I told you we should stay away from him."

The males around me really took liberties. I caught his paw but resisted the urge to backhand him in return. This wasn't a game of tennis.

"You overstep the line." My voice was a whip.

If Marina could love her veterinary clients even when they came in to have their anal glands emptied, I could tolerate an aggravated leopard. Dad had wanted me to steer clear too, but what choice did I have?

Sahil frowned. "We have a relative in London we didn't know about?"

I pulled out my phone and searched for the text Jameson had sent me days ago. "Great-Uncle Rajiv is in his eighties. He lives on a houseboat in London's Docklands. I think he could help us."

"Let us hope he is so decrepit he has forgotten his name and needs help to wash his armpits," said Echo. "Rajiv, with his faculties intact, will try to control you. I should go in and rat you out to the wolf and the vampire. But I hate rats. They are mean and will fight to the death before ending up on my dinner menu. But let it be known your grandmother would turn in her grave if she hadn't been cremated and scattered on the wind."

I couldn't fault his logic. I still hoped he'd come with us all the same.

"We'll do this without you, leopard." Sahil cupped his hands over his mouth and made a low-pitched burp.

"What are you doing?" I asked.

"No one told you about the Otherworld taxis, eh? I guess they didn't need to, given you have a vampire's hot wheels, a teleporting wizard and a dragon at your beck and call. Well, I'm not so lucky. A pigeon is not the most athletic bird. A spider and human take an age to get anywhere. That's when I found out." He belched again. It went on for so long it could have been the sound of tectonic plates shifting.

The ground trembled, announcing an avalanche, but that

couldn't be right. We were in London, not on Ben Nevis, after all. I furrowed my brow and peered into the distance. Large objects moved towards us at speed. The trembling became a roar of engines as a fleet of black cabs approached. They didn't appear to be travelling in any particular formation. Instead, lone vehicles darted in and out of the road, paying no attention to the central line markings. These weren't London cabbies. Those were a steady, dependable lot who knew the rules of the road inside out.

These were something else entirely.

"Our ride is here," said Sahil.

A grubby, black cab veered away from the rest and swerved to a halt beside us, its amber occupancy sign flickering on and off. Dark glass shielded the driver from view.

No girl would step into a random vehicle like this. Especially one hailed by a burp.

On one side, it looked like a regular London cab: gleaming black and beetle-shaped with worn leather seats and yellow handlebars. It had either been keyed by a hooligan, or claw and tooth marks marred its other side. I pressed my nose to the glass, alarmed when the taxi skirted forward slightly.

Sahil opened the door and clambered in. "Well, are you coming?"

In Marina's absence, he was my sounding board. Granted, his instincts differed from mine, but I trusted him with my life. Going it alone with Sahil wasn't ideal, even if we had somewhat made amends. I glanced at Echo.

"Don't look at me. An Indian leopard runs thirty-five miles an hour, and this city has more traffic jams than Mumbai. I have no need for taxis." Echo gave a weighted sigh. "But I am not letting you get in there alone. After you."

"This isn't creepy at all." I climbed in.

There were no seats or seatbelts inside. Instead, a double mattress and a small chest of drawers filled the interior.

Echo's rump cleared the door, and I reached out to slam it behind him and shivered as the locks clicked shut. An opaque sheet of glass blocked the driver from sight.

I knocked on the window. "Greenland Docks, please."

The engine roared to life, and off we sped through the streets of London. The cab bumped along the road, well over the speed limit. I sank onto the mattress, sighing as the exhaustion in my bones seeped out. Echo followed suit, his claws kneading the mattress, his face a picture of bliss.

"I've had some of my best naps in these alternative London cabs," said Sahil. "And the best thing about them is that you always turn up at your destination ten minutes earlier than your departure time. Like some weirdly punctual time machine. Think of it less as a taxi and more as a rejuvenation centre. One that takes you from A to B but leaves you feeling all spruced up. See the chest there? Open the drawers."

Rolling reluctantly off the mattress, I edged my way to the pine chest of drawers, taking care to hold the yellow handlebars on the inside of the cab door. When I tugged open the top drawer, I found a neatly folded pile of women's clothes, some trainers in my size and an airport-style freshening pack of wet wipes, toothpaste, toothbrush and an eye shield. The second drawer held a pile of men's clothes, shoes and another freshening pack. The third drawer held a cashmere blanket and a plate of cubed steak covered with a bell-dome.

"This is for us?" I asked.

Echo's nose twitched. A purr rolled from his throat. "I smell steak. My nose never lies."

I handed him the steak and then plucked out the items the cab had magicked up for Sahil and me. We changed in silence, keeping our underwear on, although I would have given anything to whip my bra off and hang loose. But giving my estranged great-uncle an eyeful probably wasn't the best move. Still, it was a relief to peel off my skirt and blouse at last and get into clean clothes. I dry-brushed with the toothbrush, enjoying the grainy mint taste in my mouth, and then collapsed onto the mattress for some more sore muscle therapy while Echo munched the last remnants of the steak.

Sahil placed our dirty things in the chest and snapped the drawers shut. The low roar of an incinerator met our ears, heat pulsed through the cab, and embers rained down on us. "Watch this. It doesn't do things by halves."

"Oh, my god. I liked that blouse." How easily we had entered a new rhythm. It still bothered me that we couldn't see into the front section of the cab. "Who's driving?"

Sahil shrugged. "I don't know. Does it matter? Never look a gift horse in the mouth. Shut your eyes for a few minutes, sis. Our long day isn't over yet. And you'll need to be at full strength to rescue Dad."

He nestled beside me.

I felt a pang for when we watched cartoons together as kids, and my head would drop onto his shoulder, or we would laugh uproariously at something silly. Then I closed my eyes and allowed the swaying and surging of the cab to lull me to sleep.

I YELPED as Sahil ripped a hair from my head. "What did you do that for?"

Sahil's smooth face loomed over me. "We're here, Alisha. Payment for the Otherworld cab is a hair each. Pluck one out, and leave it on the mattress. And woe betide anyone who forgets or refuses to pay."

I rubbed my scalp. He'd obviously lost his mind. It took a minute to remember where I was. Then it all came flooding back. Marina in the Celestial Library. Ezra's preoccupation with the senate. And worst of all, a goddess on the rampage with Dad in her grip.

Sahil set his jaw, a wary look in his eyes. "Come here, leopard."

Echo hissed. "You dare touch a hair on my head, werepigeon…"

"If you don't pay, the doors lock, and the taxi dumps you in the East End of London. Didn't you notice the claw marks on the exterior?"

"No leopard in his right mind ventures there. Still, I feel as fresh as a daisy, and I pay my dues. It's a shame to ruin my zen seeking out the wily old codger I've avoided for decades." Echo's lips curled, revealing a string of steak between his jagged teeth. He offered Sahil his rump. "Do your worst."

The black cab jerked to a halt, and the locks flicked open. I heaved myself off the mattress, turned the door handle and stepped into the starry night. Free of occupants, the cab reversed down the street, executed a three-point turn at breakneck speed and disappeared into the night.

I stared at my watch. Just as Sahil said, we'd arrived ten minutes earlier than we'd departed. As if we'd stepped from Dad's living room straight into London's Docklands. "Come on. The sooner we get this over with, the sooner Dad is back with us."

Greenland Dock was the city's oldest wet dock, situated south of the river Thames. At one time, a commercial dock, home to warehouses and passing cargo ships, it had played a key role in the whaling trade. Now it was a residential area with townhouses, luxury apartment blocks, a watersport centre, and once even a floating boozer called the Wibbly Wobbly. The dock had a village feel, despite the imposing high-rises from Canary Wharf looming in the distance. We kept our voices down as we walked through the dock at a steady pace, avoiding a drunk man whose comical footwork almost took him clean over the barrier into the water.

"I think that's the one." I pointed to a maroon narrowboat called Sitting Duck bobbing gently on the water.

The barge was no more than forty feet long, with yellow trim. A lamp shone from behind drawn curtains. We stepped from the quayside and onto it, packed as tightly as sardines on the small deck. I raised my fist and knocked lightly on a set of slim doors. A litany of curses ensued, followed by a stomping across the barge that threw my balance off.

"Just our luck. He's not only got his faculties, but he's still a grump," purred Echo.

I flicked him on the head. "Shh."

The doors flew open, and a man popped his head out with a scowl on his brown, weather-beaten face. His words were thick with mistrust, and he had retained his Indian accent, despite decades in London. "I wondered how long it would take you to come knocking." He raked his eyes over us. "Well, you two better come in. The leopard is no friend of mine. Either he apologies for his past behaviour, or he can stay out in the cold."

Echo's emerald eyes glinted dangerously. "You have my apologies, Rajiv."

"That will do." Rajiv turned his hunched back and left us to follow him into the cabin.

I sighed and ducked my head under the door, treading carefully past a small desk with a large sketch pad, a murky jam jar of brushes and a pallet of water colours. Furniture and utensils filled every nook and cranny of the barge.

The limited head height forced Sahil to slouch. "Nice digs."

"You think I'm too old to understand the sarcasm in your tone, boy? Living on a narrow boat means I'm in tune with the seasons." A pause. "*I've* never hidden from myself. *I* embrace my druid heritage."

What was it about men meeting the first time that always led to willy-waving? Like dogs in the park establishing dominance by how high they could cock their legs.

I couldn't shake the feeling we'd met before. "Uncle, we're here because—"

He spun to face me in the galley kitchen. He wore white harem pants and a plain, taupe T-shirt that may have once been cream. Although age had taken its toll on his posture, he had a full head of white hair and the inner fire of a man half his age. "I know why you are here. My nephew has himself tangled in a goddess's nets, and you need my help." His eyes —their watery blueness showing signs of cataracts and unusual for an Indian—held mine. "We talked once at your mother's grave."

A chill ran up my spine. I remembered thinking how hard it must have been for an elderly man to carry out such physical labour. "You're the gravedigger."

His jaw tightened. "I've always been good with my hands. Boat dwellers are a practical sort. I might be an artist, but I can also fix the engine, empty my bog and stoke the fire. A spot of grave digging suits my temperament. Plus, a surge in deaths tells me the Otherworld is out of control. It's an early warning system for an outsider like me."

Echo growled. "I thought my nose was playing tricks on me, but you've been hanging around like a bad smell."

Rajiv raised his chin, prideful hackles rising. "My family turned their back on me, but I knew a time would come when you needed me. It gave me a reason to live."

Sahil frowned. "All this time, you've been keeping tabs on us?"

"He's a stalker," said Echo. "Would you like me to sing that song by The Police?"

It didn't matter if Rajiv was an arsehole. We needed him. A woman in her midlife knew that sometimes the way to a stubborn man's heart was to flutter his ego. "Great-Uncle

Rajiv, you're right that we need you. Our dad is in great danger, and we have no time to lose. But the goddess stole my catalogues, and I have nothing to work with." I glanced at his desk in the corner of the barge. "Will you draw for me?"

His blue eyes glinted. "I've drawn for you before, granddaughter of Rajika. You just didn't know it. You think every drawing in Rajika's catalogue of creatures was your father's?" His dry lips curled into a sneer. "I was her illustrator for decades before he came along. The swarm of bees you animated in your bedroom? You didn't give them a purpose. They came right here and whispered in my ear."

It didn't matter that I didn't like him. Dad came first. "I know better now. I always assign a purpose."

Rajiv's blue eyes narrowed. "That's just it. You have to know what rules to bend and which to follow. You are only as good as your teachers. And your teachers have taught you to be fearful of your power. But when you animate, it isn't fear that should fill you. It is freedom. In the Otherworld, every situation is different, and you must rely on your instincts to survive, not blind obedience. Why do you think I outlived my sister? You need to lean into your power, and I'm going to show you how. And when we bring your father home, I'll spit in his eye and tell him to his face that everything he has taught you is wrong."

Echo emitted a theatrical sigh to ensure everyone knew he wasn't a fan.

"Sounds like the training wheels are about to come off," said Sahil. "When do we start?"

I swallowed down the sense of unease bubbling in my stomach. "Right away."

14

Hours passed in the dead of the night. Exhaustion crept into our bones, but Rajiv pressed on.

Rajiv had lived on the barge long before owning a houseboat was something cool eco-warrior millennials aspired to. One thing was clear: inhabitants of the docks embraced an alternative lifestyle. They were rebels, rule breakers and rule benders by nature. He was no exception.

"Nowadays, those who teach magic focus on community, teamwork and obeying the rules," he said. "Well, hear me good and clear because I don't like to repeat myself. That's a pile of old crock."

"Tell us, oh wise one, what is magic about?" Echo purred.

"It's about doing the hard thing." Rajiv held up his ring finger. "Even if you lose a finger."

Echo honked with laughter. "We all know how you lost your finger."

"Actually, I don't." All the times Echo had harped on about juicy poodles and deer rumps, he really could have shared his encyclopaedic knowledge of the Otherworld with me.

"Lucky you're not married, Uncle," Sahil grinned. "Or you'd have to wear the ring on your pinkie."

"Can the mockery unless you want to enjoy a night swim," said Rajiv coolly. "You're here to learn or can get lost."

I glared at Sahil and Echo, daring them to do so much as to twist their mouths or blink in an exaggerated manner.

Rajiv leaned back from his desk, where he was working on a set of watercolours. He wiped paint on his T-shirt in a way that made me ache for Dad. "Those cretins at Wildwoods haven't even taught you the most important thing for all magic users to know, the thing my own father drilled into me and my sister." His eyes glazed over. "There is a cost to all magic. All you bring to life, Alisha, is mirrored somewhere in death. The universe needs balance. For every creature you animate, others die. A swarm of bees animated here, a swarm of bees dies in a meadow elsewhere. A dragon is born here, a dragon in another corner of this universe perishes. A rooster crows, a rooster must die. It is the way of the world. Your father didn't tell you that, did he?"

A heaviness settled over me. "I don't believe it. Someone would have told me."

And yet inside, a seed of doubt took route. Dad, Echo and Ezra weren't animators. The only animator I knew was my grandmother, and she was dead.

"Don't listen to him," said Echo. "There has never been any proof of that theory. Rajika herself ruled it out. There is only one person who could know that, and it is the goddess Gaia."

I bit my lip. "Yeah, well, Gaia's not been so forthcoming recently."

Rajiv picked up his brush again and waved it in the air. "I am not telling you this to make you fearful. Once you accept the unique darkness that comes with your magic, you can unleash your true potential. And then there'll be no stopping you. You could power this barge without an engine. You could float up into the sky. You could break down walls. You could create whirlwinds and twisters. You could create armies of creatures bound to your purpose. Or you could animate creatures with no purpose at all. All that matters is your potential and how you are underusing it. I am telling you this as a friend, darling girl. We are kin, after all."

His endearment made my skin crawl, but his words pierced into the heart of me.

In the back of my head, I heard Dad's voice. *That's what fathers are for. A little bit of support, a little bit of elbow grease and belief in your brilliance.* He'd preached careful steps and a sense of responsibility, but had he held me back?

It was hard living a double life. I walked through the humdrum world pretending to be normal. I abided by the Magical Constitution and put a tight rein on my magic when I could feel it churning inside me, yearning for release.

Rajiv was right. I hadn't embraced the fullness and potential of my druidry.

A small smile played around the corners of Rajiv's mouth. He set down his brush.

"It's time, druid. My morning ablutions await." His bones creaked as he stepped out of his chair and made his way to the small bathroom next to his sleeping quarters.

I swallowed a gulp of lukewarm tea. By now, the hands of my watch showed seven in the morning. I opened the doors for some air. Outside, the sky hung heavy with thunderous clouds as the people of the river community stretched their legs on the quayside in their autumn knitwear. My phone buzzed in my pocket.

"I've been pressing the buzzer at your flat for five minutes," said Jameson.

"I'm at Rajiv's." The barge rocked as I paced the deck.

"At the docks? Oh, shit. You should have said. Do Ezra and Orpheus know?"

"I'm a grown woman, Rob. I've been out of nappies for decades."

"Touché. Sorry about that."

I rubbed the back of my neck.

"You have something for me? I sent a search party in the sewers. There were indications of activity down there. We found the discarded water bottle Ezra brought Joshi and some clothing we identified as your brother's. There was some singing further down the chambers, but I told my search party to turn back."

"Dammit, Rob." The chill air sent goosebumps up my skin. I ducked inside and immediately regretted it. Rajiv hacked in the bathroom as he phlegmed in the sink—men's washing rituals at their most appealing. I pressed the phone to my ear to block out the sound.

"Look, I know you're disappointed, but it's not been twenty-four hours yet. Joshi might look weak, but he's tough as old boots." A pause. "You're going in, aren't you?"

I turned the page of the book of creatures Rajiv had painted until his eyes had been too bleary to fill the lines with colour. I sensed the threads of the bronze animal below my fingertips, its lifeforce pulsing within the page. "Yes, Rob. I am. This will be over soon."

"I'm worried, Alisha. According to legend, she has a terrible temper. This isn't just about Joshi. It's about the other men. You need back up. Let me call Lavinia. At least tell Ezra what is going on."

"No. It's okay. I've got this. Thanks for your help, Rob." I hung up the phone, irritated when it buzzed again with a text message. My face softened when I saw the sender's name.

A peace offering, as promised. From my aunt's box of tricks. Ezra.

Ps. I missed you in our bed last night.

I put the phone in my pocket, my heart lighter despite what we faced. I turned to Sahil and Echo. My instincts said, unlike Pan, we'd not be able to convince Mami to follow her better instincts. That she had all the markings of a woman scorned. Someone who would burn it all down. "This will be dangerous. I don't even have my wind powers down there."

Sahil put his arm around me as the heavens opened. "I'm like Uncle. I've always fancied going down in flames more than a fizzle."

Rajiv exited the bathroom; his hair slicked back with water, a grizzled stubble on his cheeks. He crossed the barge to his desk, his skinny legs visible through the harem pants. He didn't bother hiding that he'd overheard our conversation through the paper-thin walls of the canal boat. "It might not be windy in the sewers, but air is not only found in the elements. It is found in the very breath that we breathe."

He handed me the book in a bag-for-life, together with a screwdriver and a spade. I put the tools in the bag and slung it over my shoulder. It was all he could manage in a night, but it would have to do: a cobbled-together book of creatures we thought might stand a chance against Mami.

"Remember, child. Trust your darkness. Without it, you cannot beat a goddess who is lost to hers."

Echo smiled, his voice muted by the din of the rain against the roof of the boat. "I sense it is time to wage war."

My anxiety reached a new peak with the heavy rain.

"Come on. We have to get back down there." I gathered my things. Who knew where Dad was by now and if he stood, hands and feet bound, in a flooding chamber. My voice quivered as I pocketed the book Rajiv had painted for me. "Thank you for your hospitality and your advice, Uncle."

"You are a weapon, granddaughter of Rajika. Don't forget it," said Rajiv.

"What about me?" said Sahil.

"History repeats itself. You are what I was. Of minor importance," said Rajiv. "Now go."

A dark cloud washed over Sahil's lean face as he led the

way onto the quayside, with Rajiv's blue eyes boring into our backs. Echo's fur darkened with every passing second in the rain. I folded my arms over my bag, protective of the treasure it held. This didn't feel like any battle I'd faced before. With Ra, Pan and the Ravenmaster, as unpredictable as our encounters had been, I had always been a member of a full contingent. Now, our ranks had been vastly depleted. I swallowed the ominous sense that we might fail and knelt at a manhole. Sahil and I used Rajiv's tools to lift the rusty cover on a quiet street, and we dropped into the sewers.

Echo hit the slushy ground first, groaning. "It smells like faeces and rotting bodies down here."

Sahil pulled the manhole cover shut with a clank. "The leopard's not wrong."

I clung to the hope that Dad was okay. That wherever he was being held hadn't filled with rainwater. Forging ahead of Sahil and Echo, I pulled out my phone torch, alert to the scuttling of rats and sloshing of water around us, until we came to a cross junction. I had no idea in which direction to go.

Echo pressed his ear to the slick tunnel wall, his green eyes darkening in concentration. "There's a humming. At first, I thought it was the gush of water or the rattle of a train, but it's a woman's voice. I'm certain of it. I have learned to recognise all variants of the human octave during my studies of song. I would place this woman in between Ella Fitzgerald and Janet Jackson. She's perhaps in the vein of Amy Winehouse."

"She wishes," I muttered. "Sahil…"

"You need me to shift and check it out," said my brother.

I nodded. "But keep a safe distance."

I turned my back as he undressed, and when he passed me his clothing, I placed them on a ledge to spare him the humiliation when he shifted back.

Behind me, a pop and churning and shrinking of matter.

"That's disgusting," said Echo.

Sahil let loose an indignant coo. "No need to look at my sausage and eggs when you say that, mate."

He flew off in a puff of feathers, his bowels firing in Echo's direction.

Echo leapt backwards. "I feel quite certain he wouldn't have done that if Marina were here. I feel quite polluted by the stench."

When Sahil returned, he landed between Echo's shoulder blades as if the leopard were an ironing board, not a ravenous big cat who'd swallow him as easily as a throat lozenge. His claws dug into Echo's still-damp fur as he clung on, panting to regain his breath. "I found him. West down this tunnel, about three nautical miles as the crow flies. I saw him, Alisha. He's only just holding on. And the goddess is with him." A pause. "It's you she's waiting for."

Echo's tail swished in alarm. "If this is true, it is a trap. We should wait."

I swallowed hard and switched my torch off. "Let's go. You know the plan. Distract her while I work."

I pushed through ever-deepening water, the leopard bounded, and Sahil flew through the tunnels towards Dad, every fibre and cell in my body stretching towards him until my throat clogged with bile and my legs burned with lactic acid. I clung to the secret Gaia had once trusted me with: the gods were weakened when the heavens had crumbled. They were weakened by the lack of prayer and worshippers.

Even if they weren't, I'd still do this. For Dad.

When we reached the chamber in question, I realised it was a mirror of the other one. Just another orientation, another cesspool of misery, the water now thick, cold and waist-high.

I spotted him, even though his body was draped in shadows. That was what happened when you loved someone. Even the outline of their body in the dark or under sheets or a snatch of a laugh or creak of a chair alerted you to their presence. He cowered, his usually bowed body stretched tight against the wall.

"Dad," I said in a panicked whisper.

He groaned, heartbreak in every syllable. "No. You shouldn't have come back."

She came. Mami Wata.

A shimmering light around her, like she was made of seashells or corals, her dark skin glittering with an otherworldly luminescence.

I shivered as she neared us, her dark eyes gleaming in the half-light, restrained anger pulsing through her.

"You dare to come here without an offering?" she said.

Steel laced my voice as I stared at her through prison-like bars. "We are not worshippers. We're here for my father."

"Of course you are. Mortals and their worldly bonds are so predictable. Why do you think I tugged the strings to ensure you returned from the Celestial Library without your best friend? To toy with the werewolf's mind so you felt it safer to come here without him? To target your father so soon after you've lost your mother? It's called divide and conquer. A strategy as old as time itself. I have learned my lessons from colonisers and conquerors. It's why I will succeed where gods have fallen before me."

A chill ran up my spine. She had isolated me on purpose.

But I wasn't alone. I had a leopard and a werepigeon at my side, plus an ace up my sleeve. "We can end this peacefully."

Mami threw back her head and laughed. "But why would I want that? I'm having so much fun."

Her hips swayed as she came forward out of the shadows, gliding through the water. Braids hung down her back. The tattoo of the snake no longer adorned her stomach area. Instead, a thick snake hung about her shoulders, its serpent tongue flicking in and out, as if the tattoo had slithered off her skin and into reality, at home curved around her uncovered breasts. A horror. An abomination. A suckling child.

But it was the bottom half of her that frightened me most of all.

Gone were her human legs. She had a fish's tail below the waist, visible under the waterline. A mermaid with iridescent scales of green and blue that mesmerised me and my brother too, given how even in his werepigeon form, he swayed on my shoulder.

Yet she lurked in the sewers.

Mami smiled, her voice like silk, melody personified. "I see the scales have fallen from your eyes, druid. I warned you I would meet your father. You heard the promise of my threat. Yet you ignored your female intuition."

Echo growled, and the sound reverberated across the cabin. Men shouted out in response. Men, captured by Mami, who deserved to return to their lives as much as Dad did.

My stomach quivered in fear. The cold had set in, from my prune-like toes to my chattering lips. "That was foolish of me. I know who you are now."

"It is of little matter," said Mami. "You may have bested gods before me, but this time you will not succeed. I am a river that never rests. I run, but I never walk. I have a bed, but I never sleep. I have a mouth, but I never eat."

I raised an eyebrow. Didn't she know I had deciphered the Ravenmaster's message without breaking a sweat? "I'm an English teacher. You can riddle me all day long, and I will always come back with an answer. You are a river goddess. And I am a druid."

"Oh, I am the goddess of many water bodies. I have mourned my people in the oceans. And I have sent people to their death there," said Mami. "But you, Alisha, are much more than a druid, aren't you?"

Dad lifted his head. "What is she talking about?"

Mami pouted. "I told you, Joshi. Just as you kept secrets

from your daughter, she has been keeping secrets from you. Such a shame. All your yearning for children, and it's turned out like this."

Sahil cocked his werepigeon head. "Don't listen to her, Dad."

I itched to take her down, but I needed to understand. "Why are you doing this, Mami?"

She rose to her full height, appearing to grow three inches. The snake slithered into a new position around her body, angrily flicking its tongue, close, too close to my defenceless father.

The water in the chamber rose with the rain, inching ever upwards. My heart engorged inside its cage, aching with the need to free Dad.

"Why am I targeting your father?" She pouted. "Joshi's been a naughty boy. We had a deal, didn't we, Joshi? It was very greedy of you to seek the riches you forfeited."

I searched Dad's face, but I found only defeat there.

Mami's mermaid tail swished in the water as she floated, breasts like buoys above the water. "I came to this country to accompany those in peril, enslaved peoples wrenched from their homelands. But their descendants have forgotten the debt they owe me. They have forgotten the riches I provided, the men I schooled in pleasure, and the wombs I blessed. I have worn endless faces and taken countless roles. To what end? Have my worshippers grown in number? Has their love deepened? Has the Holy Father seen to it that we, his children, flourished in his absence?" An eerie smile lifted the corners of her mouth. "When the heavens crumbled, I was devastated at first. It is lonely when you don't feel the divine light. And then it came to me—why give humans free choice when they can be compelled to serve us?"

I sighed. "That's why you're kidnapping the men? Because you're angry at God?"

You'd think meeting gods and goddesses would make me

want to embrace religion, but they were so messed up, they made me thankful I was an atheist. It turned out that deranged gods and goddesses were ten a penny. I was tempted to wag my finger and send them all to therapy, but who was I to judge an immortal being? At least this encounter solidified my view. I liked being right. It was good for a women's ego to be right in a world where so often we're told we're wrong.

Mami stroked the serpent. "My anger is all-encompassing. I am angry at God. At people. At women who choose a phoney filter or go under the knife instead of asking me to enhance their natural beauty. At children who choose endless hours with computer games over drawing a picture. Most of all, I'm angry at the men who have led us here with their decisions. Their priorities. Their values. Men who have led us to this world without love or beauty. Think what this world could be if women led it."

She waved her hand, and the gate separating us dissolved into water and melted away.

We'd planned this moment. The moment Sahil and Echo would distract her.

"Now," I yelled.

Echo raised his chin, opened his mouth and crooned a tune.

The goddess froze.

"What are you doing?" I hissed.

"I'm distracting her." Emerald eyes sparked in the shadows. "If 'For Those in Peril on the Sea' isn't to your liking, I could try 'Sittin' on the Dock of the Bay'."

I clenched my teeth. "Save it for karaoke night, okay? Go, Echo."

Echo leapt into the air, taking a cresting wave with him, his claws and teeth extended, determined to get his first taste of a goddess. She flung the serpent at him, almost casually, as if he wasn't the slightest threat. I guess the singing softened his impact. The snake, olive green and hissing as it swam through the water, cornered the leopard, and they began a dance I willed Echo to win.

I sloshed my way to Dad, my legs toiling in the lifeguard move I'd seen time and again on *Baywatch*. I held Rajiv's book of creatures above the water line, keeping it safe. I kissed Dad's tear-streaked face when I reached him. His Superman costume hung in shreds about his shivering body, but my worry had to wait. I ran my fingers over the pages of the book, working one page at a time, determination in every tiny movement of my hands, in the set of my mouth and in the words going through my head.

The spell that Ezra had sent me by text. All my energy went into imbuing the creatures with the singular purpose of chanting the spell and freeing Dad and, if that succeeded, the other men beyond this chamber.

I willed it with the purity of a child at their first confession and with the darkness of a witch's hex. Every part of me, good and bad, pulsed from the pads of my fingers into the creatures my uncle had painted. All the winged water creatures we could think of to accomplish our goal: a devil ray, with its wing-like pectoral fins designed to glide through both the water and air; a flying seahorse, its dorsal fins making it a candidate; a flying fish with pectoral fins that allowed it to be airborne; and a flying squid whose tentacles had a wing-like power as it spiralled out of water.

I didn't know if our plan would work. After all, I had tasted failure before when I had tried to animate creatures beyond my repertoire. I had humiliated myself on the Wildwoods stage. This time, there was more at stake than just my dignity.

Dad's life depended on it.

Behind me, Sahil flapped in the goddess's face, more a nuisance than a threat, despite his protruding teeth and sharp claws. All he needed was to buy me some time.

They came to life, one by one.

A devil ray, with its distinctive, black, crescent-shaped stripe extending shoulder to shoulder. A bronze flying seahorse, not more than twelve inches in size. A shimmering, silver torpedo-shaped flying fish, its wings as sheer as chiffon. And with a final push and pull of the threads of the universe, a flying squid the length of my forearm with eight legs and two tentacles.

I stepped back as they encircled Dad, these weird and wonderful creatures I had managed to pull from the page. Their mouths moved as they chanted, their purpose bound to mine.

Dad's eyes widened. "What have you done? You've condemned them to death, here away from an ecosystem in which they can survive. When this chamber drains, they will die, gasping for air. I taught you better."

My heart filled with joy as the chains melted away, and the creatures swam away together, off to seek the other bound men. It was working. "But we'll have you back."

"She wants *you*." Dad jerked, filled with terror. "Sahil—"

I swung around.

The goddess had tired of my brother. He squirmed as she caught him in her hands and squeezed until his beady eyes bulged.

"Stop!" I called.

Rajiv had taught me to think outside of the box. How air exists not just around us but in us. How I should embrace my darkness. I lifted my hands, visualised the breath in Mami's body and pulled, pulled with all my might.

Mami went slack, mercifully releasing my brother. Sahil splashed into the water and then re-emerged, jubilant, his eyes trained on Dad.

I held the gathered energy for a moment, like a sphere between my hands, and then I slammed it hard, sending the goddess spiralling back into the depths of the water. Heart racing, I called to the leopard through the echoey chamber. "Find the nearest manhole and get them out of here."

The snake hung limp between Echo's teeth. He spat it out, blood coating his chin, a dangerous gleam in his eyes.

"You can count on me." A strong swimmer, he paddled to Dad and Sahil, herding them with fierce determination back towards the main tunnel of the sewers.

I turned back to find the goddess upright, cradling the snake in her arms, her dark eyes fiery coals. "You dare to use my own body against me? I underestimated you, druid." A coy smile played on her beautiful lips. "But my aim was never to kill your father. A woman harbours a fondness for a man who has painted her. And vice versa. It lends itself to a certain intimacy. It's you I wanted to destroy for your incessant meddling with the gods. But this is much better than even I anticipated."

I frowned, every cell in my body alert to her, every sinew urging me to escape.

"You see, I could have killed you, but corrupting you is so much sweeter." She smiled. "It took me a while to realise your successes so far had been an inside job. That's why Ra, Pan and Hermes didn't see you coming, of course. Scheming Gaia had tooled you up. The other gods won't believe me without proof, of course, but I don't need proof. My intuition is enough. I've watched her work for millennia. Her fingerprints are all over this. She still fights for what we have lost. Just wait until she finds out about the darkness in you. A darkness that even scheming Gaia hasn't accounted for. I can't wait to see this all play out, druid. I've seen it countless times. A mortal touches darkness, and they can't withstand the magnetism of it. I can't wait for Gaia to find out that her little lamb is as flawed as the rest of us." A sultry laugh as she soaked her hair in the water and pulled it over one shoulder. "You could be the key to corrupting Gaia herself."

A shudder ran through me. I had flaws like any other

person. Mami sounded like they could be prised open into a chasm.

But I was in control, wasn't I? My fate wasn't written. It was still in flux.

She turned her back on me.

"Mami!" My voice echoed as I called out to her. "What did you do with my catalogues of creatures?"

She pirouetted in the water, playful, gracefulness personified. "They were rather good, but I dipped them in water, of course." Diving into the water, she resurfaced further into the chamber. "I'll see you soon, druid. For now, I have other toys to play with."

Mami Wata swam away, cradling the olive serpent still, leaving me breathless with fear in the chamber.

15

Delirious with relief, I caught up with Dad, Sahil and Echo as they waded through the stinking sewers.

Only Echo had the strength to speak, invigorated by his performance during the battle. "I didn't think I would, but I missed you, Joshi. I even gave the koi in your pond a reprieve in your absence out of respect for you. Those little pea-brains will not escape me this afternoon, though."

Dad grunted, leaning hard into me as I supported him through the tunnel. His legs collapsed from underneath him as soon as we climbed out of the manhole, his last wisp of strength fading. At street level, the heavy rain had settled into the pitter-patter of drizzle. I pulled the cover shut, ignoring the stares of pedestrians crisscrossing the street on their way to work. A soaking-wet woman, a bedraggled superhero-clad pensioner, a Bengal cat and a muscly pigeon weren't everyday sights, not even in a city with as many faces as London.

Dad had been standing for hours. I lowered him into a sitting position on the kerb to give his legs a rest.

My mouth dry, every sense heightened, I called Ezra, "We need you. We're at the pie stall in Borough Market."

"I know where you mean." He came before I hung up, cavalier about discovery by commuters or vendors setting up their stalls. He wore jeans and a white T-shirt, his hair unkempt, like he'd not yet had his morning coffee. His eyes raked over me. A growl of admiration as he curled a protective arm around me. "You did it."

"Thanks to your spell." I curved my body to his, knowing he could be the strong one now.

His grey eyes brimmed with concern. He bent down to Dad. "It's good to have you back, Joshi. Let's get out of here, shall we?"

Dad looked up. "Thanks, son."

Ezra blinked at the endearment, then scanned the market, his gaze settling on an empty side alley. "This way."

We pulled Dad up between us and made it to the alley. There, we stood in circle formation, with Sahil riding on Echo's back. Ezra teleported, and we spun through the threads of the universe. We emerged at Dad's front door, with Dad—worn out from his ordeal and uninitiated in teleportation—gasping for air.

He pressed the doorbell, fingers quivering.

Alma flung the door wide open, her face painted in the bright colours of joy. "Oh, Joshi."

She launched herself at Dad and took his head in her hands, plastering every inch of his face in chaste kisses. They walked into the house, him trembling in her arms. Alma only had eyes for him, like an old, black-and-white Hollywood movie. Like love could strike at any age.

Ezra touched the small of my back, sending a shiver up my spine. "I'll wait for you here."

A spark of mischief in Echo's eyes. "The koi have waited for me long enough."

Sahil flew up the stairs, presumably to his childhood bedroom, given his stashed clothes remained under a distant manhole somewhere. He tumbled down moments later, barefoot and still pushing his arms through his T-shirt, his eagerness to see Dad superseding everything else.

Alma beamed. "You really are wonderful for bringing him home."

We hovered a small distance away while she brought Dad past Mum's shrine into the living room. There, she stripped Dad out of his wet clothes, leaving on his underwear to preserve his modesty, and wrapped him into a fluffy dressing gown. Next, she settled him on the tartan sofa and covered him in a blanket to stop the shivers.

"It's like watching a matron work," said Sahil in a whisper.

I nodded, knowing we were both thinking of Mum. "He seems comfortable with her. We wouldn't have found the portal in the painting without her."

Sahil shuddered. "But there are doilies everywhere."

Dad lifted his head from the cushion and croaked in our direction.

Alma put a finger to his lips. "You just rest up, darling. There'll be plenty of time to speak after you've had some sleep, soup and a shower. You can never go wrong with the three Ss. And maybe a paracetamol to take the edge off the shock."

Dad pushed her finger away and propped himself up, his voice barely a whisper. "I need to speak to Alisha. You went to see him, didn't you? You went to see Rajiv. That was his art in that hellhole. I recognised it."

I knelt by his side and put my hand on his. "It was the only way I could think of to save you."

A shudder ran through him. "How could you? How could you let him turn you into his image? I taught you better. I warned you to stay away."

Sorrow and anger rose like a wave in me. "How can you say that? We rescued you."

He met my eyes. "I would rather die than let that man make his mark on your soul."

His words cut so deep they could have been a physical wound.

"Dad, it wasn't her fault. We decided together," said Sahil.

I searched Dad's eyes. "Back when we found you in the first chamber, why did you say Mum's death was your fault?"

A sad smile flitted across his lips. "We were so in love. It would have been enough, but your mum, she'd dreamt of you two for so long. She didn't want to give the dream of you up even though she couldn't conceive. I don't know. Maybe it was a throwback from the Gallizenae, the virgin priestesses."

He dissolved into a coughing fit.

Alma rushed to the kitchen to get a glass of water.

Dad pressed on. "Then we met Mami. She had this ritual. All I had to do was promise to forfeit any riches I'd make from painting, and we'd have children. I thought it was all hocus pocus. You know what it's like at university. You're all smoking pot, doing Ouija boards, the odd seance to scare the bejeezus out of each other. It was just a laugh to go to Mami's dorm room. But then your mother became pregnant with Sahil. And you came along a few years later. And I always wondered."

"You said we were made from a good old tumble between the sheets," said Sahil.

Dad nodded. "You were. After Mami blessed your mother's womb and mixed around some fish guts in a bowl with some crushed herbs."

Relief flooded Sahil's face. "Phew. Glad it wasn't some alien conception because that would have been weird."

I frowned. "Mami said you'd been naughty."

"I let my ambition fall away. I couldn't exhibit my art after I stepped away from the Otherworld anyway. The senate didn't like it. But after you two became fully-fledged peculiars, I thought to myself, why don't I reach out to my old contacts and put on an art show? Prove to the world I still have some life left in me. But I'd made a Faustian bargain. And that's why she came. Because I didn't keep my promise." His face crumpled. "If we hadn't crossed the gods, Rosalie would still be here."

I reached out to him, my heart sore. "It wasn't your fault."

His eyes blazed. "You should have listened. You should have let me die down there. Instead, you betrayed everything this family stands for. I told Mami you would always make the right decision." His voice broke. "You failed this family."

"Steady on, Dad," said Sahil. "I know I like being golden balls, but that's a bit harsh."

Dad's anger rolled on, crushing in intensity. "What did Mami mean when she said that you're much more than a druid?"

I splayed my hands. Even Orpheus knew. How could I keep it from Dad? "Gaia said I'm the eternal girl."

"From the prophecy? Is my family always doomed to be torn apart by magic?" Dad's head sank into his hands. "Get out."

Sahil's eyes flitted between the two of us as recognition dawned. "Damn, this family has secrets. Dad, let her stay. Please. You can't send her away like this."

Dad raised his dishevelled head. His wiry moustached drooped. "Get out now."

Alma bustled into the room. "Is that any way to talk to your daughter?"

I swallowed the painful ball of tears in my throat. "Rest, Dad. I'll check on you later."

Sahil followed me out of the room. "Alisha, don't mind him. He's in shock. Traumatised. Whatever you want to call it. I'll get him a therapist. I would have done the same down there. We made the decisions together."

"It's okay. I can hold his anger. He's home. That's all that matters." I kissed my brother's cheek.

Shadows played in the hollows of his face. "Are you really the eternal girl?"

"It's what the goddess said. Nothing more, nothing less." I shrugged and walked into the waiting arms of my wolf.

EZRA'S deep voice tickled my ear. "I'm an important man, you little minx. I've got the pack to lead and laws to draft, yet here I am, spending the day in bed with a druid."

"Is that a complaint?" I stretched, revelling in the feel of freshly laundered sheets.

He might be a wolf, but I had him well-trained. He'd even started using fabric conditioner at the cottage. Outside the window, the trees stood bare, and autumn leaves carpeted the ground. But inside, the sheets smelled of spring meadows and wolf. That was the scent of earth and roll-ups and mountain air that was uniquely Ezra's. I sighed heavily, contentment held at bay by Dad's reaction.

"Joshi will come around, Alisha. Your brother's right. Look what he's been through. He's in shock. He was just lashing out. You'll see, it might take a little while, but he'll be proud Gaia has such faith in you." Ezra paused. "You know, I'm still a bit irritated that Orpheus knows about your place in the prophecy. I trust him, but I'm cursing myself for not training you in the fine art of Jedi mind tricks before he plucked that secret out of your head."

"My mind is a fortress. I'll have you know."

He laughed, more relaxed than I'd seen him in weeks. It had done us good to spend some time together cocooned away at the cottage. "You, my love, are an open book. Have you noticed the vampire's more tender with you than with others? Even his own clan."

I had definitely noticed. I poked him between the ribs. "Do I sense a touch of jealousy?

"I don't care if Orpheus is interested in you." A storm in his eyes. "I mind if you are interested in him. You're mine."

"Say that again." I rolled on top of him, pressing my nose to his chest and then trailed three kisses down his bare chest, stopping at the waistband of his boxers.

His grey eyes darkened with desire. "Oh, oh. The lady means business."

I looked up at him from beneath my lashes. "Maybe."

"Maybe?" He beckoned me closer, daring me to defy him.

I inched closer until his breath mingled with mine.

He kissed me with bruising intensity, almost a punishment, as if he couldn't get enough of me. As if I were his alone. As if he wouldn't ever let me leave.

God, he was hot.

I threaded my hands through the hair at the back of his neck. When he pulled away, I almost begged him to carry on.

Copper flecks danced in his eyes.

"Are you ready to talk about what happened down there? She could have killed you." He bit my lip. "Stubborn woman."

I sighed and rolled back against the pillow. "Yeah, well, she didn't. We've been through it, Ezra. My power felt incredible. I animated four creatures in a matter of seconds. I floored a goddess. I've never felt that strong before." A pause. "Not even when you mentored me."

He took the dig lightly, confident in his abilities. "I helped you get grounded in the Otherworld, but our magical skills are worlds apart. That's why it's important for you to train with Rayna Willowsun. Only a druid can help deepen your skills. You are talented, Alisha, but it's your courage and leadership that have seen you through so far." Ezra's bicep curled up as he cradled his head in his hand and slung a rock-hard thigh over me. "I like that you're your own woman. I like that you forge ahead despite what I think. That you outgrew the lines I drew in the sand when I first took you to

Wildwoods. That you now teach there yourself. There is no limit to who you can be as long as you're true to yourself."

I bit my lip. "Mami Wata said that my flaws would be my undoing. That they would be Gaia's undoing."

A growl. "Who cares what she thinks? Nobody expects you to be perfect, hellfire."

I still smarted from Dad's criticism, but Ezra's words soothed the sting. I drew in a shaky breath, knowing there was one person I couldn't hide from. One person who could give me answers. "I need to see Gaia."

Ezra sighed. He pulled me into a bear hug. "I thought you might say that. I'll let you go on two conditions."

It wasn't even worth the effort to raise my head. I was well and truly trapped. Not that I was complaining. "Name them."

"You come with me to a coven dinner tonight. Lavinia's invited the senate, and a few others, and it'll be more bearable if you are there."

My mouth twisted into a frown. There was nothing I fancied less. Even though I fancied him rotten and judging by his general standing to attention against my belly, he definitely felt the same way. "It's been a long week. I have a night class to prepare for, my hair to wash, my feet could do with some TLC, and my bikini line *really* needs doing."

"There is nothing wrong with your bikini line. I like yetis. I even like chin hair and love handles. There's just more of you to love."

I struggled against his hold. "You jerk!"

The teasing note left his voice. "If I'm honest, it's important to me. With Gunnolf gone, I don't have much family left. And Lavinia…she's been more attentive to me without Gunnolf around. I don't know. Maybe it's because I'm a senator. Or maybe because there's no longer this tug of war with them fighting over me. But it feels good. Like I belong. She's been teaching me spells. And bending my ear about Defence Minister stuff. She trusts me. And I really want you and her to get along. I want you to be a part of it."

"Then I'll come. And I'm honoured you want me there," I said. He still hadn't let me go. "What's the other condition?"

His voice rumbled through his chest, full of purpose and desire. "I want to hear your special moan."

I blushed. With a failed marriage behind me, I hadn't known it was possible to start all over again in middle-age and have butterflies in my stomach. "Well then, cowboy, what are you waiting for?"

A half-hour later, I collapsed onto the mattress, utterly blissed out.

Ezra lit a post-coital roll-up in bed, his brown hair flopping into his eyes. A sheen of sweat covered his chest. He smirked. "Too soon to go again?"

I grinned. "You are relentless. An animal."

"Why, thank you, ma'am." He took a drag from his cigarette and blew the smoke away from me towards the open window. "Sorry. I try not to smoke in front of you. It's been a hard week."

Raising my hand, I sent a current of air to aid the rings of smoke on their way. "At least you look hot doing it. I might think twice if you had a beer belly and blew it in my face."

His eyes twinkled. "That's a hell of a lot of pressure to keep in shape, hellfire. The things a man does for love."

My phone rang. Ezra cursed as I dragged the duvet with me across the room, shielding him from a full moonie. I liked my arse, but our relationship was still too new to wave it in his face. On the other hand, I'd left him exposed and wasn't averse to a sneaky look at him in his full naked glory as I answered the phone.

"Jameson." I giggled as Ezra, with his cigarette hanging from his lips, took a pillow and writhed against it. The man would ace a Magic Mike audition.

"Alisha. Three bodies floated up from the sewers this afternoon."

The smile dropped from my face. A vice tightened around my heart. "What?"

Ezra dropped the Magic Mike act and came closer, his brow furrowed. "What's wrong?"

"Gordon Stevens. Henry Radcliffe. Ali Sheikh. Three men we'd identified as possible victims of Mami Wata. Three bodies matching their description. Recently dead. They're with the coroner, but initial reports suggest drowning," said Jameson.

My chest grew tight. I struggled to breathe. "No, that's not right. I sent my creatures to free them. They knew the spell."

Why hadn't I gone with them? Why hadn't I checked the men were safe?

I didn't need to ask the questions to know the answer. They had always been an afterthought. Our priority had been rescuing Dad. I hadn't even really thought of the other men as my problem.

"Then I don't know what went wrong, Alisha. And hell, I'm glad your dad made it. But those men, those men are dead. Mami Wata is nowhere to be found, and more men are missing. So I'm asking you for your help. We need to bring her down. That little girl, Annie, you found alone outside Black Lotus Inkings? We think Mami might still have her father."

Ezra faded into my peripheral vision.

I sank onto the bed. The cloud of words in my head wouldn't make sentences. Punishing thoughts of self-hatred and loathing churned through my mind. How on earth had I let this happen?

"There's one more thing. We found unexpected sea animals in the sewers in our search, completely out of their habitat. I have them listed here. Hang on." A rustle of paper.

"Yes, here it is. A flying fish. Devil ray. A seahorse. A squid. They're not yours, are they?"

A strangled noise from my throat that didn't sound like me. "I animated them. Are they safe?"

"Alisha, I hate to break it to you, but they're all dead. Partially cannibalised, by the looks of it. My team are down there right now. I have a marine biologist on it."

I dropped the phone, lurched forward and vomited on the floor as Ezra held my hair back.

16

I cleaned the floor and took a shower. Recriminations snowballed in my head. I'd never been someone who only thought of myself. I believed in the common good. I'd never even pick up the last doughnut at a bakery. I wouldn't accept favours without returning them. I'd stayed in my marriage for so long because I'd put Alex's happiness before my own. Even when he always left the toilet seat up, treated me as a live-in maid, and never once made me a cup of tea during our marriage.

So how could it happen that I'd been so focused on getting my own dad back that I'd not given a second thought to the other men at risk? Not only that, I'd animated the sea creatures without caring what would happen to them once they'd fulfilled their purpose. Without caring that they'd perish in that environment.

A chill ran up my spine.

The dead men's names reverberated in my head. Gordon Stevens, Henry Radcliffe and Ali Sheikh. Their deaths brought Nita's murder flooding back. And Melissa's. How many people had I failed? My fingers twitched with the memory of the sea creatures coming to life at my command.

Shuddering, I changed into clean clothes, although every instinct told me to creep under the bedclothes again and hide away. "Two days without Marina, and it's like I don't know myself. What on earth was I thinking?"

She always believed every interaction we had with the world was an opportunity to do good.

"It's not your fault." Ezra tugged on his jeans and pulled me against his bare chest.

I didn't deserve his understanding. "Dad was right. I messed up."

He tipped up my chin. "Then put it right."

"How? Those deaths are on me." I choked back my tears. "More men are missing."

"This is on Mami, not on you." A steely edge to his voice.

"And the sea creatures?" How was I ever going to tell Marina what happened? She'd never look at me in the same way again.

"Yeah, you fucked up there, hellfire." Sighing, Ezra reached for his shirt. "I'll speak to Rayna at the coven dinner tonight and get that training date fixed for you. I'm not leaving your side today."

"You don't need to babysit me."

His eyes met mine as he buttoned up his shirt. "The hell I don't. My girl's had a knock. I'm sure as hell going to stick around until I know you're okay."

I shook my head. "I don't want to mess with your plans for a pack day. But maybe you can give me a lift to Gaia's first?"

A vein throbbed in his jaw. "If you're sure."

I tidied my hair. My face in the mirror was wan. "I am."

Ezra held out a hand. "Then your carriage awaits."

He didn't even have to ask where Gaia lived. Senators were privy to such information, where available. His palm swallowed mine as the world shrank to a point, and we hurtled like two people clinging to each other on a rickety rollercoaster with no tracks in sight. I squeezed my eyes shut, allowed my thoughts to blur to nothingness and drank in the mountain scent of him as he propelled us to our destination.

The world spat us out near Broadway Market in Tooting, where Gaia lived in social housing on an estate. Her ground-floor flat included a small, fenced garden that brimmed with flowers despite the cold autumn downpours in London. But then, I hadn't expected anything less. She was the Earth goddess, after all.

Her front door, painted a sunshine yellow, was open. Not ajar. Literally wide open.

A goddess had no need for deadbolts or security alarms.

"Gaia? Can we come in?" I said.

She didn't answer.

I stepped into the hallway of her flat and then into the adjacent living space, with Ezra close behind me, and called out again. My steps plodded against the thin carpet, deliberately heavy to announce our arrival. I imagined she'd flatten intruders like a pancake.

Ezra pointed. "There."

A chink of light fell over the goddess. She dozed in an armchair in the corner. Her arms were folded across her belly, which spilt out above the folds of her coral-patterned sari. She woke, opening one eye that was yellow with age.

My bladder almost emptied with fright.

"How wonderful that you have come to visit, Alisha and her wolf," said Gaia.

For a moment, it seemed to me that the roles had been switched in Red Riding Hood. This time, the wolf was my protector, and the grandmother would eat me. But then she smiled, and a rush of love came over me. I always felt safer with Gaia around. Like she could wrap her wisdom around the whole globe, cocooning us from harm. I pressed a kiss to her wrinkled cheek, noting how long her earlobes were, as if centuries of gravity had taken their toll.

Ezra inclined his head. "We don't mean to intrude, goddess."

"Nonsense. No need to be so formal. You aren't in a senate meeting. Come in, come in. Make yourselves at home." Gaia beamed. "She made a good choice with you, Mr. Neuhoff. I was worried she'd have a dalliance with that undead vampire instead. It's always better for the living to avoid dwelling too much on the dead." She heaved herself out of the armchair and made her way into the kitchen in a rustle of silk. "You're just in time for some curry. I was getting forty winks after making a pile of chapatis. I hope you're hungry."

We watched her disappearing back and then nosed around. It wasn't often mortal eyes could witness the small details of how a goddess lived. What we found was beautiful for how unremarkable it was. Magnolia walls, patchy green carpet, dusty ceiling lamps. Photos of children and small, potted succulents graced a dented sideboard, the children themselves a range of ages and ethnicities. Two armchairs faced each other across a small, round coffee table, home to a smooth, marble chess set. A cassette player and a stack of tapes hid behind a spider plant on the floor. Her home smelled of coconut hair oil, curry powder and caramel pudding.

Gaia popped her head out of the kitchen. "It's homely, isn't it? I've lived in many homes, but this one is my favourite. I have my own garden, and the council looks after me when my electrics play up or if I have a water leak. St. George's Hospital is nearby in case I have any aches or pains that need seeing to. I am getting on a bit, you know." She pulled her thick, black plait over her shoulder. "There are latchkey children who pass through every day for a kind word, a signature in their school diaries or a hot plate of food. Poor things are always ravenous after battling through a school day. I'm a stone's throw away from Indian grocers where I can get chapati flour, turmeric, saffron and a dozen types of lentils, and there's always someone to help me carry my bags home. This community is always changing. Who needs a television when there is so much to see in the world? And best of all, I walk to Safia's Chai shop each night for the perfect masala chai." She wound the train of her sari around her body, tucked it in at the waist and gave us a look that would wither daffodils. "Now, do I need to ask again? You know I won't be happy if you come to my home and don't eat."

Ezra wavered for a second. It took balls to disappoint a goddess. "Actually, I have pack business to see to." Sparks flew between us as our eyes met. "If you're sure you'll be okay, hellfire?"

Gaia pursed her bow lips—whether at Ezra's name for me or the fact he'd refused her food, I did not know—then moved faster than an old lady had any right to move. She stuffed a laddu, an Indian sweet ball, into Ezra's mouth with the determination of a bowling champion going for a strike.

His eyes widened, and he swallowed the yellow ball and even pretended to like it, but his revolted expression gave him away. Ever the gentleman, he thanked the goddess while still retching, then kissed the top of my head.

His voice dropped a notch. "Love you. Ring me later, and I'll come to get you."

Then he disappeared.

Gaia waggled her eyebrows. "He's a hunk. Enjoy yourself before your bits go south. There's nothing more disconcerting than finding your breasts behind you in the bedroom."

I spluttered. Sex talk with your best friend was one thing, but sex talk with a pensioner who happened to be a goddess was downright weird.

Gaia clicked her tongue in annoyance. "Now, can we sit down and eat?" She went to the stove, doled out a generous serving spoon of steaming curry and one chapati each and ushered me to a clap-out table against the kitchen wall. "Isn't this wonderful? Two women sitting together in perfect harmony."

I missed Marina's company and counsel fiercely. The tiny cubes of potato melted in my mouth, and I scooped up the sauce with buttered chapatis.

Gaia licked her fingers. "The children sit on the carpet in the living room to eat, but my bones are made from stars and dust these days, and they are in danger of crumbling however much yoga I do. But you didn't come here for me to talk your ears off, did you, granddaughter of Rajika Verma?"

I phrased my words carefully. Resentment bubbled through them all the same. "You've seen me grow into this new life. You've asked me to battle gods. You told me that I am the eternal girl. And then you disappeared."

She frowned, and the warmth left the room like the temperature was regulated by her moods. "Go on."

Hell, there was nothing for it except to keep digging. "Once, I could summon you as long as I had need or gratitude in my heart or a thoughtful offering. But now, I can't help feeling you've left me high and dry."

"Is that right, druid?" Eyes like burning forest fires, or was I imagining it?

"I've made mistakes, Gaia, and I don't think I would have made them if you'd been at my side." The words left a bitter taste in my mouth. I clamped my mouth shut in case I'd pushed her too far.

Gaia's eyes narrowed, and the sense of homeliness and contentment slipped from her as if the old lady was just a facade that hid a much more dangerous persona underneath. She was the mother, the crone but also the warrior. She hit the armrests with a thud to punctuate her points. "Important as you are, druid, I have other duties besides you. You think the soils remain fertile without my loving hand? How do you think the squirrels find their bounty or the trees their myriad of deepened colours?"

I winced. "Forgive me."

Her face softened. "Just because the world could burn, do we stop tending to the little things? The things that make life on this planet joyful? You have hubris indeed to be angry at me for not being at your beck and call." She sighed. "You think I abandoned you?"

I pushed my plate away. Tears of glass cut my throat. "Three men died, goddess, and four creatures, and Mami Wata crowed that my flaws, my darkness, would be my undoing. That they would be *your* undoing."

Gaia's face lost its angles and shadows and became cherubic once more. "Have you forgotten what I told you? You are still learning. What a gift that is to still have the capacity and time to learn. Mistakes happen to us all, child. I've made my fair share. But not as many as that fishy songstress Mami Wata." Sadness filled her voice as if she had a never-ending well of compassion, despite all the acts of wickedness she'd witnessed. "Believe me, those dead men are not your fault. Mami Wata has been chewing up men and spitting them out since the dawn of time. And as for you *feeling* alone, you weren't really alone, were you? You had your brother. Getting him on our side is going to be key to this whole debacle. Chanakya did a marvellous job with the snake. And then there was—"

A knock sounded at the open front door.

Gaia clapped her hands excitedly. "Right on time. Come along, druid. I love it when a plan comes together."

17

———————

In came Alma. She waved her hands with a flourish. "Surprise!"

My mouth fell open. This Alma had a clever glint in her hazel eyes. All hint of the doddering doilie-obsessed lady was gone.

"Are you two friends now?" I asked. The two of them had met over lunch at Dad's house when poor Alma hadn't quite known what was going on, between Gaia being herself and Sahil coughing up sawdust.

Gaia threw her plump arms around Alma. "I sensed you were coming and invited Alma over for us to have a chinwag. Sometimes a chat amongst women is just the ticket to unlocking progress, don't you think?"

"We've been friends for *years*," said Alma. "In fact, Gaia bought me my goldfish. Not the diseased kind trapped in a sandwich bag at fairs. These ones glow with happiness. I've never known two goldfish to live so long."

Gaia chuckled. "Wasn't it a hoot, pretending we didn't know each other at the Verma house? Your face was so funny when I called Sahil a pigeon. You should have gone to acting school. You could have given Sigourney Weaver a run for her money."

"Oh yes, I love *Alien*," said Alma.

I gawped at her. "You do? But you like baking and doilies."

Alma stared at me like I didn't have all my marbles. "People don't just have to like one type of thing, Alisha. I'll never give up my love of doilies, but I also happen to like science fiction movies." Her eyes sparkled. "And I like heroes and heroines. Just being in their orbit. I like being there to make sure everything works out smoothly for them."

I exhaled in a whoosh. "All the tiptoeing around we've done, and you've known about the Otherworld all along."

Alma shrugged. "Well, of course, dear."

"So you know Echo isn't a Bengal cat?"

"Even a humdrum would notice the amount of water he displaces from the koi pond when he's leaping about in there."

"Holy shit. You deserve an Oscar."

Pride emanated from her face, making her seem younger than her years. "I'm many things: a Spaniard, a doilie-maker and a baker. Maybe I should add amateur acting to that list. Oh, and I'm a peculiar. A seer, to be precise."

"Except she works with flour instead of a crystal ball," said Gaia helpfully. "I could have done with a hand making the chapatis earlier, Alma. You're so good with a rolling pin."

That explained the baking and all the clouds of flour. Dad had fallen in love with Mystic Meg.

Alma frowned. "I ran out of flour on the day your father went missing, so I didn't see that coming. My visions only give me a heads-up of a minute or two, and they're very specific to who I care about, so not much use, really." She brightened. "But I have a big heart, and I'm never lazy about tidying up after my flour readings. And I've seen you grow up. When Gaia approached me to ask me to keep an eye on you all, it didn't seem much of a leap."

Gaia smiled. "I knew Alma was a good fit as soon as I found out that she's a baker. Bakers are very caring people. There are no exceptions. And realising that her surname is Bluejay was the cherry on top. Bluejays are very protective. you know."

My heart sank. "So you're in Dad's bed as part of a job?"

"No, it's more than that, dear. And it's more a calling than a job." She giggled. "I don't get paid for it. I'm certainly not a hooker. More power to those ladies, but that's not me. It's quite simple, really. Your mother's death brought us closer together, but I already cared about you all. It's hard not to care when you see a family grow up. Your father says I'm a softie. What we have is the real deal. He's quite a catch." Alma made a squeezing motion with her hands. "Buns of steel. We're enjoying a new lease of life."

Hearing about Dad's bedroom shenanigans would always be grim, but I was relieved their happiness hadn't been a sham. "So we were never alone because you asked Alma to look after us, goddess. That's why you pointed us towards the loft where we found the portrait, Alma."

Alma nodded excitedly. "I noticed it the first time I was up there. Your mother told your father to throw out the painting. But he still kept it."

Gaia's eyes gleamed. "What does that tell you about men, Alisha?"

I thought of my ex-husband. "That they are full of crock?"

She shook her head. "No, dear. That they don't have the monopoly on making good decisions. The odds of a woman making the right decision are no greater or less than a man's. The world is complex, but at the heart of it, every creature fulfils its potential by trying its best and not stamping on others. So you might as well trust your gut."

Alma gave me a concerned look. "And what *does* your gut

say about the past few days? Your father is very upset about your argument."

I sighed. "That he was right about Great-Uncle Rajiv. I didn't like who I became under his tutelage. I mean, I liked the feeling of power, but I'm not sure I can live with the consequences."

"There you go." Gaia gave a satisfied smile. "I'll let you in on a secret. Not one being that walks this earth is all good. Not even me. We all have baser instincts. But striving against the darkness within ourselves makes our triumphs even more meaningful. And I have faith that we will triumph, Alisha."

"Isn't she marvellous? Just as impressive as Julio Iglesias," said Alma.

Gaia continued. "Mistakes aren't the end of a story. They are merely a point on the map. Nothing in this life is irreversible except death." Her eyes twinkled. "And even that sometimes is not all done and dusted. Everything evolves. Cells. Emotions. Seasons. Empires rise and fall. Even galaxies burn out and are remade."

Alma's tone took a contrite turn. "It wasn't fair for us to keep it from you that I was a peculiar, but we needed to gain your trust fast. I wanted to let you in on our little charade when your father went missing, but he deserved to know first. I'll let the cat out of the bag once he's recuperated."

"You've lied to him long enough, Alma," I said. "No more waiting for the right time. You owe Dad the truth."

Gaia nodded. "You have a point, druid, but we must not forget the bigger picture. You haven't been alone."

I mean, it could be argued that Alma was more hindrance than help, but it seemed churlish to point it out. I wouldn't have complained if she'd soothed my worry. I frowned. "You know what really cuts? I lost my focus because the thought of losing Dad horrified me. But in the sewers, Mami said she never intended to kill him. She said a woman harbours a fondness for a man who has painted her. And vice versa."

Alma winked. "Why do you think I offered to sit for a portrait for your father? My readings told me that Mami and your father had a bit of sexual tension at art school. Nothing on the flame Joshi carried for your mother, of course, but enough for Mami not to harm him."

I thought of those lifeless bodies, of Annie's father still in Mami's grip, and my stomach clenched. "It's not over, you know. Not for me. Not when Mami is holding a man prisoner still. Won't you step in, Gaia?"

Deep-set frown lines appeared around her mouth. "Oh no, I can't do that. It's too early for me to show my cards. That's why I have you, Alisha. You can do things I can't."

Frustration pulsed through me. "Mami said she's fed up with waiting for worshippers. She's going to inspire devotion by controlling minds. I won't be able to forgive myself unless I try to stop her."

"Your encounter with Mami could have ended a thousand different ways. Or maybe there was only one way it would have ended. We will never know. You could have gone in there without any powers at all, with just your character, and you might have won. Or you might have lost. But nothing is dependent on one single decision or one single tactic. It's about how each particle collides with another."

Why did she always speak in riddles? I bit my lip, wanting a plain answer. Something I couldn't mess up. "So what should I do?"

Gaia's smiled with the warmth of the sun. "It's your choice, Alisha. It always has been. Go forth and make your own choices with bravery. And if they don't work, adjust and try again. No path is straight. Not even the eternal girl's."

"Weren't you going to mention the thing?" Alma made a phallic shape with her hands.

The goddess bristled. "Oh, okay. Maybe take your sword along. It's a shame to keep it in your knicker drawer. It can get a bit stuffy in there." She paused. "Now that's all taken care of, how about the three of us go out for some masala chai? I can almost taste the cinnamon and cardamom on my tongue."

BOTHERING Ezra during a pack day didn't seem like a good idea. Instead, I accepted an invitation from Orpheus to visit him at his gentleman's club in Charing Cross. After some false starts burping the alphabet in my attempts to hail an Otherworld taxi, I finally managed it and crisscrossed London to pick up Echo from my flat, then head to Orpheus. It was only sensible to take my trusty leopard as back up. Being welcomed by Orpheus was a sure bet, but I couldn't say the same of his vampire clan.

Not after I had turned one of them to dust.

Orpheus greeted us at the door wearing jeans and a dress shirt, his feet bare against the black-and-white Georgian tiles. His longish dark hair was tousled and damp from a shower, and the set of his face looked sterner than usual, despite his casual attire.

"Come in." He stood aside for us to pass and led us past the central atrium, where a pale woman lounged on a Chesterfield sofa, sipping blood from a tumbler. "No one touches a hair on their heads, or you answer to me."

A painting caught my eye as we followed him down endless corridors.

"You acquired a Jackson Pollock," I said.

He sighed, evidently a bit low, his skin as white as the cliffs of Dover. "It suits my current mood."

Echo padded alongside me. "The world is indeed a confusing place. We just found out that the doddering partner of Joshi is a flour seer."

Orpheus frowned. "A flour seer?"

Echo hissed. "No one saw it coming. Not even her."

I sighed. "Turns out everyone has a secret nowadays."

"I spent this morning checking on Annie. Her father still isn't home, and the poor girl is beside herself. I had to take a chunk out of a Labradoodle's bottom to calm myself down," said Echo. "I fear the axis of the Otherworld is realigning, and Alisha is central to it all. We must protect her, Orpheus."

"No, my friend." Orpheus took the stairs to the basement at an astonishing speed. "We must ensure that Alisha can protect herself."

"Err, I am here, you know." A passing peek through a basement door revealed a row of coffins of different styles. Once, the sight would have sent a shiver up my spine. Now I was tempted to snap a picture for Marina. The need to call, text her or scoff ice cream with her was so visceral it hurt.

Orpheus stopped at the end of the corridor, his piano-player fingers lingering on the door handle. "The detective tells me Mami is still involved in fishy business. There will be more battles in the days ahead. I can feel it in my weary bones. Which is why I arranged for you to see my personal chiropractor this morning. You can't very well go into battle with an injured body. And yes, I remembered your back has been hurting."

He gave me a sheepish look and then opened the last door along the corridor.

A rush of affection filled me. "You are a good friend, Orpheus. I am glad to have met you."

"As am I, druid," he said gruffly. "I'll leave you to it. Leopard, you may accompany her if you stay out of the way."

I walked into the room, grateful for Echo's company in the dark and dinghy rooms of the club, where vampires lived and lurked. Behind me, a purr rumbled from Echo's throat. The lingering smell of sanitising spray drifted up my nose as my eyes adjusted to the dim light and found a shadowy figure.

A clipped voice devoid of emotion met my ears. "So this is the woman Orpheus has told me about. Welcome, druid. And you, Chanakya Gunbir Hredhaan of Maharashtra. It has been an age since Paris."

Echo sprang forward, leaping up so that his front paws—at full stretch—rested on the man's shoulders, and proceeded to lick his face. "Manfred the Maimed. This is where you've been hiding all these years? In the vampire's basement?"

Manfred wore a white coat, his face obscured by Echo's fawning. "Old bones need tending to, leopard. The vampires pay well, and I have a steady, long-term clientele."

Echo moved aside at last, and the man stepped forward, a hand outstretched.

My eyes widened as he swallowed my palm in his. Six arms in total fanned out from his body, each an eye-popping blend of muscles, sinew and strength. He had thighs like Thor, and his nails were clean and short. But what struck me most was the surgical scars that marred every inch of his visible skin. His square face with tufts of dull blond hair. His multitude of muscly limbs. The veiny backs of his hands. His tree-trunk neck. Like Frankenstein come to life—a sentient horror show.

I took an instinctive step backwards. And Orpheus expected me to let him put his hands on me.

Manfred's voice made me shudder. It was bleak, brittle and a little broken, just like his body. "Your reaction is not unusual, druid. This face does not lend itself to walking the streets of London. I am not one for hiding behind glamours. My time is better spent down here concentrating on the inner workings of the body."

Echo sidled up to him, and six hands kneaded my leopard, provoking purrs of ecstasy, the likes of which I had never heard before. As he worked, the veins on his forehead popped in concentration, and the skin on his biceps pulled taut, so I feared his scars would split apart.

When Manfred stopped, Echo turned his emerald eyes on me. "I defy you to find anyone better with their hands. His chiropractor's knowledge is second to none. Indeed, increasing that knowledge is the whole reason why he put himself under his own knife. You will not regret this."

"What do you say, druid?" intoned many-armed Manfred the Maimed, cracking his knuckles.

His nose was fat and crooked, and his lips dry. His disfigurements meant I couldn't tell his age, but his clear, blue eyes gleamed with kindness and purpose. His work brought joy.

I shuddered. "What the hell. Do your worst."

His face cracked into a smile before he hoisted me onto the therapy bed. My leg flew up behind my head, and as his six hands found the sore spots on my body, I braced myself for more.

18

The coven dinner was in full flow that evening when Ezra and I arrived in our evening wear at Baba Yaga's Gym. These dinners occurred more frequently than a cloudy sky in London, possibly because the rat familiars doubled as a personal army of chefs. Even now, they scurried to and fro with tiny plates of canapés, topping up wine glasses, taking great care not to cause havoc with their tails. In the far corner, four rats—including Ignacio, the familiar who had wept over Elvira's body—wearing nothing but bowties, played in a string quartet.

At the heads of the table sat Lavinia and the Prime Sorcerer, Phinnaeous Shine, like mummy and daddy with a whole host of children between them, but it was Lavinia who held court. The diners, numbering fourteen in total, listened to Lavinia. Her table plan had interspersed witches between members of the senate. Enemies between friends, like she approached even a dinner party organisation wearing the hat of Defence Minister. As if every occasion happened to be an opportunity to play games, uncover secrets, divide and conquer. This was her home, after all. Her guest list. Her menu. Her snooping rats.

As usual, umbrellas lurked in unexpected places, the coven's weapon of choice. They were always prepared for bad weather, an impromptu spell, a spot of fencing or a harried flight across the London rooftops.

Ezra and I slipped into the empty seats between Orpheus and Isadora, Ezra's red-haired aunt.

"I saved a seat for you both," said Orpheus.

Ezra nodded in greeting. "I hear you paid for my girlfriend to have another man's hands on her today."

A small smile from Orpheus. "No need to get your hackles up. Manfred's approach is clinical rather than romantic, Neuhoff. How do you feel after seeing him, druid?"

"As good as new. I had no idea my body could be bent into those positions. It was like he knew exactly how to manipulate me to release the pressure. He was a revelation. Thank you, Orpheus."

"There are other ways to release the pressure," murmured Ezra.

"Stop it." I slapped his knee and glanced around to get my bearings.

Opposite us sat Ravynne in a lacy negligee. It would have been a pleasant surprise to see her fully dressed, but she'd left it out front and centre as usual. The detective, seated next to her, was painfully underdressed for the occasion—a plaid shirt amidst a row of crisp, white ones.

I leaned forward. "Any word about Annie's father? Or the other missing men?"

Jameson shook his head. He blamed me, even if he didn't say it out loud.

Orpheus rolled his eyes and slid my wine glass towards me. *Honestly, woman. I'll hand you a whip if you enjoy self-flagellation. If I carried the guilt of my mistakes with me, I'd never leave my coffin each day.*

I don't think anyone expects a vampire to be perfect. Your transgressions are priced in. I can feel the Prime Sorcerer's eyes boring into me from here. I forced myself to tune into the ongoing conversation about the latest curriculum adjustments at Wildwoods. The past few days had been enough to send me to bed with a paracetamol and a hot water bottle, but I hadn't wanted to disappoint Ezra.

Lavinia's tapered nails toyed with the stem of her wine glass. Her silver curls had been preened to perfection, and her navy dress showed off her toned shoulders and tiny waist. "All this talk of Wildwoods. How rude of me not to welcome you, Alisha. My nephew was adamant that we should spend more time together."

I tried to relax my shoulders. "Thank you for the invitation, Minister."

Amusement filled her cornflower-blue eyes. "Oh, you must call me auntie in informal settings."

It's like a spider trapping a fly, said Orpheus.

Lavinia checked a non-existent chip on her bubble-gum pink nail varnish. "The rats tell me you've had quite the week. It pleases me that my spell came in handy. Not everyone was as lucky as Joshi. I wish you'd come to me directly. I would have told you that, in all likelihood, that spell was only for one person. Like a single-use plastic. Very wasteful, really. Particularly wasteful of those three men's lives."

The rats, having just delivered the main course, froze in their duties, well-tuned to the slight shift in the mood of their mistress.

My heartbeat accelerated. It hadn't been my fault those men had died.

The diners proceeded to fork lasagne into their mouths, their eyes arcing between Lavinia and me as if they were watching a tennis match.

"Fuck," said Ezra. "I should have known you were playing games."

"Language, my dear boy. Spells are unpredictable things."

I told you so, said Orpheus. *Witches will give you stitches. And not the laughing kind.*

Rocking the boat was the last thing on my mind. "It seems like I still have a lot to learn," I said. "I bitterly regret the men's deaths, but it wasn't me who imprisoned them. As for Dad, the doctor checked him over and said he's doing well, all things considering."

I took a cautious sip of my wine, suspicious that Ravynne's semi-nakedness meant she'd brewed her special truth tonic again, and I'd soon be spouting how much I hated playing politics at these cushy senate meals.

Margola frowned at the delay in topping up her glass and reached for the bottle herself. "Nothing like some blood and guts to sell newspapers. Readership of *The Otherworld News* spiked nicely this week."

Two lizards scuttled from the Bestiary Minister's sleeve and across his plate. Helio picked them up and popped them back in his sleeve. "'Men Murdered by Sewer Monster'. That headline had quite a ring to it."

Margola tucked her flame-coloured hair behind one ear. "Didn't it? All thanks to the detective. He's very forthcoming with information. Once the investigation is over, of course."

Jameson swirled his glass as if it held the most fascinating beverage in the world.

A puzzled look crossed Orpheus's face. "It's not over yet, as I understand it. The perpetrator is still at large."

The Prime Sorcerer glowered. "And it will remain so. We have our laws. The humans have theirs. If Jameson wants to go after the goddess, it is on his head."

The detective stared blankly into the middle distance.

Jameson is unusually quiet this evening, said Orpheus. *Perhaps he's pining for the empath. I was going to ask him to arrange a guard around your flat and your father's house until everything is resolved, Alisha, but it might be better in this instance for me to arrange my own vampire guard instead.*

I choked on a mozzarella ball. *Don't be ridiculous. You destroyed the portal painting, and that's quite enough. We don't need your blood-thirsty crew lurking in dark corners outside our homes. I can just imagine what would happen if we took out the bins.*

The Prime Sorcerer went on. "We cannot continue to turn a blind eye to infractions. Neuhoff, it pains me to question your integrity, but the druid here has fallen foul of our rules once too often."

There had been a shift in power since the night at Wildwoods when, for all the power he possessed, the Prime Sorcerer had hurried to safety instead of staying to fight. When he spoke, he no longer had a captive audience of fawning listeners. Instead, his authority had been punctured by the seeds of mistrust. His reasons for leaving might have been the Pragmatist's Law—that mortals should not meddle in the affairs of gods—but fleeing Wildwoods when it was under attack marked him out as a coward under all the glorious trappings of his power.

Ezra's hackles rose. "There are many amongst us who break the rules. Some deliberately, some by chance, and some because a minor infraction would save a far greater evil. Parts of the Magical Constitution are not fit for purpose."

Warmth filled my stomach. Ezra jumped to my defence more than my ex-husband ever had. He was like a knight charging into battle.

Orpheus's voice reverberated in my head. *The wolf senses the shift in power. This is a pre-emptive strike. I'm quite enjoying the spectacle.*

I didn't really care for the Prime Sorcerer's criticism. Once, I might have lost sleep over it, but he had paled in my eyes. Still, I spoke for myself so Ezra didn't have to defend my honour. "Each time I have had a run-in with the gods, they have meddled with me. I have finished what they started."

The Prime Sorcerer's eyes narrowed on my face as if he wanted to glean every last secret of mine.

"Hmm." Margola's engine-red lips curved into a smile. "That's not strictly true. You infiltrated the Ravenmaster's home. Just like you did with me. You are the reason he targeted our magical home."

She just wasn't going to let that go. I sighed.

I didn't want to be the centre of attention. I wanted to disappear into the background. Forget the now cold lasagne on my plate. I was being served up as the main course. "Does the law have to be black and white? I hold up my hands. My love for my father meant I couldn't help but go after Mami. However, there is a middle way. Pan saw fit to see reason. He stopped the tremors when I appealed to his better nature." I hesitated, fearing a slap in the face, but it was worth a try. "There is a missing man yet to be found. Perhaps you could intervene with the water goddess, Margola. An approach from a selkie might just be what's needed to appeal for mercy."

I would think the detective would baulk at you appealing to a murderer for mercy, but he has the look of a man who has puffed the magic dragon. And yet, his policeman's pride makes him suspicious even of talcum powder, said Orpheus.

Incredulity washed over Margola's pale face. "I would rather help a mosquito than you, druid."

Next to me, Orpheus shook with silent laughter.

Isadora bravely intervened. "I've always found it discourteous to throw insults at the dinner table."

"Oh, leave it be, sister." Lavinia popped an olive into her mouth. "It's handbags at dawn, not a knife fight."

Ezra reached for my hand, his nostrils flaring. "You forget who returned your selkie skin to you, Margola. Perhaps you are worried Alisha is a better match for the goddess than you would be."

A cold stare from behind Margola's cat-eye glasses.

"Would you forgive so easily if the pack farmhouse disappeared? Be careful who you bare your teeth at. The previous wolf also showed flawed judgement, and we all know what happened to him."

"I could argue that the Ravenmaster appeared at Wildwoods with such unrestrained power that, despite the yew tree's shielding capacities, it risked exposing our whole school. The very centre of our community." Ezra directed a pointed glance at the Prime Sorcerer, Margola and Helio. "Yet you, and others here, decided to walk away rather than stay and fight."

Margola clamped her mouth shut.

A tinkling laugh from Lavinia. "My nephew's not wrong. My dear guests, the gods are becoming more and more presumptuous about the boundaries between the worlds. Can we tolerate these indiscretions when the Ravenmaster desecrated our haven at Wildwoods itself?"

Rayna, her long, grey hair intertwined with berry vines, had sat quietly through the discussion. "I could not stand by while blood was spilt at Wildwoods. Will you sanction me too?"

"Neuhoff might sit on the senate, but he has yet to earn the respect of his colleagues," said Phinnaeous. "If he is convinced our laws are outdated, he should settle the business at the senate, as per our norms. Not throw missives across the dinner table like a wronged wife."

Ezra growled. "I wasn't the one to start on politics. That was you."

The Prime Sorcerer's smiled coldly. "Perhaps you should look a little closer to home when you consider who starts the trouble."

Maybe it hadn't been a good idea for me to tag along. So much for the sense of togetherness Ezra had longed for. I squeezed his knee and picked up a bowl. "Anyone for a tiny pickled pepper? How about you, Prime Sorcerer?"

Orpheus spat out his wine. *You are priceless.*

Ezra leaned closer, dipping his mouth to my ear. "Are you trying to make a correlation between the size of his penis and those peppers?"

I stared at him in mock horror. "I was just trying to move the conversation along."

Orpheus's mouth twitched, his voice droll. "Next time, maybe go for the garlic baguettes to save confusion."

19

———

After dessert, Rayna and I escaped downstairs into the gym, leaving the other guests to split into cliques and nurse their drinks. The sanitised, peaceful vibe of Baba Yaga's gym contrasted with the bustle of the flat upstairs. Judging by Rayna's expression, she found it as much a relief to have a breather as I did.

"It must be your upbringing," said Rayna, her voice devoid of judgement. The most straightforward senate member, it appeared she had neither hidden motives nor artifice. "Druids tend to avoid confrontation. You are a curious mix of compassion and fire, much like your grandmother."

I turned on the bright lights in a yoga studio, wondering if a poor rat in the basement was now peddling furiously on a bike to generate energy. Lavinia had revealed once the coven quarters were self-sufficient. "I hope you won't find yourself out in the cold, given you invited me to teach at Wildwoods, Headmistress."

A beatific smile played on Rayna's lips. "You may split opinions, but you inspire the students, and my priority is to them."

She was perpetually unruffled and hadn't touched a drop of alcohol.

I felt like a positive gas-guzzler in comparison. "I never thanked you for staying to fight when the Ravenmaster entered Wildwoods. Especially given the philosophies of druidry. Druids are natural peacemakers, after all. They are priests, teachers and judges, not warriors. It must have cost you a lot to stay."

She waved a dismissive hand. "Even druid history is awash with blood. No culture is without its transgressions. Passivity, too, can be an evil. You don't think I wear this knife on my hip as an ornament, do you? It reminds me that sometimes there is no other course of action but to defend that which is sacred."

Though Rayna had faded into the periphery within the senate dynamics, she had a quiet steel and fortitude I admired. Giving attention to the loudest in a group meant I had missed out on noticing her strengths before.

Her eyes sparked with curiosity. "You have broken our rules with abandon but always with good cause. I admire you for that. It's why I voted for you to receive the Wildwoods Medal of Honour. Where is your medal, by the way? Where one keeps one's awards reveals much about the character. Is it on your mantlepiece? Do you have an altar of your achievements? Or have you lost it altogether?"

I grinned. "It's hanging from the knob on the inside of the guest loo."

Rayna blinked, then gave a bark of laughter.

"Headmistress, I always pegged you as the Prime Sorcerer's deputy. But your decisions do not always mirror his."

A smile floated across her wrinkle-free face. "To follow someone blindly is to be a fool. Phinnaeous Shine is a talented peculiar with unique skills. He's a strong leader and a good communicator. But while he understands the art of war, he is less proficient at the art of peace. And his instincts are to reject progress and conserve the past. He reminds me of the established religions, so sure of his intellectual and moral superiority. So different to druidry with its pragmatism, its worship of nature over power, its comfort with diversity, and its dismissal that there is one truth. I am my own woman, Alisha, just as you are yours." She tied up her hair at her nape and slipped off her shoes with the fluidity of movement of someone in their twenties, though she was in her sixties. "Let's get to work, shall we? Neuhoff has been whispering in my ear, urging me to make good on my promise to turbo charge your druid training. There's no time like the present."

She rolled out two yoga mats.

We stood barefoot, facing each other in the mirrored studio. My heartbeat accelerated as she took off her belt of potions and spread her feet wide. Rayna wore a grey shift dress in a viscose material. I wore my go-to forgiving black dress with a balcony bra not built for exercise, my hair loose about my shoulders. When she started her yoga practice, a wave of self-consciousness washed over me.

This was not what I had expected when she spoke of turbo-charging my training.

She frowned at my hesitancy. "What's the matter? Too proud to learn?"

"No, of course not." I bit my lip. "It's just… I'd expected us to be in the Wildwoods arena or on a mountain top, with the elements coursing around us. I wasn't expecting yoga."

Rayna sighed and stopped short. "Alisha, yoga is a vital tool. There are still gaps in your training. You have gained the basics from the wolf. You have learned some spells. You have studied history with Orpheus." She glanced at the potions. "You will learn herbology, healing and perhaps even wilding from me. But first, you have to reach your potential in weapons training. You haven't yet realised how magic doesn't have to be extraordinary. You can find magic in the most ordinary things."

I scanned the studio, noting a pile of yoga blocks and a few dumbbells. Pink, of course, given how Lavinia stamped her taste on everything with dogged persistence. "I don't see any weapons here unless you want me to throw some dumbbells at you."

"You forget, Alisha. Your body is a weapon, and you've not yet worked out how to optimise it. You are impressive but unpredictable. You have yet to learn how to rely on your body and what it can achieve." Calm eyes on mine. "Clear your mind. All the nagging worries about your mistakes and your enemies, your loves and your losses: forget them at this moment. Choose to be present. Listen to your body and copy my movements exactly."

I did as I was told, widening my stance, seeking extension in my limbs and fingers. I found the curves and shapes in movement as Rayna did, arching my feet and finding poise and resistance with my arms. I grounded myself through the floor, flowing through sun salutations and forward folds to balletic movements with an ease that I marvelled at.

My inhibitions fell away. My body grew lighter. My breath deepened, and drops of perspiration formed in the valley between my breasts.

Rayna circled her arms. I watched, transfixed, as the vines in her hair slid out like ribbons and grew longer, although they were unrooted to soil. They twirled around her, elegant and vicious all at once, snaking through the air at her command.

"Don't stop your movement, Alisha. Nature is about fluidity, continuation, perseverance."

I nodded and emulated her arm movements, one foot arched outwards as support.

When the winds came in through the slither of the studio window, I gasped. They came thick and fast, building to a crescendo around me, a whirlwind of dumbbells and yoga blocks that had come from a place of calm. Not anxiety. How many times had I called the winds without fear?

The power energised me, and the whirlwind raced around me, yet I was still in control. It was completely in tune with what I needed from it. It was a part of me rather than a force stemming from me.

"That's good, Alisha. Very good." Rayna's vines threaded themselves back into her hair, no longer weapons but a caress. "Return the projectiles to their places. See them in your mind's eye and guide them back."

The dumbbells and blocks returned to their places without a bang or a knock. I dropped my arms at last, beaming with pride at my accomplishment.

"You see, power doesn't have to be reactive. Real power is not grasping or vengeful. It is quiet, but it is still fierce. It is a whisper you hear inside yourself that is louder than your doubts. That is aligned more with truth and beauty than fear or anger."

I exhaled, still sensing the thrill of power in my palms. "That felt different to Rajiv's way."

"Destruction is unnatural for a druid. Your grandmother understood that." Her hazel eyes lit up as she collected her potions belt and dagger. "A druid who stands on the side of love will always be more powerful than he who chooses death or vengeance."

This was what Dad had meant. This was why he'd been furious at me.

Rayna's slim eyebrows drew together in thought. "I have trained many druids, Alisha Verma, and you have been the quickest study. I'd wager that has more to do with you than my teaching abilities. Now come along before we fall foul of the witches."

I needed the toilet, so she returned to the party before me. In the ornate coven washroom, I found seven cubicles, although, after Elvira's death, only six coven sisters remained. It was more a boudoir than a lavatory, with marble sinks and gold-rimmed mirrors, plus an array of potions, creams and powders that would rival a department store. The scent of thick perfume hung in the air.

I chose a cubicle, pulled down my knickers and breathed a sigh of relief at a moment's solitude. All too soon, the door to the washroom creaked open, and a gaggle of witches entered.

"Watch you don't make that ladder on your tights any bigger. A bit of nail varnish will help," said the first voice, tart and self-assured.

"You have lipstick on your teeth, Ravynne," wheezed the second voice.

A third voice, older than the other two. "I could do with a rejuvenation spell. My eye bags have resurfaced."

By their voices, I recognised them to be Ravynne, Agatha and Chandra, the gentlest of Lavinia's sisters. Nothing good came of eavesdropping. I stopped my flow midstream—pleased at the condition of my pelvic floor muscles compared to the horror stories from my childbearing friends—and quietly finished up. My hand was on the flush when I heard my name and stopped in my tracks.

"Did you see Ezra tonight, jumping to the druid's defence like a well-trained puppy?" said Agatha.

I peeked through the chink between the cubicle door and its frame. Ravynne assessed her reflection in the mirror and tucked the waterfall of her hair behind one ear. "I noticed that too. Why would Ezra choose her over poor Rashida? Rashida's *gorgeous*. I suppose Rashida has an in-built advantage with all the late-night pack runs. And the druid...well, there's a little middle-aged weight gain, *c'est vrai?*"

I checked my curves, hating myself for my self-doubt. It had taken me a long time to love my body. I didn't want to hear her voice inside my head. I curled my hands into fists. I wished people would keep their unhelpful opinions to themselves.

"The druid's not bad, all things considering. Forty years old without the advantages of magic to prolong her youth, unlike the wolf suitor. She looks like a yoyo dieter, though." Chandra smoothed her silver gown down her tall, slim frame and swept aside her blonde fringe. "I think she'd be spectacular if she had access to your potions, Agatha. Or a few spin classes."

Agatha giggled. "I bet she spends a fortune on Vitamin D, E and cod liver oil supplements and *still* looks like that. Our rats have glossier coats. Maybe I should offer her a makeover. From the dregs of South London to the cover of *Vogue*. Or at least, *Mum's Weekly*."

My simmering anger became rage. Marina would waltz out of the cubicle and give them an earful, not cower next to an unflushed loo. We both hated it when women were critical of other women. I held my breath all the same, cringing at the thought of a confrontation when I didn't have my wingwoman with me.

Ravynne laughed. "Oh, you are wicked. I want to know what hold she has over Ezra. You don't think she's cast a spell over him, do you?"

"Don't be silly." Chandra gave herself a spritz of perfume. "Alisha's a druid, not a witch. We all know love spells are the most difficult to master. In any case, Lavinia wants us to give the druid a chance. She's enjoying this newfound closeness with Ezra since they've been serving on the senate together."

Notes of vanilla and bergamot floated up my nose, threatening to unleash a sneeze. I pegged my nose, my eyes watering.

Ravynne batted her kohl-ringed lashes in the mirror. "Well, my sympathies are with Rashida. It was so humiliating when the druid escaped the pack house. She's devastated to lose an almost sure-fire chance of children after Isadora went to such trouble to prove compatibility." A pause. "Rumour has it the druid can't have children."

To hell with it, I thought, my sense of injustice overpowering me. I might be eavesdropping on a conversation in their house, but it was them that deserved to be ashamed. The dead witch Elvira was worth ten of them. I let rip the most orgasmic sneeze of my life, flushed the toilet and exited the cubicle with my head held high.

Colour drained from their witchy faces. Agatha darted a look at the exit.

"You've been in there all this time?" said Chandra.

"Uh-huh." I washed and dried my hands. "I thought a coven would understand that women should support women. I guess I was wrong. You should know Ezra's his own man. He's *very* particular about his tastes. He likes my body, and I do too. So it doesn't matter that you criticise me because it took me a long time to be comfortable in my skin and I won't be shamed by you." I revelled at their horrified faces. "You spend your life in either lingerie or a barely-there towel, Ravynne, but I'd challenge anyone who tried to slut shame you. Your body, your choice."

Ravynne's mouth opened a fraction, then shut.

I knew a retreat when I saw one and stood a little taller. "For the record, it's true I can't have children. But I distinctly remember Lavinia telling me once that a vagina has more uses than childbirth. But then maybe you wouldn't know that, given the body parts you are most concentrating on are your arses. As in, talking out of them."

I hid a grin. Marina would be so proud of me.

"I apologise for our unforgivable rudeness. I fully expect you to claim your pound of flesh when the time comes," said Chandra. She was clearly the only one of them with any shame.

I almost felt sorry for her. Almost.

"Oh, I will," I said breezily. "Anyway, I have a man to cast a spell over. I'll see you in there." I couldn't resist pointing to Ravynne's jaw. "Is that a curly chin hair I see? Your first one? I don't want you to leave here with egg on your face."

She scrabbled for a pair of tweezers.

I walked away, closing the door to the bathroom with a beautifully controlled breeze. In the main party room, the Prime Sorcerer huddled with Ezra and Orpheus. Jameson slumped in a corner. He'd obviously started on the sauce too early. Ezra spotted me, excused himself and made a beeline in my direction.

I melted into him, my buoy within shark-infested waters. "That was some revelation your aunt made. I keep thinking I might have been able to save them all."

"I'm sorry, Alisha. Old habits die hard. Lavinia always has some trickery up her sleeve. Years of being Defence Minister have only made that trait worse. I think she convinces herself that constantly testing those around her makes the Otherworld safer. All she does is destabilise potential allies. Her orchestration around that spell resulted in the death of innocent people. It is unforgivable."

I shivered with relief. "But I'm sure as hell glad the blame doesn't lie with me. I couldn't live with myself. What was Phinnaeous whispering in your ear about?"

"Senate business. I've been wrangling for a vote on the Pragmatist's Law." Grey eyes on mine. "Rayna returned fifteen minutes ago. I was about to launch a search party for you. She's been waxing lyrical to Lavinia about how talented you are."

"She's a good teacher." I plucked a wine glass from a passing rat and curled my arm around his waist. "Do we have to stay much longer? I just had a run-in with Ravynne, Agatha and Chandra in the bathroom, and I'd like to leave on a high note."

A low laugh rumbled through him. "A run-in was a high

note? Next time I might think twice about bringing you here. It's like putting a match to tinder."

I ran my fingers through the hair at his nape and pulled him close enough to murmur against his lips. Lips that would definitely work some magic on the knots in my shoulders. "I'll try to be better behaved."

He stole a kiss. Wine and chocolate and a bitter edge of roll-up cigarettes. "Hell, no. I'm not going to keep a good woman down." Frown lines appeared on his brow as the trio of bathroom witches stormed past us. "Although the three of them look like they're on a mission."

A shiver of apprehension crawled up my spine as the women joined Lavinia and Rayna's group. My ears burned, a premonition that their conversation centred around me. I hadn't been that much of a cow in the bathroom. I thought my retaliation had been quite measured.

Rayna's eyes found mine from across the room, a moment of compassion before her face shuttered.

"Something's going on, Ezra," I said.

He sighed. "Something's always going on in this witches' hovel. Why do you think I prefer the simplicity of the pack farmhouse or our cottage?"

Hardly a hovel, given the rat butlers and the fact the coven flat dripped in jewels. Still, I hugged that *our* to me. The fact that he considered the cottage mine too, the last piece of the world his parents had left for him.

"Let's finish our drinks and go home," I said.

Ezra nodded as the bathroom trio of witches withdrew to a corner, no longer cowed as they had been when I'd confronted them but gloating. I saw it in the toss of Ravynne's hair, Agatha's simpering smile and the set of Chandra's shoulders. Lavinia turned aside and beckoned the senate members to her. They conspired together: Rayna and Orpheus still and stern, Lavinia, Margola and Helio animated, Phinnaeous with a dawning smile. Only Ezra stayed at my side as if his opinion didn't matter at all.

Orpheus, taller than the rest, sought my eyes above their heads. *They know, Alisha. Lavinia has been suspicious since the night you tore the Ravenmaster to shreds at Wildwoods. And with the little titbit her coven sisters just told her about your inability to bear children, she has stumbled upon the truth.*

My heart raced, trying to decipher what he meant. *Now's not the time for riddles, Orpheus.*

Then, Lavinia broke from the group and clapped, asking for the attention of those congregated: five witches, the detective who had slumped in a corner, Ezra, and me. "It has come to our attention that a rather exceptional woman in our midst might be the hallowed creature from the Chameleon Tale."

Oh, shit. I thought.

Oh, shit indeed, said Orpheus.

Next to me, Ezra cursed, and power pulsed through his body. "The vampire must have told them."

I placed a hand against his chest. "He did no such thing. Your aunt is as clever as they come. We'd known it was only a matter of time before they worked it out."

He growled. "Do you want me to whisk you out of here?"

Shaking my head, I took a slug of my drink, grimacing as I swallowed it. I wasn't running away with my tail between my legs.

A smile. Lavinia relished these performances. "Ignacio and the rest of the string quartet, can I have a flourish from your bows?"

A nod from the rodents, followed by a swell of sound that didn't help my rising nerves.

"You all remember the Chameleon Tale, don't you? It is one told to peculiars when they are babes in arms. It features in the very first lesson for magical students at Wildwoods. It is the very reason female initiates in our magical community enter a tank with Kraglek. And what is that tale, pray tell?"

The witches chanted in unison, led by Isadora. The macabre edge to their tone told me each of them had suffered through the ceremony at one time or another. "The Chameleon Tale speaks of an eternal girl who blends in even though her talents are brighter than the sun. When Death opens the door, only the eternal girl may stop the coming Dusk, with a disintegrating tome lost to the world."

Lavinia beamed. "It turns out one woman amongst us hasn't yet undergone the Kraglek ceremony. She does indeed have talents brighter than the sun. Did she not beat Ra, as we all watched? Has she not performed feats that even the experienced and powerful amongst us have not achieved?"

I piped up. "Technically, that was Gaia."

"Don't be a pedant." Lavinia swept her gaze across those gathered. As Defence Minister, she was practised at rousing speeches. "We have always assumed the eternal girl refers to a child. But could it be that the prophecy relates to a woman unable to bear children? Could we have missed what has been under our noses all these months?" A dramatic pause. "I must admit, I suspected as much when the druid tore apart the Ravenmaster as if he was a slice of pizza. Alisha Verma is of a great magical bloodline, and it is only right that she faces Kraglek."

Ezra clenched his fists. "You can't foist this on her. It's not right to ambush her like this. You've jumped to the wrong conclusions, Auntie."

Lavinia's eyes softened when she looked at him. "Oh, I don't think so. Forgive me for not including you in our rather hurried discussion, nephew, but your romantic notions towards the druid rendered your opinion unreliable. Instead, I ask you, Alisha Verma, granddaughter of Rajika Verma, will you step into the tank with Kraglek?"

"Say no," growled Ezra in my ear.

Sooner or later, this was going to happen, said Orpheus. *It's better for it to be on your terms. Succeed, and you will hold more sway with the magical community and the senate than ever before.*

I didn't know what to do. I willed my voice not to quiver. "I have demands."

A slow smile spread across Lavinia's lips. "Of course you do. I've come to expect nothing less."

"If I subject myself to this, quite frankly, obscure and horrific ritual, and if I prove I'm the eternal girl in the prophecy, my opinion will hold as much sway as the senate. As much as I am a part of this community, I have my other foot in the human world, and I will not compromise on what I think is right."

The Prime Sorcerer's voice boomed across the room. "She's asking for a set of Get Out of Jail Free cards. She wants to be above our laws."

I shook my head. "No, I just want a fair hearing. I want to be seen as an equal, not an interloper."

"Let her make this bargain. She is not the eternal girl," said Agatha. "She is too old, but the ceremony will be fun to watch."

"It is not her. She is unfit," said Helio.

"She is infertile," said Margola.

The Prime Sorcerer's eyes gleamed. "She is undisciplined."

"Then let's agree to this bargain and let her be tested," said Lavinia.

"Please, don't do it," said Ezra in my ear.

Do it, said Orpheus. *It is time.*

In my head, I heard the refrain from the Rage Against the Machine song when Wonder Woman goes into battle. All these opinions of me.

Only I knew who I was. Only I sensed my potential.

And yet, their voices chipped away at me until they became a deafening roar in my head. They infuriated me. All the doubters and the naysayers. Who didn't want me to question them or think for myself. All the ones who thought I was too loud or too old. Too unfit or undisciplined. The ones who thought I was too human and I didn't belong. I'd do it, and they'd never question who I was again. I was as powerful as every single last one of them.

I couldn't deny it any longer.

I knew deep inside that what Gaia had said was true. I'd known it for some time.

It wasn't ladylike to blow my top, but I couldn't help it.

I pushed my glass into Ezra's hand and balled up my fists. My heart thudded against the walls of my ribcage. "Will you all just shut up?"

Poor Ignacio dropped the bow of his cello in fright.

"I'll go into the tank just so I don't have to listen to you all. I'll do it tomorrow."

Lavinia clapped in delight.

Orpheus gave a sombre nod. "I suggest a closed-door ceremony inside the vaulted cabin at Wildwoods. Only senate members and family allowed."

"I will, of course, be documenting the ceremony for *The Otherworld News*," said Margola, unchallenged.

The copper filaments in Ezra's grey eyes glittered dangerously. "What have you done?"

"I'm sorry." Somehow, the anxiety in my chest had dissipated. "I'm tired of hiding. Now will someone take poor Robert home?"

20

———

After a fitful night's sleep, the day of the Kraglek ceremony arrived—my third day without Marina. I could have done with one of her hugs. She would have forced me to smuggle a four-leaf clover, a rabbit's foot or a horseshoe into the ceremony, but it was her who brought the luck. I couldn't decide if I'd been foolish or brave to agree to the ceremony. Round and round it went in my head.

I was the eternal girl. Wasn't I?

Gaia had told me it was true. She was reliable, wasn't she?

I knew what Ezra thought without him spelling it out. He always needed a moonlit run when he was frustrated or angry. He'd run through the city streets for so long that the starry night became a fragile dawn by the time he returned to the flat. But he didn't need to agree with me to support my choices.

I was my own woman, and Gaia had reminded me that I had my own mistakes to make.

That was all any of us could do.

The living room of my flat brimmed with friends and family. Dad had come, nudged by Alma, a fragile peace between us since I'd revealed to him that I was the eternal girl. He might not have agreed with my decisions, he might rail against them, but he'd always been there through thick and thin. Orpheus had come too. He sat on my sofa at the opposite end of Ezra.

Orpheus frowned. "I wish this could wait, but we have a problem. Lavinia called me this morning after the detective arrived at Baba Yaga's gym. She was worried that he appeared unusually vacant. I assessed him and…"

I searched his alabaster face. "Tell us."

A heavy sigh. "Lavinia and I are in agreement. What initially looked like the result of an over-consumption of alcohol paired with a weak constitution is something else entirely. Jameson seems to have quite literally lost his mind. He may be continuing his daily routine by instinct, but he is not all there. He is like an opera without the arias. A shell of himself. I fear his time investigating the sewers may have led to an encounter with the water goddess."

My stomach cramped with anxiety. This was Marina's love. My friend. "What can we do to help him?"

"Let's not jump to conclusions," said Dad. "Who knows what happened? Mami's anger is not proportionate, but she usually has a reason for choosing her victims."

"Joshi is right," said Echo. "Not all that smells of fish is fishy. The Shadow Squad has many seedy contacts. Any one of them could have acted nefariously towards the detective."

Orpheus nodded. "In any case, Lavinia has determined the fracturing of his mind to be irreversible with potions. I, too, tried and failed to unlock it. It might be that an emotional encounter or reliving an experience can free his mind, but for now, he is, I'm afraid to say, a cabbage."

Ezra winced. "The poor man's hardly a cabbage. He's been enchanted. We will fix this, but for now, we need to concentrate on priming Alisha for the ceremony."

Echo leapt onto the sofa between wolf and vampire, making himself impossibly big between them, a mischievous glint in his eyes. "Indeed. We must prioritise our battle plan. The day has come when all the glory in the Otherworld will be ours."

Dad set down his teacup and sighed. "Why does the cat sound like a tinpot dictator? My daughter is about to go into a tank with a vicious octopus."

Alma patted Dad's knee. "Don't worry, darling. Kraglek can't be that vicious if he's been blessed by the goddess of the Ganges. Many years ago, I went on a retreat to India, and the guru told us the waters there are healing. Immersion in the river purifies bathers of their sins. I spent a lot of time in it, atoning for my wild child days. The guru said it is impossible for such a holy river to birth a monstrous creature."

"As an Indian leopard myself, I would like to suggest that the guru simply told you what was necessary for you to empty your wallets," said Echo.

Alma huffed. "Well, as someone who endured the Kraglek ceremony myself, let me assure you, Alisha, that the octopus did not kill me or any other girls. There have been some unfortunate mishaps, but what's a few months of unconsciousness in a long life?"

Ezra deadpanned, a bleak expression on his handsome face. "That's okay then."

I sat cross-legged on the floor, my back ramrod straight. Manfred really had worked wonders on my back. "Good to know. Do you have any survival tips, Alma?"

She thought for a moment. "Take a deep breath before immersion, and don't lose your head."

Echo nodded. "Wise words. It reminds me of a catchy Toni Braxton song I have just discovered called 'Breathe Again.'"

I didn't know whether to laugh or cry.

Unexpected swings in emotion are the mark of a lunatic, said Orpheus.

Or menopause, I said.

Orpheus choked back his laughter and looked down at his hands.

Jaw clenched, Ezra's eyes darted between us as if he was alert to my bond with the vampire and didn't like it. "I'm with your father, hellfire. I think we've had enough turmoil over the past months without drawing the attention of the entire Otherworld to you, Alisha. But there is no way back now. You agreed to go into the tank, so we can only hope you can subdue the octopus."

"Maybe the octopus doesn't need subduing," I said. "Maybe he needs befriending."

Echo's gums showed as he honked with laughter. "This is why your druid family needs generations of leopard protectors. You have not yet learned the laws of the jungle. Eat or be eaten."

Orpheus bared his fangs. "The leopard is not wrong. Friendship won't save your life."

Unimpressed, I saved him the humiliation of voicing my thoughts out loud. *I seem to remember my friendship saved your life when you stood at a precipice and asked me to retrieve a holy stake for you.*

Damn you. You have a memory like an elephant, said Orpheus.

Dad's knees bounced, a nervous tick that surfaced with his worries. "You can't animate in the tank, not when you're submerged in water and with the octopus waiting to surge. But your wind powers will be an asset." His brow furrowed. "At least your mother took you to swimming lessons. When's the last time you practised? Maybe we should head down to the public pool. Better yet, we could sneak some floats into your knickers."

"Or you can wear a buoyant bikini top," said Alma. "It can provide lift in more ways than one."

Ezra sank his head into his hands. "Christ, this is the blind leading the blind."

"Never fear. She has me," said Echo. "I made an oath to

lay down my life for Vermas. I even risked my neck in the sewers for Joshi. I fought a serpent a hundred feet long with a tongue like a double-decker bus."

Orpheus's eyes rolled back so hard I feared he'd get whiplash. His admiration when he'd first met Rajika Verma's famed leopard had transformed into something much more ordinary. "That sounds plausible, leopard. You should save it for your memoirs. Tonight, however, you'll be on the outside of the tank like the rest of us." He elbowed Echo for a bit more space and shifted forward. "I might have encouraged you to go ahead with this feat, Alisha, but you have to be match fit. The octopus is fast. I seem to remember you cornered him at the last ceremony. But you are bigger than the usual girls in his tank. He may well see you as a significant threat. You must be prepared for anything."

I raised an eyebrow. "Charming."

Never one to be deterred, Echo gave a self-assured purr. "I can give you lessons in how to talk to pussies, vampire. You need only say the word. I am very experienced. I imagine, with some coaching, your baritone will open many legs."

Dad spat out his tea. "This is too much."

Orpheus raised a heavy eyebrow. "I'll bear that in mind, leopard." He frowned like he'd been assaulted by an unwelcome mental image, then continued. "Alisha, all you need to do tonight is survive a minute in the tank. None of us can change that. What I can do is use our telepathy to prompt you during the ceremony."

Ezra bristled. "I knew it. I knew you were in her head, vampire."

Orpheus raised an eyebrow. "Calm down, wolf. We are friends. That is all. That is enough."

"Play nicely, you two."

Ezra came to sit next to me on the floor and put a possessive hand on my thigh. "We have to concentrate on the matter at hand. Kraglek is a carnivore, but he is well-fed.

Helio won't let any harm come to you. Neither will I. Even if I have to break ranks with the senate."

"A knight in shining armour." Orpheus flexed his fingers. "Just what the most powerful woman in the Otherworld needs."

"That's not what I meant," said Ezra. "I have faith you can do this, Alisha. Look at us in this room. Who else could have brought disparate groups together other than you? You are born to be this pin between us all. My logic tells me you will win this battle, but my heart wants you to be cautious. I've told you before. The Otherworld is not cotton wool and cuddles. It is blood and guts."

"I think we should talk about the floats again," said Dad. "Indians aren't good swimmers, and you do have half my genes."

"I can pick some up from the pound shops if you like, Alisha," said Alma. "No one swims in autumn. They'll be a pound a dozen. You'll be positively pneumatic. Like a blow-up doll."

Dad's eyebrows disappeared into his hairline; whether titillated or rendered speechless was anyone's guess. I logged the comment to retell to Marina and Sahil.

"I think I'll be okay, Alma." I rose to my feet in a balletic movement and made a mental note to book a regular session with Manfred. "I've heard enough. I'll see you all out. I need a power nap if I'm going to keep my wits about me tonight."

<h1 style="text-align:center">21</h1>

I'd seen the vaulted cabin dressed countless times for celebrations and ceremonies, performances and school dining, candlelit first impressions and orb-lit senate meetings. Tonight, it had an austere feel, softened by small groups of flickering pillar candles on the window ledges. The moon filtered in through the stained-glass windows. I could hear a pin drop. There was no orchestra this time to lend a sense of grandeur to the occasion. I inhaled a shaky breath.

Dad, Alma and Echo darted worried glances my way from where they sat on a lone bench towards the rear of the cabin. Sahil, though invited, had wished me luck in a harried phone call just before he signed his latest property deal in the heart of the city. My disappointment that he hadn't come showed how much our relationship had changed during our rescue of Dad.

At least if it all went wrong today, Sahil and I would have parted on better terms.

Ezra pulled at his charm necklace. "I need you to wear my thistle charm. It will heal non-fatal injuries more quickly than if you go in there without protection."

I stilled his hand as he fumbled for the clasp and inserted

a note of bravado I didn't feel into my voice. "No. It won't help in there. Besides, Helio will step in if things get too rough, and Rayna is a skilled healer. I'll be safe. Don't worry."

"I hate this." Ezra's stubble grazed my skin as he pressed a kiss to my lips. His smoky voice was warm as honey around the edges. "I hate being here in the role of senator when our love comes first. I should be at your side and not on the stage."

I channelled calm, even though my mind was as choppy as a stormy sea, and hugged him. "It's okay. I've got this."

He caressed my cheek for a fleeting moment I wished could go on forever. "Good luck, Alisha. I believe in you."

Then he walked away from me to the stage, where the senate—with the exception of Calypso, who remained in the Celestial Library—sat in high-backed, wooden chairs. An enormous Wildwoods flag fluttered behind them with its golden W and nine posies of plants.

One thing was clear: I had friends amongst the senate but also enemies and a fair few who couldn't give a toss about my fate.

I was the answer to a centuries-old riddle or an evening's entertainment.

A light in the dark or a pissing torch without a battery.

A saviour or a fool.

The fates could decide either way.

A tradition as old as time. Cruel to boot, Ezra had said once.

The Prime Sorcerer's formal robe swept the dusty floor. His afro, threaded with silver, and bearing, had once marked him out to me as distinguished, but I knew now that he had feet of clay. He stood and raised his voice like a preacher. "As I have said many times in this place, the Chameleon Tale tells of our destruction and salvation. Could this be the night we find our salvation? Will the granddaughter of Rajika Verma be the one we have been waiting for all these years?"

I trembled with nerves before them, wearing—at Helio the

Bestiary Minister's insistence—a frilly, floor-length, white nightdress like a Victorian granny. As if the situation wasn't bad enough without making me look like a moron. Marina wouldn't be caught dead in this get-up.

I hadn't even thought to bring cycling shorts to preserve my modesty.

The Prime Sorcerer swirled each hand in the pattern of an eternity sign.

I'd seen this before, on the evening Miriam had entered the tank when Wildwoods was new to me. Even then, this sight had made my stomach churn.

I braced myself as freshwater gushed through the vaulted cabin. Beads of sweat pooled on Phinnaeous Shine's brow as he manipulated the water. Only he knew the source of the water. Only he knew what it had cost him to learn this magic. The water ebbed and flowed in rivulets, finally ending clumped together in the centre of the room. The sphere stretched almost wall to wall, floor to ceiling.

A sphere that would swallow me whole.

My pulse quickened to lightning speed, and I looked to Ezra for reassurance.

Grey eyes locked with mine. Ezra flexed his neck, and for one moment, I thought he might shift to his wolf and fight the world for me so I didn't have to go through with it. We could escape to his cottage or Paris or the end of the world and never think of this again. The hoops I'd jumped through since becoming a druid. The sacrifices that came with my skills.

Helio the fairy, who'd been banned from the Celestial Library for smearing pages with bogies, sprang off his chair. He shouted an introduction like a tipsy master of ceremonies at a wedding. "Behold, the most important creature in the Wildwoods Bestiary. The immortal Kraglek. Touched by Ganga, the goddess of the Ganges. The only living creature able to sense the prophesied eternal girl."

At the centre of the sphere, Kraglek the octopus writhed.

He seemed to grow with the space, filling every inch of the sphere, his tentacles reaching, feeling, and making me sick with anxiety. He had a bulbous head with ancient eyes that knew my every thought, that knew pain and how to cause it. He was deep purple with eight limbs covered in suckers. Limbs that could squeeze the air from his victims until they hung limp in his arms. Limbs that trailed blue ink. That could entrap or mangle his prey.

Today, I was the prey.

His ravenous mouth opened.

My lungs constricted. I balled my fists, determined not to let my fear show.

Breathe, Alisha, said Orpheus. *It will be over in a few minutes.*

I grimaced. *That's what I'm worried about.*

Lavinia, in yoga leggings and a matching tank top that showed off her age-defying physique, raised her voice above the din of the octopus swishing in the sphere of water. "A minute in the tank, Alisha, and we will know. We will know whether you withstand Kraglek's poison. We will know whether you are who we have been looking for." She smiled. "Of course, if you are rendered unconscious, as a druid, it will typically take you longer to recover. As pacifists, your kind has less fight than the rest of us. Should that happen, Helio has kindly offered to look after your leopard and dragon."

Helio bowed, the little shit, as if stealing and confining my creatures to captivity was something to be proud of. I hadn't forgiven him for calling me unfit.

I gave both of them eyes like daggers. "If you want me in that tank, then my father, Joshi Verma, and my best friend, Marina Ambrose, are joint guardians of any creatures affiliated to or animated by me."

No doubt they'd be fighting over my sword too.

Dad gave me a wave from the far end of the room so we all knew who he was.

The Prime Sorcerer exchanged glances with Lavinia. "Very well, druid."

Lavinia smiled. "Now get in the tank. Unless you've changed your mind?"

It was all very well standing up to bullies, but now I was at my moment of reckoning. I wondered if it wouldn't have been cleverer to accept their criticisms and doubts of me and fly under the radar for a little while longer after all. Sticks and stones and all that.

Orpheus's gravelly voice filled my head. *Be brave, Alisha. There will be many who are out of pocket tonight if you succeed.*

My eyes darted to him. *They're betting on me? You didn't join in, did you?*

He stared straight ahead, not a flicker of emotion or quirk of body language betraying his conversation with me. *I'm an immortal amoral vampire, not Mary Poppins. Of course, I did.*

"What say you, druid?" said Lavinia.

My throat was thick with panic. I exhaled, willing all my negative thoughts to exit with my breath. I took a deep breath to fill my lungs with as much oxygen as possible.

Then I stepped into the sphere of water.

The octopus didn't compress his form. He didn't shrink from me. Only one victim had entered his tank, and he was used to many more. Kraglek's clever, unblinking eyes anchored themselves on my face, on the terror that lurked there, taking in my flailing limbs, the cheeks full of air that revealed I was out of my usual environment. That here, he was king.

He surged. His mouth opened.

A scream built inside me. Instinctively, I swam. Deep breaststrokes up through the sphere of water, flinching from the tentacles grabbing at me, the suckers I couldn't escape. I was going to be eaten by an octopus, and I would never live it down. It would be written on my gravestone at Streatham

Cemetery, a few rows down from where Mum was laid to rest.

HERE LIES ALISHA VERMA
OCTOPUS PREY

I reached the edge of the sphere, bumping against it like a stupid goldfish in a bowl, too scared to make sense of its world. Already panicking at the need to take a breath, I swivelled to face Kraglek, his prehistoric brain and bulging eyes making me squirm with terror. My ridiculously long nightdress gathered around my breastbone, impeding my sightline, and my exposed bottom, in its white granny pants, squelched against the side of the sphere, giving everyone gathered an eyeful.

The shame almost killed me.

But then the octopus loomed, and I knew that my demise would be a messier affair.

Kraglek wasn't even in a rush. I caught sight of his exposed, pink underbelly, where his tentacles converged. A sharp, parrot-like beak snapped there almost lazily. There was nowhere for me to escape.

My panic rose like a tidal wave. I was a goner. He knew it. I knew it.

Reality slowed. How many more seconds did I have to endure? I didn't even bother to push down the night dress. Fear paralysed me. If a moonie was the senate's last memory of me, then so be it. Maybe it would be better to give up. There was nothing worse than an animal flailing for its life and still getting chomped on. I could just doggy paddle into Kraglek's mouth and go to my end with dignity.

Orpheus's voice pulsed in my head, urgent, laced through with desperation. *Remember the lessons Rayna taught you. Keep calm. Remember your power. Never operate from fear.*

Without warning, Kraglek's lumpy, boneless arms

stretched out, reaching for me with the speed of a cobra. Inky fluid shot from him, blackening the water and splattering my bunched-up dress like some sort of heinous ejaculation.

I couldn't hold my breath anymore.

I closed my eyes and stopped flapping, allowing the water to hold me as I pushed off the edge of the sphere, mercifully freeing my bottom. Opening my eyes, I blew the lingering gasps of air in my lungs into the water, pushing the octopus back. I remembered my kickboxing training, my years on the yoga mat, and the training with Rayna at Baba Yaga's gym.

My arms stretched, and I ignored Kraglek's surge as he swam towards me once more in an attempt to corner me. His tentacles grasped for me as I found a calmness and belief within, my limbs in harmony with my thoughts as I found a vinyasa routine in the water, found speed and length as I worked. My hands pressed out in a warrior pose as Kraglek swept towards me, tentacles billowing behind him, releasing his toxins. As I struck mountain pose, something miraculous happened.

Kraglek's ink streamed towards my hands, pooling there before evaporating.

And when I looked down at the night dress, all trace of blackness had gone.

My eyes met the octopus's as his colour changed from deep purple to blue, and he dropped, cowed to the bottom of the sphere of water, curling his tentacles closer to his body.

I trembled, coherent thought impossible when I was so deprived of oxygen. And suddenly Ezra was there, through the sphere, shouting for help, though I couldn't hear his words.

The sphere poured me out into my waiting wolf's arms.

I spluttered, vomiting water as he lowered me to the floor, coaxing me to lean my weight on him. He patted my back, pushing my wet hair out of my face, whispering sweet nothings all the while.

His anguished face appeared above me. "God, that was hell. I was so worried."

I lifted my head as a smattering of applause broke out from Rayna on the stage. Orpheus looked as pleased as punch. Margola snapped pictures for *The Otherworld News*, where I'd look like a bog troll. The rest looked on in awe.

Echo bounded over ahead of Dad and Alma, their faces pale with worry.

Dad sobbed. "That felt like a lifetime."

"You conquered the fish," said Echo. "The laws of the jungle made you victorious today."

"I'm okay." The pain in my lung eased, and I faced the stage, uncaring that the senate could see my body clearer than an X-ray machine through my soaking nightdress and undies.

Lavinia leapt to her feet, shaking her head in bemusement. "Well, I never."

I held my chin and raised my voice for all to hear. "I warned you that traditions like that belonged in the dustbin of history. All those times you put young girls through this barbaric ritual were for nothing."

Phinnaeous Shine stood up in a swish of his robes. "What are we going to do with her now?"

Rage filled me. I was the eternal girl, and they still thought they were in control, despite our deal. "Are you going to give me a fucking crown? Because that's one childhood fantasy I'd given up on."

Lavinia tutted. "Oh, get your head out of your bottom, dear. You've not won the lottery. Things just got a whole load more high stakes for you."

Ezra growled, and I felt the reverberations next to me. "Be quiet, auntie," he said. "Alisha has earned the right to speak here."

I addressed the senate. "We are equals. Do not presume to tell me what to think or how to act. I am the eternal girl, but I am so much more. Tread carefully because you need me more than I need you."

Silence ensued, which I took as a win.

Only Orpheus spoke, his eyes gleaming. "Well said, druid." He left his space amongst the senate and joined us with vampire speed that belied his usual reserved manner. "So what Gaia said was true. It's all out in the open now."

Helio approached the truncated water body, now a hemisphere, where the octopus rested, spent from his exertions. He lifted a Taser and delved a hand into the water, shocking Kraglek. The octopus jerked and went limp.

"Stop," I yelled. Anger consumed me.

The once legendary creature was almost pathetic now, his purpose now rendered useless. I'd already subdued him. There was no reason for Helio to taser him apart from a macabre sense of revenge.

I blasted Helio onto his backside. He rushed at me, but I returned him to his arse with a flick of my hand. "How could you, Minister? That creature was in your care. But he isn't anymore. I will see to it that he is properly rewarded for his service to this community."

"I like this side to the druid," said Lavinia. "It shows gumption. Perhaps the Otherworld is not lost after all."

Ezra gave his aunt a wry smile and put a protective arm around me. "What now?"

"First, I change my clothes." Hope brimmed inside of me. I had wronged the men I had left to perish at Mami Wata's hand. I had wronged the devil ray, seahorse, flying fish and squid by not ensuring their safety after animating them to serve my purpose. But I had a way to make amends. I had a way to earn back some good karma. "Then we free Kraglek, rescue kidnapped men from a rogue goddess and fix the detective's mind. Easy peasy."

22

———

Easy peasy, my arse. Still, freshly bathed and in dry clothes, with a piping hot takeaway curry in my belly, I was buzzing with my achievement. My self-belief had soared through the roof, and I hadn't even needed to ferret pneumatic aids into my knickers to get there. Even so, caution prevailed. Being cocky wasn't my style.

Though acutely aware of the need to help the octopus, we waited until those grey-black hours of the night, when adults snore on the sofa in front of flickering screens, and London was quiet apart from the din of foxes and the dull thud of bins thrown by high winds. Then, we teleported to a deserted spot at the Albert Embankment in Vauxhall, cringing at the semi-conscious octopus that hung in the tarpaulin between us.

Our feet crunched on wiry grass at the shore of the river Thames.

"I am displeased that you roped me into helping, druid. This creature smells worse than a vampire who has forgotten to exfoliate," said Orpheus. "Just because you are the eternal girl doesn't mean you can take liberties."

I huffed as we lugged Kraglek further, even though Ezra

and Orpheus bore most of the weight. *I didn't ask because of my status. I asked because we are friends.*

Oh. Very well, then, said Orpheus.

"Perhaps the octopus will make it back to our mutual homeland and find a mate. Perhaps he will tell his tale of tank warfare to the tens of thousands of eggs his mate will produce." In the moonlight, the scar at Echo's right eye glistened. "Or perhaps he will be devoured in shark-infested waters and never use one of his suckers again. It is a shame we will not know the rest of his story."

"For heaven's sake, will you shut up, Echo?" Ezra said. "You're the only one not doing the heavy lifting here."

Echo sighed. "You strike me in the heart, wolf. I thought you were more sensitive than to hold my lack of opposable thumbs against me."

We rolled Kraglek from the tarpaulin in a mass of purple flesh, bulbous megamind head and knotted tentacles. He slopped onto the grass.

"What now?" I said. "Shall we just push him in?"

Marina would have known what to do. It seemed stupid to stand on the riverbank and search the internet for an answer.

"I have an idea." Echo padded to the water and dunked his head into it, emerging with a mouthful of water. He spat it at the octopus and retreated a few metres back to clean himself.

The octopus roused at last, sensing the relief of the water, the freedom that would wash away the taste of captivity. He turned his head towards me, his clever eyes resting on my face for a long moment before a great shuddering encompassed him, then a sigh, and he slopped along the grass and fell into the Thames.

I peered over the edge. "Where is he?"

Behind you, said Orpheus.

I swung around and swatted his chest.

Ezra took my hand. "We won't see him now. He's camouflaged in the dark water. But he can thank you for his freedom, Alisha. I think, in his own way, that's what he did just before he dove in." He glanced at Orpheus. "Alisha told me what you did for her in the tank, vampire. I'm grateful."

Orpheus turned up his collar against the autumn wind. "The pleasure was mine."

Ezra paused. "So, how often are you in my girlfriend's head?"

"Be honest, Orpheus. It's pretty often." I laughed and then reached up to kiss Ezra, a few seconds more than was strictly polite in company. "But you have nothing to worry about."

"Oh, he has something to worry about, Alisha," Orpheus's Roman nose and alabaster skin stood out against the night sky. "After all, who wants another man's voice in their woman's head? But Neuhoff and I make too good a team on the senate for me to jeopardise our working relationship by overstepping the line."

Maybe I was just tired, or maybe it was telepathy, but I heard a silent *yet* at the end of the sentence, and it sent a shiver up my spine. It felt good to be the object of desire, even if nothing could turn my head from Ezra.

"Well, as long as we have an understanding." Copper flecks danced in Ezra's eyes, a dangerous promise should the vampire overstep the mark.

"Oh, I'm quite sure we're on the same page," said Orpheus.

I frowned. "Stop sparring with your cucumbers."

Orpheus chuckled. "She likes comparing nether regions to vegetables, Neuhoff."

"I mean it. We've got important things to discuss. I'm afraid I'm going to fall foul of the Pragmatist's Law again, and this time, I won't have the excuse of naivety or the actions of other peculiars or intruder retaliation or family love. I won't be able to defend myself against accusations of illegality. Regardless of the bargains I struck, not every senate member is a friend. But I'm going to go down into the sewers with the express intention of using violence to stop Mami Wata. And I don't want to end up in the dungeons with Gunnolf because of it."

Ezra snarled, more wolf than man. "Why do you think I took the position as Justice Minister, though it curtails my freedom? You do what you need to, hellfire. Orpheus and I have been bending ears behind the scenes. There's a vote tomorrow on the Pragmatist's Law, and we might yet pull off a vote in our favour to get it amended."

"I told you we were a good team," said Orpheus.

Relief swept through me. "Okay. Maybe we can just pull this off."

"Shh." I frowned, struggling to decipher noises over the lapping of the Thames against the riverbank. A scuffling met my ears, followed by muffled cursing. "Do you hear that? Where's Echo?"

Ezra and Orpheus whipped their heads in the direction of the sound.

"How dare you manhandle me!" said a male voice.

My jaw slackened as Echo dragged Great-Uncle Rajiv out of the bushes by his eighty-year-old bottom.

I bolted forward to scold Echo and help Rajiv. "Hey, go easy. He's a pensioner."

"Mutton or lamb, it's all meat to me," said Echo.

"Remind me not to entrust my care to the leopard in my old age," deadpanned Ezra.

Orpheus appraised Rajiv. "He has good hair for an aged mortal."

"Hindus eat their greens." Rajiv dusted himself down, his expression grim.

I eyeballed Rajiv's weather-beaten face suspiciously. "What are you doing here, Uncle?"

His voice was wafer-thin with age, though it still had a

hard edge. "You owe me a spade and a screwdriver, Alisha. I need them for my canal boat repairs. They were a loan, not a gift." A sniff. "I see you're cavorting with the magical community instead of coming to see me."

Orpheus thrust out a hand. "You must be Rajika Verma's brother. I've read much about you. I'm Orpheus Might, Minister for History and the Today."

"Well, la-dee-da," said Rajiv, clearly bitter and not one for pomp. Tonight, he wore threadbare jogging trousers stuffed into green Wellington boots and a moth-eaten T-shirt.

I frowned at Echo's jostling of Rajiv's legs with the persistence of a mosquito, disappearing in the darkness and then reappearing at the other side like some demented intruder system.

"I lost your tools, Uncle, but I'll arrange for more to be sent to you." A pause. "How did you know where to find us?"

"The river talks to me," said Rajiv.

Echo's emerald eyes narrowed. "He lies. I caught his scent. Stalker."

Rajiv glared at him. "Housecat." A sniff. "Maybe I have been keeping an eye on you, but can you blame me? You visited me out of the blue for help, and then I didn't hear from you again."

"That's because you revealed your true self in absentia. In the corpses of dead squids and reams of fish guts," said Echo. "Alisha stood in a sewer, but it is you who polluted her."

Rajiv's watery eyes narrowed. "I freed you. And now a little birdie told me that you're the eternal girl."

"You're not trying to correlate the two, are you?" I took a deep breath. "Without you, I might not have saved Dad. I owe you a debt of gratitude for that, but that night, I also made some of the biggest mistakes of my life. You're not the right person for me to learn from, Uncle."

Rajiv raised his chin. "So it's like that, is it? You are casting me out. I can't even come to your family home to reconcile with my nephew?"

I shook my head. "He doesn't want to see you."

Ezra's phone glowed in his hand. He had to be more reachable as a senator, and it irked him. He stared at it before turning to me, a smile on his lips. "Sorry to interrupt the family reunion, but we have to go. My aunt says Calypso and Marina are on their way back from the library."

Joy exploded inside me.

"What library? Wandsworth Library, Croydon Library? The Celestial Library?" Rajiv's eyes widened in horror. "That place killed my sister."

Echo sighed. "I will deal with this one."

I reached for Ezra's hand. "Take me to Shanghai Moon."

"Go to your friend. I have an idea and will see you there," said Orpheus.

I nodded, bidding Kraglek a silent goodbye as Ezra wrapped his arms around me, and we disappeared in the monotones between the worlds. A growth of pressure, a clinging of bodies, a meteoric hurtling, and the world spat us out on the pavement of Shanghai Moon.

"Are you ready?" said Ezra.

"I'm going to wet myself with excitement. My bladder isn't what it was." I rapped my knuckles on the shop front.

Ezra laughed. "Please don't."

The door jangled as Fei Yen and Faeza opened it. I gasped in delight at the sight of them. They wore cap-sleeved traditional Chinese dresses, known as qipaos, orange with ornate gold buttons running down the back. With their hair in elegant up-dos and a slick of red lipstick, we'd obviously disturbed a special occasion.

We followed them inside. "You look beautiful. We're disturbing you."

"At such a late hour, too," said Ezra.

Faeza smoothed down her dress, frank as ever. Her

plucked eyebrows hitched up a notch. "You did indeed interrupt us. It's date night. Usually, we treat ourselves to dinner in China Town, but we could not leave the shop in case Marina exited the portal."

Fei Yen entwined her dancer's fingers with her wife's. "Foxes are creatures of the night. And we have a lifetime of dates to enjoy before us. Do not worry yourself, Alisha Verma. The eternal girl should not burden herself with small worries when there are greater things at stake."

To be fair, over the past few days, I had expended mental energy worrying about missing bin collection day, doing a laundry load and stocking up on Echo's steaks at the butcher's. It was a grown woman's curse to multitask. Just like our destiny to kiss frogs before finding a prince.

"You know I'm the eternal girl?" I said. "I'm sorry I kept it from you."

"We all have our secrets. The rats of this city spread the news even before Margola Silver's ink dried on the page. We also know you went to see Rajiv," said Faeza.

"You know my uncle?" I said.

Fei Yen exchanged glances with her wife. "We wouldn't say 'know'. We might have chosen the path of the outsiders like he did, but we avoid him. We are outsiders because we have been burned by the establishment before. There are some who choose to be outsiders because they can't get along with others."

"Although we are concerned that it is hard to remain outsiders when your friends are central to a hallowed prophecy," said Faeza. "But tell us. What can we do for you?"

The shop door swung open, and Orpheus brought Detective Jameson, looking worse for wear in the same plaid shirt he'd worn to the coven dinner.

"There are a thousand different smells in this establishment, but the most overpowering one is sweet and sour chicken," said Orpheus. "Is the empath here yet? She is the key to unlocking this cabbage mind."

Ezra groaned. "Did no one think that the centuries-old vampire might need to go on an HR course?"

"That's why we're here." I checked the clock. Lavinia had anticipated a midnight arrival. "Marina is returning from the library."

"Well, what are we waiting for?" Faeza's relaxed demeanour transformed into a fluttering of hands and darting of eyes. "I'll light the incense. Bring the candles, my love, and the tarot card."

My best friend was coming home.

FIFTEEN MINUTES LATER, Shanghai Moon wafted with earthy, rich tones of sandalwood incense sticks. The foxes rushed about, a sheen of perspiration on their sallow skin as they prepared for Marina's arrival. They weren't just students of my English night class. They weren't just takeaway-obsessed Chinese immigrants to London. They weren't just owners of a tea and occult shop. They weren't even just shapeshifting *hu hsien*. They were midwives to a weird Otherworld portal.

They were wonderful.

And they went quietly about their business while being wonderful.

I crouched down to Jameson, who was being nannied by Ezra and Orpheus.

"Rob. Rob, are you okay?" I said.

Nothing.

"Did Mami do this to you, Rob? Did you find her in the sewers?" I shook my head. "I'm sorry. I should have been with you."

Nothing.

"Give it up," said Orpheus. "I tried on the way here. His

mind is soup. It is a shame for a man whose humdrum brain could withstand the enormity of true sight. I am afraid the second half of his life will not be so illustrious."

"He can probably hear you. I'd watch what you say." Ezra gave Jameson a manly clap on his back.

The detective flew forward. The plaid shirt really needed a wash.

I put my hand out, straightened him up and tilted his chin. "Look at me, Rob. Marina would hate for anything to happen to you."

A flicker of recognition.

I sprang up. "There. He reacted. He's in there still."

Ezra's eyes filled with concern. "Look, hellfire, we've got to be realistic."

"It's no use, Neuhoff. The druid is a romantic," said Orpheus. "She thinks love can save the day. Even after it chewed her up and spat her out the first time."

Fei Yen and Faeza came down the stairs from their flat. They had changed into white pharmaceutical wear, tied their hair in neat ponytails and wiped the colour from their lips as if they meant business, although their bickering voices gave a contrasting impression.

"Alisha would have chucked us out of her night class if we'd lost the portal card," said Fei Yen.

Faeza tutted. "Well, it wasn't me who put it there. Who told you to move it?"

Fei Yen frowned. "I figured it was safer that way. I made a mental note to remember where I put it. But it slipped my mind exactly where."

Orpheus sighed. "I am surrounded by forgetful imbeciles who prefer tea to blood."

The foxes united to give him a dismissive stare and then beckoned us all to the tarot table, clothed in a midnight blue tablecloth. This time, they didn't pull the curtain of sequinned stars around the table. There were too many of us to fit into a confined space. The candelabra flickered as Ezra and I took our seats at the tarot table, with Orpheus and the detective behind us.

"The time is nigh," said Fei Yen, opposite us. "You must listen carefully."

Faeza brought out the portal card they had kept safe, the now slightly tatty, hand-drawn Ace of Wands with its sprouting wand, hills and blood-red edges. "We do not know how Marina Ambrose might arrive or who will come with her. She will journey through the passage from the Celestial Library, and the only thing we can do is guard the portal and use our collective will to guide her here."

She placed the card in the centre of the table.

Fei Yen continued. "All of you, take a deep breath. Cleanse your mind of everything—"

"That will be easy for the detective," said Orpheus.

A thin smile from Fei Yen, like you might give to an annoying child. "—then place your hands on the portal and think only of the empath."

She placed her dainty hand flat on the card, and each of us followed suit, like a strange Power Rangers ensemble, with Orpheus vying for top position until Ezra gave an alpha's grin and his strong hands clamped Orpheus's into place.

I closed my eyes and filled my thoughts with Marina and all the silly, meaningful and traumatic experiences we'd shared over the years. Dancing until our feet hurt at a club in Leicester Square. Her support when Mum died. Laughing until we cried when my swimming costume malfunctioned at the local pool. Our periods aligning.

Good god, woman, said Orpheus.

Almost immediately, I sensed a shift in the environment. My eyes met Ezra's over the portal card.

"Now," said Faeza. "Let go."

"Step back," said Fei Yen. "She will need more space."

A rush of water from the card, a yawning gap that grew

larger, and Marina Ambrose flew into the Shanghai Moon on a Lilo with a unicorn head.

Relief flooded my body. My joy was stratospheric.

It didn't matter that she had just endured a perilous journey. I launched myself at her, squealing like a pig.

My rainbow-haired best friend stood up, shook herself off like a mutt, kissed the cross at her neck and wrenched me into a hug. Boobs against boobs. No holding back. Not a scrap of air between us.

Ezra and Orpheus patted her on the back as if Marina was one of the guys, and the foxes went to collect the mops and towels to clean up. When the detective made no move towards her, Marina flung herself at him, pressing her lips to his. When she pulled away, he cocked his head slightly to the side like he was rebooting.

I took Marina's hand in mine. "I've missed you. I was so worried. Was the journey awful?"

She grinned. "The magical oven in the laboratory taught me lots. The mind is a powerful thing. Mind over matter, you know. I just had to pretend there was a Lilo under me, and one appeared. So then I went with the flow, let the current take me, and pretended I a piña colada. Lo and behold, one appeared in my hand, the tastiest piña colada I have ever had the good fortune to sip. Although I'm bummed I ruined my catsuit between my trial, the journey and all the coffee and cake in the Celestial Library."

The leather had no give and had popped open in various places.

"Four days," I said. "Four days without you."

"I know, but isn't this a lovely welcoming committee." She looked around and gave everyone a wave before treating the detective to a flirty smile. "You're being a bit reticent, Rob. Come here, you soppy thing. Four days without me have turned you into a pale shadow of yourself."

I grimaced. "You have no idea. There's something I have to tell you."

"That's why we rushed back. Calypso and I heard about the Kraglek trial. I never doubted you or your place in the world. You are fierce. You faced a gigantic octopus. You don't even like the aquarium. I am so proud of you."

"Calypso's here?"

She shook her damp tresses, the pink and blue and purple, all the colours that added up to make her unique. "Soon. The Custodian loans magic from the library, remember? She can zoom all over the place to collect loaned items. She doesn't need the passageway we needed."

"On that note, it is time to burn the portal card," said Fei Yen with a beatific smile. She gave Marina the tarot card, lighter fuel and a box of matches.

Marina stilled her excitement for a moment to drench the card in lighter fuel and set it alight. The Ace of Wands flared and withered until she dropped it in an ash tray that Fei Yen held out.

Marina breathed a sigh of relief and reached out her hands to the foxes. "Thank you. For facilitating my journey and holding space for me. I am so grateful. And please, leave the cleaning to us."

Faeza nodded and set down her mop. "Was your journey successful?"

Marina's baby blues shone. She shot Rob a curious look at his lack of interest but continued all the same. "You're going to be so proud of me. Ta-daaaaa." She moved aside her hair, and her fingers tangled with the necklace Mum had left for me.

Its amber stone had an eerie glow.

My heart raced. "You did it? You finished Mum's work on the Rose of Jericho. Is it like Ezra's thistle charm?"

"Not quite." She bit her lip. "What do you know about the Rose of Jericho?"

"It is revered in many cultures. And is also known as the resurrection plant," said Orpheus. "Like vampires, it occupies an interesting place between life and death."

Marina nodded. "Precisely. The Rose of Jericho can be kept for years in a dark wardrobe and still be revived in water. Its roots don't need soil. It can simply grow from a base of pebbles."

"Legend says that the plant has magical properties," said Fei Yen. "Some say it brings prosperity. Others say it offers a second chance. Its ability to heal itself is miraculous."

"If you have managed to imbue the necklace with these powers, it looks like fortunes are turning in our favour," said Orpheus.

"The tea leaves this morning were indeed auspicious," said Fei Yen and Faeza in unison.

"So it is like my thistle charm?" said Ezra. "This is perfect timing, Marina."

"Not quite," said Marina. "I have only had limited time to trial the necklace, but as far as I can tell, the wearer of the necklace does not benefit from speedier healing. At least, not in the sense you mean. It won't heal a broken rib or a lacerated leg or mend a seeping wound."

My brow furrowed. "What does it do then?"

"It brings back someone from the brink of death," she said.

"Oh," I said. The thought of returning to life after death was a bit zombie-like. Or vampire-like.

Orpheus rolled his eyes. *I heard that.*

"Hopefully, I won't need that, but it's a great thing to have, just in case." I suppressed a shudder.

Marina high-fived me, eighties-style. "Think of it as a fail-safe. I don't think I would have been able to do it anywhere else. There's something about the Celestial Library. It was like every pore soaked up knowledge. I only had to think of something for it to appear in the oven." She took it off her neck and handed it to me. "There's no way I could sit around and watch you get hurt over and over."

I cupped it in my palms. It was a magnificent achievement. There was no doubt about it. "Mum would be over the moon."

"It was all her idea. I was just the gal who finished it off." She held out her arms for Robert. "Now come here, big man."

He jerked to life, crossing three metres to her embrace.

We all gawped as she stared deep into his eyes and then kissed him with tongue. This time he responded to her instinctively. It made no difference that his mind had been hollowed out by magic. Something in her spoke to him, whether it was his love for her, her empath skills or the fact Marina's love had the power to save anyone. It pulled him back from the brink.

When he spoke, he sounded like himself again. "Marina, you're here."

She gave him another smooch. "Miss me?"

I left them to their whispers and rather raunchy reunion while we finished clearing up. Then we said our goodbyes to the foxes before stepping out into the night. The breeze chased goosebumps up my arms as Orpheus idled his engine at the kerbside, waiting to give Marina and the detective a lift.

"I'll see you in the morning?" I said to Marina.

She linked her arm through Robert's. "Hell, yeah."

"Nice to see you fighting fit, detective." I gave him a teasing wink. "She's going to have to sit on your lap in the car."

He smiled. "I've been looking forward to it for days."

"Let's go home." I laid a hand on Ezra's chest. "Tomorrow, we fight."

Ezra growled. He looped his arms around my waist. "Okay. But for now, you're mine."

23

The rooftop of my apartment block wasn't the most sensible place to practice sword-fighting, but I wasn't worried. Most Londoners were so busy looking at their phones or checking the pavement for dog poo that they forgot to look up.

If they had looked up, they would've seen three women of different ethnicities and styling of attire with a Bengal cat. They might even have seen my sword Transcender in my hand, although the sun's reflection off the slim blade would have made them glance away and continue on their way.

After all, Gaia had told me to remember to take my sword to my next encounter with Mami Wata.

I disregarded Gaia's words at my peril. That wily old woman. Her words, even if I misconstrued or discounted their meaning when I first heard them, often turned out to be gems of wisdom in retrospect.

Which was why I had spent a long morning with Marina and Calypso, learning how to do damage with Death's sword.

My kickboxing and yoga training meant balance and footwork came easily to me, and my running history meant I could regulate my breath. I had the physical and mental conditioning, and my arms were strong, apart from a possible onset of bingo wings.

But just like when I trained to use bō sticks with Ezra, fighting with a sword was a whole new skill. Stabbing someone with a fork or chopsticks was quite different to the slash of a sword, however many episodes of *Highlander* I had watched. The Duncan MacLeod version, obviously. It would take more time than we had for me to learn how to fight with unpredictable rhythm. And if my opponent could predict my moves, I was as good as dead.

Of course, I'd be wearing the Jericho necklace, just in case I needed resurrecting.

Better a zombie than six feet under.

"You don't need to excel at using the sword," said Calypso. "Just for heaven's sake, don't drop your weapon. You aren't going into battle against King Arthur and the Knights of the Round Table. You merely need to be proficient. The legends of Mami tell of a cunning goddess, not a warrior. But taking your sword into this battle might make you feel safer, and it may well give you an edge. Remember, a blade cannot be dulled by water."

"Oh good." After endless bruising hours of learning to block and attack, I thrust the sword at her. "In that case, I need a sit down."

I slumped next to Marina and watched Calypso admire Transcender's shimmering, obsidian blade and ivory hilt set with a small, deepest blue jasper. Once fashioned for Gaia by her lover Death, it now belonged to me after Gaia took offence to the mammoth tusk that formed its hilt and decided to regift it. Luckily, it was slender, double-edged and light, so even an untried swordswoman could hold it.

"Made from a spirit cloud, you say? And blessed by Death?" called out Calypso.

"Yeah," I replied. "Gaia said if the strike is true, an

ancestral thrust can add power and disrupt the mind of the attacker."

"Huh. Well, maybe one day you will land a true strike. But I'd wager it won't be today."

I groaned.

"She's a toughie," said Marina. "I'm so sorry Rob isn't part of this. His memories of the past few days are full of gaps. He doesn't know whether he's coming or going. When are lover boy and the vamp going to put in an appearance?"

"They're meeting us at the Tate Modern tonight after the senate vote. I'm not sure it's a good idea for Ezra. Mami had a hold over him in her tattoo shop. We could do with Orpheus's help, though. With his undead status and own mind powers, she won't be able to control him."

"Ezra can take care of himself. We've got Calypso, too, remember. She might be bookish, but there's no one better with blades."

I lay my head on her shoulder, exhausted. It felt so good to be near her again. Like I could drop all artifice and just be myself. "Yeah, well, she's had practice with her prosthesis. Did you see her slashing at the Ravenmaster with them during the battle at Wildwoods? Who needs armour when you have silver dreadlocks, metallic eyeshadow, a well-cut trouser suit and blade runners? If I were bi, I would."

Marina gave me a shifty look.

"Ha, you've thought about it!"

"It crossed my mind, but I'm with Rob, so..." She shrugged. "Calypso's history made her a fighter. I learned a lot about her while I was up there. She's a loner. By destiny and by choice. She's not afraid to walk her own path. I love that about her. It's why she's often on the periphery of senate decisions. Why she removes herself from the politics of it but hangs about where it counts most. Even if others disagree with her." Marina giggled.

The sound of her laughter healed me more than popping a paracetamol ever would.

"She told me Nightfall taught her to be like a horse with blinders on. That blocking out the noise and focussing my attention on what I value would always be a good thing. Imagine that. Learning from an animal. It's almost unheard of these days."

"I'm glad you had a friend up there."

"It was more than that. I worked for hours, but in the evenings, she taught me things."

I searched her face. "Like what?"

"She taught me that my empath powers can reach across the psychical divide and influence people if I really channel an emotion," said Marina. "I've tried with positive emotions because Calypso was my guinea pig, but I think I can make it happen with negative emotions too. It's like an extension of what I've always done to animals in my care. I try to make them feel good. Or like me helping Elvira to find peace when she lay dying. But it's more powerful because I have to think of the essence of one emotion, kind of the colour of it, and hey presto. Calypso thinks I might even be able to do it with groups of people."

"Can you try it on me?" I said.

She nodded. "Give me your hand. It's easier to channel through touch."

An effervescent feeling of free-wheeling joy bubbled through me, and just as quickly, those emotions became thunderous gloom.

"Bloody hell, Marina, that's incredible," I said.

"The gloom was easier to channel than the joy. So how are you holding up?"

I told her what she needed to hear. "I'm fine."

The concern in her eyes told me she wasn't fooled. "Calypso said you're not animating tonight."

I blew out a long breath. "I can't get over what I did. I just abandoned these magical creatures, Marina. You wouldn't have recognised me."

"I've seen it before. People give more time to furry creatures than slimy or tentacled ones."

"I couldn't think straight after I saw Dad tied up down there."

She blew the pink hair out of her face. "Sometimes the fear of losing someone makes us act less human, you know? But when we're dealing with monsters, we have to be more human. Even if that means we lose what we love. Or we lose our own selves. You can't let this stop you from animating."

"It's not that. I know now that Rajiv's way isn't my way. There's nothing left of the catalogues, and now's not a good time to ask Dad to paint for me. It was a lot for him to find out about my place in the prophecy. I'm not going to tell him about tonight until it's over. He'll only worry."

Marina's blue eyes clouded over. "You know that saying about worrying not doing any good? I disagree. I think if someone is worrying about you, it shows that you matter enough for them to care. And if they care about you, their worries aren't useless. They're like anxious little prayers that can protect you. Little blessings that act as a shield." She burrowed into her coat and took a swig of her water. "Now, we're going to put tonight aside for a moment, and you're going to distract me with more details about the chiropractor. He sounded like a hoot. I guess matching tattoos are still out of the question?"

I spluttered. "What do you think?"

"Now I'm *really* mad at that waterlogged temptress."

NIGHT FELL like a curtain across the city. The type of night where even the owls had fallen silent and homeless men shifted deeper into the porches of city shops. The detective had informed us it was the final day of an art exhibition Mami had curated at the Tate Modern. The gallery was housed in an old power station on the bank of the Thames, a stone's throw from Shakespeare's Globe.

The street performers with their bubbles, the buskers and the living statues had long since packed up and gone home. So we stood on the embankment, in the glow of the luminous building, as the last visitors to the gallery petered away, awaiting the goddess.

For the first time, I hadn't stumbled into acting against the gods.

I had planned an ambush, and part of me liked it.

"It has been an age since I have been here," said Marina. "Inside that building, there are masterpieces by Cézanne, Matisse, Picasso, Rothko, Dalí, Pollock and Warhol."

"Oh, you can view a Pollock at Orpheus's club. Maybe after Manfred gives you a good kneading." I adjusted my sword in its baldric on my back and checked the Jericho necklace remained securely at my throat. Marina had refused to wear it, so we had a deal—any sign of danger, and she had to fall back.

Echo prowled the pavement, narrowed eyes trained on the exit to the gallery. "Surely the water goddess should be finished by now?"

"Where are Ezra and Orpheus? Their senate meeting should be over by now. If the goddess appears before they do, we'll have to go on without them." I checked my watch and turned to Calypso. "Thank you for standing with us tonight."

She shrugged. "My gut told me to stay with you. And I always follow my gut. Whatever lies in store for us tonight, you must remember all is not lost until the last breath is taken. If your grandmother had given up that night defending the Celestial Library against Muriel and the artefacts had been taken, the world would be an entirely different place."

"I like her dreadlocks and her pep talks," Echo purred. "We should invite her to accompany us more often. This is a good team, even if the wolf and vampire disappoint us. The Custodian has experience. The druid has the sword, and I have the heart."

Marina raised an amused eyebrow. "What do I have?"

Echo tilted his magnificent head to one side as he considered. "The tenderness. I could die in worse arms than yours, Marina Ambrose."

I let their repartee fade into the background and closed my eyes, recalling the darkness that had surged through me when I had used Mami's own breath against her and pledged to do better. I had to be sure that what ensued was justice, not revenge. Otherwise, I was no better than the foes I set out to defeat.

A growl from Echo wrenched me into the moment. "She comes."

We stepped out of sight behind a tree as Mami Wata, resplendent in a shimmering coral dress and stiletto heels, left the gallery very much alone. Connected as she was from her time living in different pockets of the city and doing different jobs, she seemed to be a woman with few loves.

Maybe that was why she had tried to separate me from my loved ones.

She knew the pain of being alone and that it could break you.

Calypso nudged me. "Druid, if we don't go now, we'll miss our chance."

I nodded. We sprinted after her, keeping a safe distance, our hearts thudding. Three women and a Bengal cat, striding across the Blackfriars Bridge after a beautiful woman, all keenly aware that the lives of men hung in the balance—and perhaps our own. Near Fleet Street, we held back as Mami kicked off her obviously very expensive stilettos, lifted the lid of a sewer and dropped inside.

A goddess of prosperity could buy as many Jimmy Choos or Manolo Blahniks as she wanted.

"We wait five minutes, and then we go after her. I hope the missing men are alive. Remember, locating and releasing them is our priority. But we also have to make sure Mami doesn't just move to another area and snatch more men. We need a promise she'll stop. It might be possible to get one."

Grim nods from all except Echo, who urinated against a wall.

"An empty bladder means a faster body," purred Echo. "Although leopards understand aerodynamics more than women."

"Tell that to the female pilots and engineers," whispered Calypso.

I crept forward, Marina directly behind me, Calypso bringing up the rear and Echo padding between us. The manhole cover lay ajar, so I checked for passers-by, then shifted aside and poked my head down into the sewer.

The coast was clear. I took a deep breath, lowered myself down and activated my phone torch. The stench made me heave, but I had forgotten to bring clothing pegs for my nose.

At least I didn't have a leopard's sense of smell.

My friends leapt down behind me.

Echo's nose twitched. "I have her scent. This way."

He bounded forward through the all-too-familiar sloshing water, and my nerves kicked in. I'd gone through possibilities for tonight a thousand times over, but there were a thousand more outcomes that wouldn't have occurred to me. Encounters with immortal gods and goddesses were unpredictable; the odds stacked so much in their favour that we must have been imbeciles for trying. For not hiding at home and counting our lucky stars the men *we* loved were safe.

But that would make us monsters.

I ran. I ran through the dark after Echo, with Marina and

Calypso in tow, my baldric bumping lightly against my back, every sense primed for the goddess.

A roar up ahead told me Echo had found what we were looking for.

Subtlety wasn't his strong suit. He had also simultaneously announced our arrival to the goddess.

We picked up our speed. Calypso's protheses made her quicker through the dank, foot-high water. She reached a corner first and recoiled at the sight.

My heartbeat clamoured in my ears as I reached her and swept my phone torch across the area.

In an off-shoot chamber, a dozen men sat happily in a circle, unfettered and unsupervised.

These weren't sewer workers. They had no high-vis jackets on or thick boots or helmets with torches. They sat together, like children in a story circle, with a haul between them. A haul that included bananas and apples, kiwis and oranges, porcelain teapots and Victorian dolls, handheld mirrors and combs, strings of pearls and pretty shells.

Weirder still, they were covered in a dusty, white powder.

It scared the bejeezus out of me. I almost ran screaming out of there, but I had a job to do.

"They are as vacant as the detective, but at least he escaped the water goddess's clutches. These men could walk freely out of here," said Echo. "Yet they are as stupid as huddled gazelles on a vista, still unmoving though a big cat prowls nearby."

The men reacted slowly to my torchlight, blinking with the speed of sloths as if enchanted or perhaps dehydrated. When they finally stood, I realised a pillar candle burned amongst their bounty.

An altar.

Marina frowned. "I think there's something wrong with them."

"They appear to have bathed in talcum powder," said Calypso. "It's one way to avoid a shower."

I tried again and swung my torch over their faces, lingering on a man who resembled Annie. "I know your daughter," I hissed at him. "She loves hot chocolate with marshmallows and wishes you would come home."

"He can't hear you, Alisha Verma," said a melodic voice.

My body trembled with terror.

24

Mami Wata emerged from the shadows behind the men. Her coral dress had been peeled downward, so it hung as a skirt around her slim waist. Her feet—no fishtail this time—and breasts were bare, and the snake tattoo had returned to her belly.

I squared up to her. There were fewer than five metres between us. "Let them go."

"That man's only concerns are *my* desires. That is why he wears the sweet-smelling powder. That is why he sits here quietly, waiting to satisfy my needs rather than his own daughter's."

Calypso sized up Mami. "So you are the water goddess."

"And you are the Custodian," said Mami. "Hardly an adversary when I fooled you so easily with my message to the stars. I see you're here, muddled up in a druid's mess rather than taking care of your home. Tell me, what happens in history when a Custodian abandons the Celestial Library?"

"It is not abandoned," said Calypso calmly.

Marina's voice quivered. "You turned out to be a real disappointment, Mami. I'm going to have to get rid of this awesome tattoo you gave me because you were a shit to humankind *and* my best friend."

"So feisty. Even though you are defenceless. Who are you to judge, empath? You endured in my tattoo chair for less than half an hour for a minuscule clover tattoo, spilling all the secrets of your best friend and the people she relies on," said Mami. "It was so easy to pick them off one by one after that."

"Oops," said Marina.

That was her smallest tattoo. She had enormous ones too. But I guess her empath skills didn't extend to sensing the darkness in a god.

Mami ignored her. Her dark eyes promised pain. "You do realise, druid, that if I let the men go, they would still do my bidding. They have been branded."

"Rob wasn't. I've searched every inch of him, believe me," said Marina.

I locked my eyes on the goddess, trying to decipher the secrets hidden in the slight curl of her lips and the narrowing of her eyes. "Why are you doing this?"

Mami's finger traced her snake tattoo. "The world has forgotten its deities. Do you blame me for finding new ways to be relevant and remembered when worship has fallen out of favour?"

"I don't need the whole world to remember me," I said. "Just a few."

A pitying smile. "Oh, druid, you haven't lived. Tell me, what did my old friend, Gaia, say when she learned of the darkness in you? Was she disappointed? Is that why you are down here, desperate to make amends? I hate to have missed the fireworks. Be a darling and give me a blow-by-blow account, will you?"

"If you must know, she said that we all make mistakes and to get back on the bicycle," I said. "It's not too late for you to turn a new leaf, Mami."

"Gaia is worth ten of you, you fishy wench," growled Echo.

Mami played with her beautiful braids. "You will pay for wounding my snake, leopard. This time you will not be so lucky. I will make you my slave, and when I tire of you, I will feed you to the fish."

Calypso unsheathed the daggers strapped to her thighs.

Echo raised his head, as haughty as a prince. "You'll never hook me. I am neither marine life nor man, and I am loyal only to my druid. And to Gaia. Not in that order."

"Are you so sure your friends can't be turned, druid? Are you so sure that you yourself are immune to my charms? Wouldn't you all be happier if you joined my congregation? Come closer, and my ink will fulfil your deepest desires in exchange for your devotion." She raised her hands, and her nails had become gleaming, black talons. "You'll never be rich."

I shrugged. "Perhaps."

She sashayed closer. "You'll never be beautiful."

"You think a woman in midlife relies on her beauty?"

Mami's eyes narrowed into slits as she fingered a string of pearls around her neck. "You'll never be a mother."

I clenched my fists. That one hurt. "Stop baiting me. I've long since accepted that."

The snake on her belly curled around her breasts. "You'll always have bad sex."

"Fuck no," said Marina. "That's where we draw the line."

Mami started singing.

Echo unleashed a mournful growl. "What the hell is this? It's worse than Bono in the early years."

I clamped my hands over my ears. Not because I was scared of being enchanted. I was pretty sure her powers stemmed from tattooing—and tattoos could be erased—but because it sounded bloody awful. Like this time, she wanted to deafen us into submission.

"Release those men," I said. "They deserve to choose their fate."

To my sweet relief, she canned her tortured tones. "How ridiculous you are. You may save these particular men, but the world is full of men who are tempted by a beautiful woman. Your interference is not the end of the world. All I have to do is find a dozen more and a dozen more. I can walk down the embankment like the Pied Piper, and they would follow me just because I desire it, and deep down, they desire me. Even though they have wives and lovers, they always choose me."

I shook my head. "You have to see what's right. Aren't you supposed to be godly?"

The snake on her belly writhed. "A god is many things. We are creation and destruction. Life and death. Love and hate. We are everything distilled into one being."

I drew Transcender from the baldric. The sound of its unsheathing sent a chill up my spine. "I'm warning you, Mami. You'll force my hand."

"You're a pesky thing. It looks like I'll have to kill you as I first planned." The snake slid off her belly, becoming real—olive, green and pulsating—and wrapped itself around her neck.

I turned to Marina and Calypso. They worked well as a team, and Marina's empath powers meant she could perhaps get through to the men. If not, we'd call Gaia. "Get the men out of here and to the nearest police station. Ask Rob to meet you there."

They started towards the men, but whenever they neared, the men foiled the rescue attempt, snarling and throwing projectiles from the altar as if they were in a pub brawl.

"It's all right," said Calypso. "We've got this."

Mami smiled and turned into the tunnel. Then she raised her taloned hands, and gushing water began to fill the chamber, filled with endless shoals of sea bass, sole, perch and carp that made me recoil.

Echo roared and leapt deeper into the water with the gusto of his koi pond antics, only with more teeth and aggression.

Here, he didn't have to worry about Dad scolding him for butchering his prize fish.

"Get out of here," I shouted to Marina and Calypso before re-sheathing my sword and diving into the rising water to go after Mami.

Wading in the dank water was one thing. Being submerged in it was quite another. I gasped as the cold hit me. Fish slapped me in the face and hindered my progress through the tunnels as I swam.

Swimming lessons hadn't prepared me for this.

Marina's powers of imagination couldn't conjure up a Lilo and a piña colada in this stretch of water.

I abandoned the breaststroke to switch to the dreaded front crawl, putting my head underwater in my effort to catch up with the water goddess, spluttering at the fishtails that threatened to put me off sushi forever. A surge to my left showed that Echo accompanied me, powerful swimmer and loyal friend that he was.

It buoyed my courage to know he was still by my side.

We'd lost sight of the goddess. I didn't know if her legs had transformed into a fish's tail and she had swum masterfully ahead, away from me and my need for assurances that she would not jeopardise further lives. The darkness in the sewers overwhelmed me, and with my whole body drenched, my phone was pretty much a goner. Not even plunging it into a bag of rice would help. There was precious little chance of my torch still working, even if I got to dry land.

Just when all hope seemed lost, will-o'-the-wisps appeared ahead of us, hovering guides, lighting our way. On and on, through endless tunnels with floating debris and shoals of fish, driving at us. Echo and I pushed through a dead carpet of bream to an end of a tunnel, where our glowing guides slipped up and out through an open manhole.

I gasped for breath. "Come on."

We heaved ourselves up the ladder. Echo went first and, despite being a strong climber, needed me to push his rump. Leaving the rancid air of the sewers behind us, our burning lungs adjusted to the surface air. I scanned the roads around us, searching for the goddess. I found her a hundred yards away on the Millennium Bridge, a steel suspension pedestrian-only bridge that crossed the Thames, now deserted.

She was breathtakingly beautiful. Her bare feet against the asphalt, clenched fists, and bare breasts made a striking silhouette against the night sky, devoid of stars. The olive-green snake, manifested from her stomach, looped around her shoulders, unscathed once more even after Echo's ravaging. Strong winds whipped her braids into a frenzy, autumn leaves skirted past, and Mami's eyes flashed with wild fury. Like nothing mattered except striking me where it hurt. She waited for us to reach her.

I didn't think to question why she had chosen the bridge to confront us.

"How dare you, druid?" said Mami. "You wouldn't exist if I hadn't laid my hand on your mother's womb. Where is your respect? Where is your gratitude?"

This had to end. I pulled out my sword and prayed I wouldn't be arrested by the Metropolitan Police, especially out here in the open. Especially given that the detective was hardly in the right frame of mind to pull strings.

Echo hissed at my side. "I hate to ruin your moment, but there's a merry member of the public giving the wench's bare bosoms an eyeful, the dirty scoundrel. You know the laws about magic and humdrums."

"Get rid of him, Echo. He's not safe here." I hadn't taken my eyes off Mami. "Remember, without true sight, he sees you as a Bengal cat."

"Oh, I know," Echo purred. "I've got a great Puss in the Boots act. Big eyes, licking my paws, being all cutesy. The punters can't get enough of it."

"Go." He scampered off, and I slashed the sword through the air, finding the balance of the hilt again.

A sound met my ears. I froze, listening hard, and deciphered a voice through the spirit sword—a calm, lilting, contented voice.

My breath hitched in my chest.

I would know my mother's voice until the end of my days.

The scent of her Estée Lauder perfume—white lilies, rain and leaves—hit me right there in the middle of Millennium Bridge.

The goddess sashayed ever closer. "And so it ends, Alisha Verma, like I planned it. With you all alone."

She underestimates you, Alisha. You are not alone, Mum's voice said.

My fear evaporated, leaving only a feeling of wonder.

"Did Gaia not tell you?" Mami taunted. "You can't kill an immortal."

"Maybe not, but I've sure as hell found a way around that sticky wicket before. You have two options: either you see the error of your ways, or I'll send you to the bottom of the river in pieces. It's your choice, Mami." I readied Transcender, eyes darting, eager to take my chance to incapacitate the goddess. Once she was down, I could call for Gaia, and we'd decide what to do with her.

Mami's dark eyes gleamed like she already tasted victory.

"There it is. The hubris that is my duty to crush. You do not hold power over me, druid. And you are utterly friendless."

"I'm not alone."

"You're nothing."

What the hell. *The Otherworld News* would be out by morning anyway. "Oh, didn't you know? I'm the prophesied eternal girl."

Mami's face twisted into something monstrous.

She lurched forward, and her snake flew forward, arrow straight, fangs bared.

Channelling Uma Thurman in *Kill Bill*, I lifted Transcender and swiped that worm's head off. It landed with a dull thud on the steel bridge. In two parts.

Mami gave a wail of anguish and launched herself towards me, talons outstretched. I'd crossed a line. She really seemed to have cared for the serpent. There was no doubt she wanted to rip me to shreds and feed me to the sharks.

I raised Transcender again, swiping diagonally, once, twice, leaving a deep, criss-cross welt across her stomach.

She clutched her belly, howling in pain.

At that moment, she didn't look immortal. She looked like death. Mami eyed the sword, a look of astonishment warping her face.

"No mortal blade can wound me." Desperation crept into her voice.

"Tell me you'll stop, Mami," I said. "And I'll lay down the sword."

"I won't." Her dark eyes blazed like the coals of hell as she pushed herself to her feet and hoisted her hands aloft, despite the blood that gushed out of her wounds.

Then you have your answer, said Mum through the spirit sword. *And you know your path.*

Mami Wata's hands jerked upwards, and, at last, I knew why she had chosen the bridge.

The river responded to her summons, and its waters

surged in two great waves on either side of the bridge and collapsed onto us.

I sheathed my sword, urgency making my hands fumble. Barely in the nick of time, I raised my palms to send the water driving back with my winds, though my face dripped with water, and I could hardly see.

The waves came again, beckoned by Mami, mingling with her blood and powered by her fury. They swept me off my feet—salty, turbulent, swollen waves—sending me sliding across the wobbling bridge.

I regained my foothold, barely, only for another wave to crash on top of me, swift and black and wintry. I gasped for breath as I ricocheted over the barrier, clean over the suspension cables, and plunged into the murky river.

Bubbles streamed from my nostrils as I sank deeper into the dark water, and the currents caught me. I was too tired to fight. This time my brain started to slow.

Maybe I wouldn't make it.

But I wasn't alone.

My mum was with me.

And others had accompanied me every step of the way.

With my last ounce of strength, I used my wind powers to push off the riverbed, driving me up to the surface. I emerged from the depths of the river, wheezing and coughing, treading water to stay afloat, my limbs tiring with every second.

There was Mami Wata, with her fishy tail, anticipating her victory already, her talons raised.

About to finish me off.

I flinched as a huge shape surged past, torpedo fast. A prehistoric brain inside a bulbous head with sprawling tentacles, toxic poison and a beak-shaped mouth.

He was purple and fleshy and covered in suckers.

Kraglek wrapped his tentacles around the horrified goddess and dragged her out toward the open sea.

"Holy shit." Euphoria surged through me. Had we really beaten the water goddess? Had my kindness to Kraglek led to this moment? Had he been lurking in the Thames, anticipating this moment since we had freed him? Kraglek was blessed by the goddess Ganga. He was extraordinary.

Mami definitely hadn't seen him coming.

I closed my eyes, exhausted. The cold crept into my bones. Is this what it felt like to flatline? Maybe the necklace would work, or maybe this was goodbye.

I had nothing to be ashamed of. I had done my best.

I smiled. It was nice floating. The sword was talking to me again.

My brain processed a splash nearby. Then Echo's jaw closed around my upper arm, and he tugged me to the embankment.

25

I waited for Ezra across the road from The Ritz in Green Park. He'd made a weekly pilgrimage to visit his disgraced former alpha, the only member of the pack to do so. Gunnolf languished in the dungeons under the hotel, utterly human, after his werewolf self had been bound by a witches' potion. He was a murderer and a liar, but he was still the closest thing to a father Ezra had left.

His posture sunken, and his hands stuffed deep into the trouser pockets of his suit, Ezra crossed the lofty chandeliered hall of the hotel and nodded goodbye to the doorman. Stepping into the sunshine, he loosened his tie and undid the top button of his shirt.

Only then did he notice me. His face broke into a smile, and he darted across the road, dodging buses and cars, and swept me into his arms.

"You didn't say you were coming." His lips found mine, despite the tooting and cursing of an irate driver who'd swerved to avoid him.

I grinned. "I know seeing him is hard. I thought I could be an antidote."

We loitered on the pavement, oblivious to tourists jostling past.

"How'd it go?" I asked.

A wry smile. "I'm not sure how many card games he can take, but it's The Ritz. Even the food in the dungeons is good." His posture straightened like he'd mentally reset himself. "You did it. Even though you were alone, and I couldn't be there to help."

"I wasn't alone," I said. "*You* did it. You persuaded the senate to amend the Pragmatist's Law."

He ran a hand over his stubbly jaw. "The first change to the Magical Constitution in three centuries. I couldn't have done it without Orpheus. The Prime Sorcerer filibustered the senate session for so long. It wasn't just that he was determined to prevent change. It felt like he wanted to keep us there."

My body tensed. "You don't think he's in the pocket of the gods, do you?"

Ezra shook his head. "No. He's an old codger. A dinosaur. A sly fox. But he's not corrupt."

"Just your average wanker then. What with him keeping succubi as house slaves."

Ezra chuckled. "He did everything he could to water down our suggestions, but in the end, we passed the New Pragmatist's Law. It implicitly allows for the fact that the gods are not as powerful as they used to be and states that 'attempts to thwart a god may only occur where there is a significant threat to peculiar or humdrum lives.'"

"A new law for a new age." I pressed my lips flat, trying to cork the dread that bubbled in me. "Because you know Mami wasn't the last one."

"I know." Ezra tightened his grip around me. "I wasn't going to do this here, but things are changing so fast, I just want us to have some stability. A piece of the world where the ground doesn't move." He dug in his pocket. "I picked it up this morning."

Butterflies darted in my stomach.

Ezra missed a sense of family. He'd been an outsider in his pack, and now as alpha and senate member, the power he wielded made him remote. A cut above the rest.

I'd spent so long in a dead-end relationship, longing to be loved. I wanted a strength of love that matched mine. I had finally found it. I loved what we had and didn't want it to change.

And holy cow, I really wasn't ready to get married again.

He retracted his fingers and held up a metal object that caught the midmorning rays.

I giggled with relief. "A key."

Ezra raked a hand through his hair. "What do you think, hellfire? Want to make the cottage our permanent base? I don't want to decide every night if we sleep at your flat or the cottage. I want it to be a given that we belong under the same roof. I want to do the normal things couples do. Like cook for you, run you a bath, fight about who's going to do the dishes."

A warm thrill ran through me. It was such a big step, and somewhere between my divorce and this moment with my suited, handsome wolf lover, I'd worked out that being alone wasn't a bad thing.

I kissed him. "I love you so much it hurts, but I don't want to rush into a decision. It's been a whirlwind week. Can I think about it?"

"Get a room," shouted a stranger.

A shadow of disappointment clouded Ezra's chiselled face. "Sure thing, hellfire."

Echo sidled between us. He'd been roaming the back streets of Green Park when he'd caught Annie's scent and bounded off.

"You protected Alisha well, leopard," said Ezra.

"Why does your face look like a slapped arse, wolf?"

"Never you mind," I said. "Did you find her?"

Emerald eyes softened. "Over there. I am glad her faith in him was not misplaced."

A man and child walked past, hand in hand. Annie wore her blonde hair in bunches. Polka-dot tights peeked out from between her wellies and a pink rain jacket. Her blue eyes tracked Echo.

"That's the cat, Daddy. The one I was telling you about," said Annie.

"Don't be silly, honey. There are hundreds of cats like that in London," said her father.

"Not like this one."

I LEANED into the crook of Dad's arm, enjoying the late burst of autumn sunshine before winter arrived. Our legs were outstretched on a picnic blanket in my parents' back garden.

Echo lurked at the edge of the koi pond, his jaw wide open. A bored Orpheus watched him while sipping Kraken Rum from a tumbler. Our friendship had pushed him out of his comfort zone. This family knees-up in the sun was a far cry from the dark, dinghy rooms of his gentleman's club.

Dad clinked glasses with me. "Here's to Kraglek, the brainiac with a soft core."

"To Kraglek, a friend when it counted." I sipped my drink. "Oh, I almost forgot." I handed Dad a brown paper bag that held new moccasin slippers. "I picked them up for you at Broadway Market after you lost yours in the sewer."

"My thoughtful girl. What would I do without you?" He peeked inside, beaming, and stuffed his feet into them immediately. The memories of his kidnapping had faded due to Alma's cheerful fussing. She was exactly the right tonic for his anxious heart. "I hate arguing with you. Who am I to stand against fate or the will of a strong woman? You might as well be prepared. I'll have a new catalogue for you soon. I started working on it as soon as my strength returned. I only needed a little nudge from Alma."

"Don't you mind that Alma lied to you?"

He sipped his rum, a thoughtful expression on his creased face. "People lie for lots of reasons. I learned that when your mother died. All that sneaking around was because she wanted to protect us. Alma used to be an amateur actress in her youth, you know. Very good at it, by her own account. And you can't hold a person's talents against them, can you?"

I reached for his hand. Remnants of blue paint curled at his cuticles. "Dad, when I had the sword, Mum told me that seeing you happy meant everything to her."

Tears filled his eyes. "She said that? She really said that?" A sigh. "It meant so much to me that you girls showed me the Jericho necklace. It was so wonderful that Marina could finish your mum's work. Like her death wasn't in vain."

I swallowed the lump in my throat. "I know, Dad."

He hiccupped. "I don't know what I would have done if Mami had hurt you. The funny thing is, if it wasn't for her, Sahil and you might not exist. Where is he anyway?"

"Trying his luck with Marina for the hundredth time, I think."

"That boy never learns." A flush crept up Dad's neck. "Do you know what the worst thing is? Mami gave me a tattoo on my behind."

I stared at him. "She did what?"

His wiry moustache twitched. "I'm not showing you. I looked in the mirror this morning."

I sat bolt upright, my heart racing. "What is it? Did she want to control you?"

"No, I think she wanted to humiliate me. It's a tattoo of a shocked, toothy beaver on my right cheek. I daren't even undress in front of Alma. She thinks I've lost my mojo." His downcast eyes were my undoing.

My attempt to hold back peals of laughter failed. "Well, it could have been worse. At least it's not 'bad boy' or 'thug life' in biker font. Or worse, a butt cheek on your butt cheek."

Dad looked at me aghast. "This isn't a joking matter, Alisha. I am branded for life. Like a cow."

"Goddess," I called. "Goddess, we need you."

Alma and Gaia raised their guilty eyes from the cheese board and hurried over. I wept tears of laughter as I explained the predicament.

"Joshi, my poor darling," said Alma.

Gaia laughed until her belly wobbled through the sheer material of her vibrant sari. "I can get rid of that for you. Bend over."

Dad turned pale. "With my trousers off?"

"Of course. Don't be shy. I've seen it all. Rabbits doing it like the world is going to end. Bulls ejaculating. Flamingos defecating on themselves to keep cool. Koalas riddled with chlamydia. And fruit flies having orgies. It can't be any worse than that." She winked. "And if it is, I promise to never think of it again."

Dad reached across to hold Alma's hand and bent over.

I averted my eyes, but further afield, Echo, Ezra and Orpheus were transfixed.

There was a flash of light, a zap and a yelp from Dad.

"There you go. All gone and nicely exfoliated, if I say so myself. It will take the hair a while to grow back. Alma will rub some aloe vera in, and you'll be as right as rain." She dusted off her hands and turned her cherubic face to me. "Now, Alisha, it's time we caught up."

We walked through the garden that still bore the mark of Mum's labours, despite Alma's pots lurking in random places.

Gaia hooked a plump, papery arm through mine. She

grew unnaturally still, and her brown eyes bored into mine. Her voice held a rare note of sternness. "I told you everything would be okay. You should never have doubted me."

I couldn't hold her gaze. Her irises weren't normal. If I stared into them long enough, they revealed the turning of the seasons, the shifting of continents and the burning of stars. "I doubted myself."

She smiled. "Yes, you did, foolish woman. It's such a female affliction. You'll have to keep on working on that. It's not the sort of thing that disappears overnight. It's more like a deep-rooted fungus. Come now, let's walk."

Our arms remained linked, and she urged us on.

"Thank you for removing the tattoos for those men," I said. "Mami's intention was to take away their choice to worship her."

"Oh, the Father of the Gods wouldn't have liked that." Gaia's sari swished through the grass. "He's big on choice."

I frowned. "I thought you said the Father of the Gods died when the heavens crumbled."

"Silly me. Of course, He did. You know how it is. In our hearts, we always think of those we have loved in the present tense." The joy fell from her face. "Beware, druid. Now you've used the sword against an immortal, Death's eyes will be on you." She brightened. "But that's a battle for another day. You should go and check on the pigeon. Something tells me he's up to no good."

I frowned and ran up the stairs, my heart pumping.

The box with the necklace was empty. I dropped to my knees, checked underneath the duvet and threw open the closet. My brother's clothes lay scrunched up there.

I pelted to the window.

On the sill, I found a pigeon feather and a splatter of excrement—the absolute prick. My head jerked up.

Sahil cooed in a tree at the bottom of the garden. Muscly,

monstrous, his head cocked to one side. He carried the necklace in his beak.

Fury coursed through my veins. What a fool I'd been to trust him.

I pointed at the werepigeon, sorely tempted to wring its neck. "Sahil's taken it. He's taken the Jericho necklace."

Ezra caught my eyes from across the lawn, expression grim. "I can catch him."

Orpheus bared his fangs. "He's going to pay for that."

"Alisha…" Dad pleaded.

"No," I sighed. "Let him go."

"I wouldn't worry," smiled Gaia. "All might seem lost, but it could be that under the surface, you forged a new connection with your brother that might well save us in the future. The smallest butterfly, the smallest choice, impacts us all. That is the way of the world. It bodes well for us that you've stopped drifting. I think you finally understand who you are." She listened to something in the distance. "I hear the patter of small feet in my hallway. Time for me to take my leave. Until next time, Alisha Verma."

Her sari rustled, her hair flew back, and then she was gone.

"I hope the neighbours didn't see that," said Alma.

Marina looped her arms around me. "It's all going to be all right, you know. The goddess is right. He just doesn't know who he is yet."

I planted a kiss on her cheek, just in case she didn't know I loved her.

"So, are you going to do it, then?" said Marina. "Are you going to move in with Ezra? Make him your personal bodyguard, bedwarmer and taxi service?"

"I could do with some undivided wolf attention after the ride we've had." It would be good to hold the darkness at bay and concentrate on something pure for once.

She waggled her eyebrows. "Atta girl."

Echo padded over, his ears erect. "Tell me it isn't true. You wouldn't give up our flat, would you?"

I fussed over him, then dug out Ezra's key from my pocket, a small smile on my face.

I'd fought hard for my independence, but being with Ezra felt like home.

I cherished that sense of belonging, despite the challenges ahead.

ACKNOWLEDGMENTS

First, thanks to my readers. Alisha's world has come to mean so much to me, and I'm honoured you choose to spend your time in it.

To my editor Jeni, words cannot express how much I appreciate your gentle encouragement and feel for story and words. Thank you, Toni, for your eagle eye and patient work. A big thanks also to my cover artist Maria, whose island and home were hit by a typhoon in the midst of this project. I'm in awe of your resilience and talent.

For my beta readers Debbie and Sheri, who are always ready to read for me at the drop of a hat. Your enthusiasm and belief in my stories give me courage. Thanks for picking up on things I miss and pushing me to do my best. A big thank you also to Joe at GoIndieNow, who is a brilliant champion of indie creatives.

Mum and Dad, you didn't think I'd be writing about druids, werewolves and vampires, but you brim with pride when you tell your friends about me all the same. Thanks for being there for us through thick and thin. Your kidney bean curry will always be my favourite thing to eat.

For our children, Hana, Raiyan and Noah, we couldn't be prouder of you. Our love for you is so all-encompassing that I almost don't mind how noisy you are or how many trousers you wear through.

To my husband Jan, my weathervane, my first reader, my favourite person. You know how to read my moods from a flicker of emotion across my face and instinctively say what I need to hear. None of this would be possible without you.

FREE SHORT STORY

If you enjoyed this book, please leave a review online to help other readers find this story.

The Druid Heir novels are written in Alisha's perspective, a 40-year-old teacher living in London. The short stories explore the world from an alternate character's viewpoint.

You can get the Druid Heir short stories for free by signing up for my fantasy newsletter at www.nillunasser.com.

MIDLIFE PORTALS: DRUID HEIR BOOK 5

I've earned the grudging respect of London's Otherworld, and I'm ready to enjoy my second chance at love with Ezra. But trouble still comes knocking. The old gods are rising, even the ones I've defeated before. They haven't forgiven me for thwarting them. I might be a druid wielding Death's sword, but without the Jericho necklace, I'm as exposed as a middle-aged jogger without a sports bra.

Not even Wildwoods is a haven anymore. Especially when suspicions mount up that the Prime Sorcerer is acting against us. A woman in her midlife knows how to stand her ground, but confronting him is a dangerous game and risks ripping a chasm through the magical community.

When my friends are sucked into the orbit of danger, it's clear that none of us can escape unscathed and I'll have to take greater risks than ever before. Will we walk away with our lives, or will I be left with a knicker drawer full of regret?

If you're a fan of Paranormal Women's Fiction and magic-wielding heroines over forty, continue this journey with Druid Heir Book 5.

ALSO BY N. Z. NASSER

DRUID HEIR

Midlife Dawn, Book 1

Midlife Tremors, Book 2

Midlife News, Book 3

Midlife Drift, Book 4

Midlife Portals, Book 5

Midlife Eclipse, Book 6

Midlife Battle, Book 7

Druid Heir Collections

MAJESTIC MIDLIFE WITCH

To Save a Sister, Book 1

To Curse a Rival, Book 2

To Trick a Raja, Book 3

To Hunt a Foe, Book 4

NEWSLETTER EXCLUSIVES

The Magical Grandmother, Druid Heir Short Story 0.5

A First Date in Paris, Druid Heir Short Story 1.5

Midlife Battle, Druid Heir 7 Bonus Epilogue

To Become a Witch, Majestic Midlife Short Story 0.5

Biryani Junction, a Majestic Midlife Witch Cookbook

ABOUT THE AUTHOR

N. Z. Nasser is a writer of paranormal women's fiction. Her stories are about women who change the world, filled with magic and rooted in friendship.

A lover of barefoot walks along the beach, she is glad to have left behind her career in the civil service and to never wear heels again. Whether she is writing in her garden office or wrangling laundry, she is happiest with a cup of tea at her side.

She lives in London with her husband, three children, two cats and a fox-mad dog.

For new release alerts, you can follow her at Bookbub or Goodreads. For a more personal touch, join her Facebook reader group Nasser's Book Nymphs, say hi on social media, or visit her online store at www.nillunasser.com.

facebook.com/nillunasser

instagram.com/nillunasser